T0096240

AMONGST THISTLES AND THORNS

ALSO BY AUSTIN C. CLARKE

Novels
The Survivors of the Crossing
The Meeting Point
Storm of Fortune
The Bigger Light
The Prime Minister
Proud Empires
The Origin of Waves
The Question
The Polished Hoe
More

Short Stories
When He Was Free and Young and He Used to Wear Silks
When Women Rule
Nine Men Who Laughed
In this City
There Are No Elders
Choosing His Coffin

Memoirs
Growing up Stupid Under the Union Jack: A Memoir
Public Enemies: Police Violence and Black Youth
A Passage Back Home: A Personal Reminiscence of Samuel Selvon
Pigtails 'n' Breadfruit: The Rituals of Slave Food, A Barbadian Memoir

AUSTIN C. CLARKE

AMONGST THISTLES AND THORNS

INTRODUCTION AARON KAMUGISHA

PEEPAL TREE

First published by William Heinemann Ltd
in Great Britain in 1965
This new edition published in 2011 by
Peepal Tree Press Ltd
17 King's Avenue
Leeds LS6 1QS
England

ISBN13: 9781845231477

For my children
Janice Elizabeth and Loretta Ann

AARON KAMUGISHA

AUSTIN CLARKE'S BARBADIAN COLONIALITY:
LANGUAGE, HUMOUR AND VIOLENCE
IN A CARIBBEAN COLONY

The republication of Austin Clarke's *Amongst Thistles and Thorns* (1965) after forty-five years marks the welcome reappearance of a powerful book that has been much misunderstood and neglected by Caribbean critics. It is an early contribution by an author who now, at the height of his powers, is being belatedly recognised as one of the giants of Caribbean literature. It is also a work that contains much of aching relevance for contemporary Barbadian society. The second of my three claims may be the easiest for readers to assess, as Clarke's 2002 masterpiece, *The Polished Hoe*, has been awarded the Giller Prize, Canada's top literary honour, and the overall Commonwealth Writers' Prize. The first West Indian to publish a novel in Canada, Clarke is now firmly seen as part of a Canadian *and* Caribbean literary tradition.

The reasons for the comparative neglect of Clarke, author now of eleven novels, six short story collections and three memoirs, are complex. They range from his location in Canada outside of the London-Caribbean nexus of much of the Anglophone Caribbean's literary development – at least in the 1960s and 1970s – and its related organisations such as the Caribbean Artists Movement (CAM); the limited space for Black Canadian and Caribbean studies at Canada's universities; and his conflicted relationship with, and reception in, Barbados. This official Barbadian discomfort with Clarke, closely linked to his controversial role as general manager of the island's lone television station, the Caribbean Broadcasting Corporation, in 1974[1], and his satirical recounting of that affair in his novel *The Prime Minister* (1977), has waned considerably, and his later work has gained him a new audience in his home country. Close attention to Clarke's first two novels, *Survivors of the Crossing* (1964) and *Amongst Thistles and Thorns* (1965) – the former also shortly to be republished by Peepal Tree Press – sheds a tremendous amount of light on the preoccupations of Clarke's later work set in Barbados. Above all, both novels provide a subtle and devastating indictment of the reproduction of coloniality in that country, an indictment whose relevance is far from diminished.

It has been argued, perhaps most forcefully by Frantz Fanon, that the order of the colonial state, imposed with a searing violence that was both material and epistemological, meant that decolonisation could never be other than a disorderly phenomenon.[2] *Amongst Thistles and Thorns* was published in 1965, the year before Barbados's flag independence, and at the time of warnings by Fanon, C.L.R. James and other anti-colonial writers that the legacies of colonialism, cultural and material, would haunt the newly emerging nation-states of the Caribbean and Africa. A generation later, and in response to these legacies that just will not lie down and be still, theorists such as Sylvia Wynter and Aníbal Quijano have utilized the term "coloniality" to refer to a global order of knowledge that has emerged over the last five hundred years. Coloniality, as defined by Nelson Maldonado-Torres, is a particular form of power with its genesis in the colonial relation, which now defines "culture, labor, intersubjective relations, and knowledge production well beyond the strict limits of colonial administrations".[3] Coloniality lies at the heart of the post-colonial Barbadian state and this perception is central to the tone and focus of Clarke's Barbadian fiction. Whilst *Amongst Thistles and Thorns* is quite different in organisation and mood to *Survivors of the Crossing*, with the latter's narrative structured around a tragic-comic attempt at revolution on a plantation and the humour, vices, passive aggressiveness and violence that characterise the late colonial state, both novels share a barely suppressed anger over how white economic and state power still circumscribe the lives of the black majority and over how contradictory the response of the black majority has been. In comparison to *Survivors of the Crossing*, *Amongst Thistles and Thorns* relies far less on a plot with progressively unfolding action, and much more on characterisation, and here Clarke's masterly handling of Barbadian nation-language in the conversations between characters already has a confident maturity. It is also Clarke's first narrative of childhood, a theme he would return to in his memoir, *Growing Up Stupid Under the Union Jack* (1980), and his novel, *Proud Empires* (1986). In this respect *Amongst Thistles and Thorns* follows such Barbadian novels as George Lamming's *In the Castle of My Skin* (1953) – to which a significant intertextual reference is almost certainly made – and Geoffrey Drayton's *Christopher* (1959) which deals with the life of a white Barbadian child at the opposite end of the social spectrum from Clarke's Milton Sobers.

The story of *Amongst Thistles and Thorns* unfolds over a couple of days, and tells the tale of Milton Sobers, a nine-year-old boy, and his marronage from his family home during that time. What the novel connects most tellingly to is the social order of late colonialism, and the treatment of children in Barbados. It does this very effectively through Milton's consciousness and the characterisation of those closest to him, principally the quartet of his mother, Ruby, the competing "fathers", Nathan and Willy-Willy, and Mr Blackman. Before I consider these themes in some detail, it is worth examining the responses to this novel by its critics. According to Clarke's biographer, Stella Algoo-Baksh, *Amongst Thistles and Thorns* attracted positive reviews,[4] which often compared it favourably to his first novel, an assessment echoed by Edward Baugh.[5] However, an examination of the more influential critical treatments that attempt to place *Amongst Thistles and Thorns* in the wider context of the Caribbean novel points to how the novel has been misread and, as a consequence, subsequently overlooked. In his chapter "Novels of Childhood" in *The West Indian Novel and Its Background*, Kenneth Ramchand mentions *Amongst Thistles and Thorns* as a counterpoint to his main interest, Michael Anthony's *The Year in San Fernando*, but purely to dismiss it as an example of a novel in which social protest overwhelms the voice of Clarke's young protagonist.[6] While I am sympathetic to Ramchand's distaste for those reviews of *A Year in San Fernando* (1965) that insisted on a readily identifiable social meaning, or demanded that it have a trajectory that supposedly

marks the "traditional" bildungsroman – that is that the protagonist should arrive at a state of "maturer" awareness – the effect of
Ramchand's defence of Michael Anthony's novel seems to work
towards a double erasure of Clarke's book. For Ramchand, its
"impurity" of voice (in which we hear both the young Milton,
and a suggestion of an older self) suggests that it can't be a true
novel of childhood, while for others, the novel's inevitable
indeterminacy (because it is socially and psychologically realistic)
about where it leaves Milton leaves them unsatisfied that a
coming to consciousness has been achieved. Lloyd Brown's more
considered discussion of *Amongst Thistles and Thorns*, though it
deals with the novel in its own terms, still has a major area of
silence.[7] In contradistinction to Ramchand, Brown sees the novel
as Milton's "experience of... (the) world, and his imaginative
response to it" and he has many keen insights on Clarke's style.
Yet, he manages to occlude one of the central concerns in the
novel, by utilising the language of seduction to describe headmistress Brewster's and Girlie's behaviour towards Milton. In the
remainder of this introduction, I will attempt to provide a correc-
tive to these readings of *Thistles*, through a consideration of the
novel's treatment of the social order of late colonialism, and the
place of children within it.

In a 1970 essay titled "The Social Framework", the prominent
Caribbean historian Elsa Goveia declared that the most critical
integrating factor of Caribbean society has been the "acceptance
of the inferiority of Negroes to whites".[8] The symbolic value of
whiteness and negation of blackness is certainly not just a Caribbean conundrum but part of a global order of knowledge. In the
late colonial period in which Clarke writes, Barbados was still a
society where the white hegemony of the past three hundred
years persisted in the ownership and control of the land and the
commanding heights of the economy by an elite that was pre-
dominantly white, even though political control had largely
passed out of white hands. One of Clarke's achievements in this
novel is his incisive portrayal of the overpowering ubiquity of
whiteness both as an actual presence – a key element in the
overarching system of domination that the black community
faces – and as a deeply embedded and self-restricting element in

the consciousness of many of the novel's black characters. In church, for instance, there is "a smell of whiteness and richness" (p. 177), and Ruby's and Girlie's discussion of the strangeness of white folk – here specifically the excessive quantity and selection of underwear that white women choose to buy – is a telling moment to consider. If white people, who in the colonial symbolic order are their social betters in a society so evidently organised in white interests, can behave so irrationally, what hope is there for a rational order of things in the colony and the wider world? This is a cause for more than passing anxiety to Ruby and Girlie. Whiteness must, after all, be defended, both from attacks on its claim to a rational integrity, and from encroachments on its space in a community split by a colonial geography, lines that can only be crossed when the exploitation of the black working classes' labour is required. Thus Milton, on account of his perceived rudeness, can be forced to inhale a semi-poisonous substance by a pharmacist, followed by a beating from his mother for venturing, without legitimate reason, into "the white people district".

Perhaps Clarke's most biting depiction of coloniality comes in his account of the deliberate attack on Milton by a young white boy's dog. As Milton wriggles on the ground desperately trying to free himself, and the dog's owner watches with interest and nary a word, the hotel watchman, Chandler, comes on the scene:

> "You black boy! Get up to-arse offa the white man' dog!" Chandler took the dog off me; and he patted the dog and gave it back to its owner. "You little black fool, what the hell right you have hanging 'round the white man' hotel? You ain' belongst *up* here! You belongst down there!" (p. 56)

After Chandler rescues the dog (which is, after all, white property) he hurls abuse at Milton, promises violence if he should ever see him in this area again, and entreats the little white master to call on the (R.) S.P.C.A. to prosecute Milton. This story will only sound extraordinary to someone who has not lived in a colony, existing or with a "post" affixed. And even the more oblique moments of *Thistles* reveal the vivid texture of colonial domination. The long description of Ruby's work as a washerwoman for a white woman from the "Front Road" is telling in its detail and its sympathy for the labour of working-class women, a theme recurring in Clarke's fiction and memoirs.[9] The "quick-tempered nervousness" (p.52) of Ruby's hand, her "strange uncontrollable nervousness" (p.64) are symptoms of the nervous condition that is the native's plight under colonialism, first sketched by Fanon and beautifully rendered in novelistic form some three decades later by the Zimbabwean novelist, Tsitsi Dangarembga.[10] There is never a doubt about the authority that both produces and sanctions violence in the colony. As cruel as the headmaster, Mr Blackman, can be, the white school inspector, on his annual visit, shows a brutality towards the boys that is distant and unmediated even by Blackman's misguided notion of moral and social uplift. The production of good citizens of the empire, wrested away from the vices born of self-produced poverty and the heart of heathen darkness, requires violent action on young bodies, and an epistemological violence on their minds, through the instillation of a consciousness that Britain is the source of all light and learning – colonial violence begets more colonial violence. It is a reminder again of Fanon's reckoning that "colonialism is not a thinking machine, nor a body endowed with reasoning faculties. It is violence in its natural state, and it will only yield when confronted with greater violence."[11]

★   ★   ★   ★

When that tam'rind whip crash-in in his backside, he fly-up in the air like a piece o' lightning!
                                    Headmaster Blackman
Confuse myself with Milton? If he dead, I will hear.
                                    Ruby, Milton's mother

The treatment of children in colonial Barbados is the most omnipresent theme in *Amongst Thistles and Thorns*. Here the power of Clarke's treatment of adult behaviours that encompass both physical brutality and sexual abuse gives the novel a painful vitality for the contemporary reader, even if what is being portrayed could be shown to be a purely historical phenomenon. But the truth is that this most wrenching legacy of colonialism continues to bedevil the Barbadian state today. It is apt that this book is being republished at a time when Barbadians have been having perhaps their most serious (and divisive) debate about the possible abolishment of corporal punishment in schools.

Clarke is hardly the only Caribbean novelist to explore these questions. The fairly substantial body of Anglophone Caribbean novels of childhood, from *In the Castle of My Skin* in 1953, to novels such as Jan Shinebourne's *The Last English Plantation* (1988) or Diana McCaulay's *Dog-Heart* (2010) – though here the violence has moved from the classroom to the police station – are full of descriptions of the beatings of children.[12] Indeed, the descriptions of brutality towards children, cloaked as discipline, in *Amongst Thistles and Thorns* are by no means the most explicit in Caribbean literature; amongst those I've read, a scene in C.L.R. James's *Minty Alley* (1936) stands as the most horrific.[13] What Clarke shows best is the sadistic glee and righteous satisfaction felt by practically every adult participant in this ritual of coloniality. And it is here that we see coloniality's violence unmasked.

It would be irresponsible to suggest that many Barbadian children's lives mimic Milton's at this point in time, almost half a century later. However, given the polarisation of debate around banning corporal punishment in schools, and the scepticism of many towards the idea of children's rights, it is evident that deep cultural beliefs in the efficacy of physical punishment persist in Barbadian society. Barbadians may not enjoy hearing stories about physical brutality towards children. But we don't quite *dislike* these moments enough either. To misquote Bob Marley, when we hear the crack of the whip, our blood *doesn't* grow cold. There is an overwhelming sense of nostalgia that is evident in the stories that Barbadians – and Caribbean people in general – tell about the discipline they received at home and school. It is commonplace to hear boasts about the floggings and punishments taken, particularly from beloved headmasters, recounted with joy and laughter. It is, particularly among men, part of the fashioning of themselves into adulthood; the ability to "hold the blows" is a sign of prowess and devilish outlawry. The sheer variety of phrases in Anglophone Caribbean Creole that refer to these beatings make it clear how yoked to the culture of the Caribbean physical punishment has always been. A sampling: "share blows", "hot lashes", "warm blows", "licks like peas", "cut he/she tail", "a good cut ass", "hard ears won't hear, hard ears going feel", "give you something to cry for", "domestic discipline", "a stiff beating", "roast yuh with licks", "show yuh which God yuh serving", "unmek [unmake] yuh with blows", "catch a fire in he/she tail", "wash he away with blows", "burst ya ass", "roast ya behind", "cut you down to size", "raining blows", "blind yuh with licks", "lather yuh tail with blows", "You-feel-you-is-a-man-well-handle-man-blows [each word punctuated with a lash]", and "I going beat you now so the judge don't have to hang you later". And that is a mere sample. It is not to suggest that tremendous changes have not taken place in Barbados in the almost half-century since *Thistles* was published, or that there are not widely divergent views on disciplining children in Barbados. The fact, though, that I could receive a list of over thirty terms when I put out a request on Facebook, all from friends under thirty-five, certainly shows that dismantling the ideological edifices that perpetuate violence as the preferred means of discipline – which range from perceptions of increasing deviance among young people and the belief that physical violence is the answer, lack of knowledge of alternative means of discipline, and acute parental stress – will need a concerted societal effort.[14] Coloniality's violence, as Frederick Douglass once noted, will never give up without an earnest struggle. Its enactment on the bodies of Caribbean children demands a response. In this respect, *Thistles* still has much to say.

Almost every potential type of child abuse is experienced by Milton in what we deduce is not – apart from his running away – an extraordinary two days. He is beaten savagely by a sadistic headmaster. When curiosity gets the better of him at the public bath, he is called a savage, an African, a "black cannibull". He witnesses threats of violence between his purported father (Nathan) and his girlfriend, who turn him away when he arrives at their door late at night for shelter. His biological father threatens him with death if he does not corroborate a story on his location the previous night. The beating at the hands of Mr Blackman is so much a part of Milton's daily world that when he thinks he has exhausted the headmaster, he feels as if he has defeated him (though he also silently pledges revenge). Physical abuse, neglect, abandonment, threats to life and limb, psychological abuse, and hints towards the end that he may be sent to work as a child labourer are welded into a story of such commonplace experience that provides support for Christine Barrow's assertion that there is a "historical tradition and cultural acceptance of child abuse in the Caribbean".[15]

I omitted from the above list another form of abuse Milton experiences, which is one of the more important themes of the novel: the sexual abuse of boys. Other critics have passed over these moments in *Thistles* with silence, while Lloyd Brown strangely describes the most telling episode as an attempted seduction. It is, however, a moment whose significance should not be missed. On two occasions Milton turns to women in the community for help. In the first instance his vulnerability is exploited when he asks Girlie to mend his pants after the attack by the dog. Then there is the episode with the aged headmistress, Miss Brewster, whom Milton meets late at night after fleeing his mother's blows. Girlie, a woman of thirty-five, is a rogue, known by Ruby and Willy-Willy to be interfering with boys; she humiliates Milton in a manner he regards as "unbearable". The scene itself has a simple directness, but its context demands a more complex reading. At one level, Willy-Willy (Ruby's temporary live-in man) describes Girlie's behaviour as "worthliss" and, largely for Ruby's approval, berates Girlie for "robbing the cradle" and says "That hard-back woman love boys" with such "horror" that Milton feels forewarned. But then he confuses Milton by saying, when the two are alone, and observing that the boy's pee now froths, that he should leave school and "help me breed the womens in this village" (p.58), and that "I going make Girlie give you a piece! Girlie slightly more older than you... but she sweet. And she would give" (p. 59). Milton is seen by the adults in his life (though perhaps not by Mr Blackman, for whom Milton belongs to an unregenerate sub-species of boys) as a miniature adult, though Clarke makes us see, through the creation of Milton's voice, his powerless vulnerability as a child. Willy-Willy expresses a version of Caribbean masculinity (which sees itself as commendably roguish) that can't countenance the idea that a boy can be sexually exploited by a woman. If Willy-Willy is at all shocked, it is that a hard-back woman like Girlie prefers boys to hard-back men like himself, rather than thinking that there is anything inherently wrong in what Girlie is doing. Contemporary Caribbean sociologists have noted how often boys' first sexual initiation is by women substantially older than themselves, and it is evident that many in society still appear to find this scenario amusing – and a welcome early antidote to the possibility that a boy may become gay.[16] Here hegemonic masculinities and predatory sexualities collide, resulting in abuse retaining its common fate: it is silenced, ignored, but not forgotten.

Milton's perceptions of adults are refracted through a lens of trauma and suspicion through which he has come to see them. How he processes the often inappropriate information he is offered by the adults in his life is suggested in the scene when, on the run from a beating by his mother, he is rescued by the elderly headmistress, Miss Brewster. She, on the evidence of an earlier meeting, is the one person who cares for him as a child, though because of the frailties of age, her own inappropriate behaviour and the distorting vision that Milton brings to the encounter, even she seems to him to be nothing more than another predator. We can see this as the combined product of a lonely boy's night terrors, his accumulated suspicions of adult behaviour, and the confusions about sexuality that the likes of Willy-Willy have sown in his consciousness.

The episode begins with Milton thinking that "I never wanted to be inside a house as much as I wanted to be inside Miss Brewster's house" (p.84). The estranging incomprehension starts when Miss Brewster breaks a lamp which has some unexplained sentimental value to her and begins to cry. At this point Clarke wants to show that she has some awareness of her position as an adult in relation to a child. Milton sees her as "Crying like an old woman would cry; so quiet, so ashamed of herself for crying in front of a small boy" (p. 85). This is perhaps not quite plausibly Milton's perspective, though it is a necessary starting point for charting what happens next. More plausible is his utter puzzlement over why she should be crying "in such a comfortable house, filled with furniture that my eyes had never seen before…", a response that reveals Milton's emotional impoverishment. After Milton is fed, Miss Brewster readies for bed and begins to undress in front of him. Her responsibility for his distress is complex. Milton knows from a story his mother tells him that Miss Brewster is severely forgetful, so his first thought that "Perhaps she did not remember that I was still there" may well be the fictional truth. This also affects our ability to judge whether or not Miss Brewster has any predatory sexual designs on Milton. One has to consider here her disrobing in front of him, and her persistent questions to Milton about whether he "like girls", if he "ever see' a girl yet" and if he likes seeing girls running on Gravesend beach naked. Milton's response is quite evidently sexualised. He does not see just the body of an old woman, but her gross fleshliness in the violently disgusted way that Willy-Willy might see it: "and as she unzipped the zipper her heavy bowels and breasts fell out into her underslip, like the entrails of a pig spurting out when the knife of a butcher had ripped it in twain" (p.86). This is the vision of a child who has seen too much. Thereafter, Milton's perception of Miss Brewster reaches into fantasy and the tales Willy-Willy has told him about women who suck little boys' blood. He sees her now as "thin as a razorblade", as a vampire or a witch. As he runs from her room he bumps into her and knocks off her wig to discover that she is bald. All Willy-Willy's homophobic stories come to mind and Milton cries out, "You is a man! You is a man. I wanna go home!" and runs from her house into the lesser terrors of the night storm – and Nathan's refusal to let him into his house.

Violence towards children is frequently an intimate violence – intimate based on the relations that exist between the child and the perpetrators, often parents or in *loco parentis* to the child; intimate in that it is almost always couched as the supposed means towards fashioning a new, more responsible, adult self – and hence, more than any other type of interpersonal violence, often claiming the language of love as its purpose and meaning. Children are an adult project and property, rather than their own beings, and parental love becomes twinned with menace. As Nathan asserts:

He is all we possesses. So, we have to sp'il him with goodness
and kindness. And this is something I intends to put to that
blasted racoon when he march' his arse back inside this house.
(p.115)

Yet it is in their dealings with children that Clarke reveals the
incomplete adulthood of many of his "adult" characters, and this is
the other side of the connection he makes between the condition
of coloniality and the particular story of this child. There is the
persistent juvenility of Milton's competing "fathers", Nathan and
Willy-Willy, two "worthless", idle men who prey on Ruby's
loneliness, constantly on the cadge for money for cigarettes, rum
and a temporary bed and sex when one of the other women they
haunt has had enough and thrown them out. As Willy-Willy
advises Milton: "One thing. Never… *never* let a piece o' woman go
to you head. Never. A piece o' woman regular every night, could
put a man in great health. But when it go to yuh head, *bram!* out goes
you!" (p. 59). Even Ruby, who struggles to do her best by Milton,
fails at crucial points to defer her immediate pleasures to his best
interests. There is the gloriously funny, but ultimately sorry scene
where Nathan comes to Ruby (he has been thrown out by his
girlfriend) to claim Milton as his son (he has never paid a cent of
support) declaring his "begrievement" for past sins, and the pair
(after Nathan has wheedled his way into Ruby's lonely bed) engage
in an orgy of turning over a "brand new-brand leaf", and visions of
happy families in which Milton, en route to a professional career,
will be singing in a chorister's ruff in the cathedral (p.116). A day
later the pair are proposing to take Milton out of school and send
him to work in the quarry. Childrearing practice in the novel veers
between immature irresponsibility and neglect, and impulsive
authoritarianism, the other side of coloniality where the culture of
colonial authority and dependence is reflected in the interpersonal
relationships of the colonised. But there is nothing of the case study
or overt political preaching here. What Clarke conveys very pow-
erfully is the tyranny of intimacy, the intimacy of tyranny.

In conclusion, it is worth briefly considering Clarke's role as
a Caribbean diasporic writer now resident in Canada for over fifty
years. Clarke had been in Canada only ten years when *Amongst*

Thistles and Thorns was published, and the focus of his concerns, as in *Survivors of the Crossing*, remains firmly focused on Barbados. But as other Caribbean writers have revealed (for instance Clarke's fellow Caribbean-Canadian, Cyril Dabydeen), from as early as the 1940s and 50s, Caribbean childhoods were infected by ideas of the possibilities of "elsewhere". For Milton Sobers that elsewhere is Harlem, a place he has heard spoken about in adult conversations, which comes to signify for him a more spacious world than the cramped cell of a racially constricted Barbados. That sense of constriction is expressed in what must be a deliberate reference to George Lamming's *In the Castle of My Skin*. Repeatedly Milton refers to his hiding place in the cellar under the church as "his castle of dirt", "the castle of my cellar" and of being "cramped in my little shallow castle" (pp. 110, 122, 140). Apart from the metaphor of social space, the allusion to Lamming's novel, set in Barbados of the 1930s and 40s, and published a dozen years earlier than *Thistles*, perhaps asks what has changed for Barbados's black and working-class majority, as the politics of nationalist awakening turn into the compromised politics of home-rule Barbados and the politics of succession and coloniality. When one reflects on Clarke's literary journey, from *Survivors of the Crossing* (1964) to his latest novel *More* (2009), you are struck by the movement back and forth between a novel on Barbados to a novel on Canada and back to Barbados again, a cycle that has repeated itself a number of times, and belies the stereotype that immigrant writers first write about their native land and then relatively exclusively about their adopted home. Some Caribbean writers use characters whose journey to the metropolis reveals the radicalised consciousness that a different experience of racism and coloniality engenders, and the dream of international working-class solidarity. Clarke would rather consider what gets lost in translation – or the authority that idle (and untrue) boasts about worldly experience and knowledge can bring. Thus a character in *Thistles* can declare "I have see' with my own two eyes, Stalin drinking vodka outta a chamberpot!" (p.83) Clarke never loses an opportunity to simultaneously entertain and provoke. And somewhere between the pathos and despair, the wit and humour, a fine novel evolved.

ENDNOTES

1. In an interview with Daryl Cumber Dance (*New World Adams: Conversations with Contemporary West Indian Writers*, Leeds: Peepal Tree Press, 1992, 2008, pp. 76-77) Clarke reports how he was fired from his job with the radio station and that: "There were threats against my life and I used to carry a .38 revolver. There were bomb threats at the place that I worked."

2. Frantz Fanon, *The Wretched of the Earth* (Translated by Constance Farrington), London: Penguin, 1967.

3. Nelson Maldonado-Torres, "On the Coloniality of Being: Contributions to the Development of a Concept," *Cultural Studies* 21. 2&3 (2007): 243.

4. Stella Algoo-Baksh, *Austin C. Clarke: A Biography*, Mona, Jamaica: University of the West Indies Press, 1994, p.74.

5. Edward Baugh, "The Sixties and Seventies," in Bruce King ed., *West Indian Literature,* London: MacMillan, 1995 2nd edition, p.65. The field of Caribbean literary criticism is now quite vast, but studies of Caribbean childhoods in literature as a separate genre, or children's literature are rare. However, note the forthcoming edited collection by Giselle Rampaul and Geraldine Skeete, *The Child and the Caribbean Imagination*.

6. Kenneth Ramchand, *The West Indian Novel and Its Background*, London: Faber and Faber, 1970, pp.206-7.

7. Lloyd W. Brown, *El Dorado and Paradise: Canada and the Caribbean in Austin Clarke's Fiction*, Parkersburg, Iowa: Caribbean Books, 1989, p.45, pp.134-5.

8. Elsa Goveia, "The Social Framework," *Savacou* 2 (1970): 7-15.

9. See Brinda Mehta, "The Mother As Culinary Griotte: Food and Cultural Memory in Austin Clarke's *Pigtails 'n Breadfruit*," *MaComère* 5 (2002-2003): 184-204.

10. Frantz Fanon, *The Wretched of the Earth*; Tsitsi Dangarembga, *Nervous Conditions,* Berkeley: Seal Press, 1988.

11. Fanon, *The Wretched of the Earth*, p.48.

12. See for instance, in addition to the novels mentioned, Edgar Mittelholzer, *Shadows Move Among Them* (1952); Jan Carew, *The Wild Coast* (1958); Peter Kempadoo, *Guiana Boy* (1960); Ismith Khan, "The Red Ball", in *A Day in the Country and Other*

Stories (1994); Rooplall Monar, *Backdam People* (1986); Lakshmi Persaud, *Butterfly in the Wind* (1990); Opal Palmer Adisa, *Until Judgement Comes* (2007). Roger Mais's *The Hills Were Joyful Together* (1953) and Michael Thelwell's *The Harder They Come* (1980) make the connection between the colonial brutality of a punishment rooted in slavery and the brutality of much interpersonal behaviour between the strong and the weak, adults on children, men on women. Corporal punishment is still lawful in Jamaica's schools, as it is in Barbados.

13. See *Minty Alley* (London: Secker and Warburg, 1936 and reprint edition London: New Beacon Books, 1971, pp.43-47) for the episode in which Nurse Jackson beats her son, Sonny.

14. Thanks to Christine Barrow, for sharing her thoughts and work in this area with me. See Christine Barrow, *Caribbean Childhoods: 'Outside', 'Adopted', or 'Left Behind'*, Kingston, Jamaica: Ian Randle Press, 2009.

15. Christine Barrow, "Children and Social Policy in Barbados: the Unfinished Agenda of Child Abuse," *The Caribbean Journal of Social Work* 2 (July 2003): 36-53.

16. Barry Chevannes, *Learning to be a Man: Culture, Socialization and Gender Identity in Five Caribbean Communities,* Barbados, Jamaica, Trinidad and Tobago: University of the West Indies Press, 2001.

Aaron Kamugisha
University of the West Indies
Cave Hill

Acknowledgements
Thanks to Brian, Cindy, Joanna, Marsha, Nastassia, Reynold, Sade, Sergio, Shevannese and Therese for help with the Anglophone-Caribbean creole punishment expressions, and Jeremy Poynting for an excellent and thought-provoking contribution to this introduction.

1

Large pearls of sweat were pouring down the headmaster's neck and his face, as he held the whip above my head. I saw his wrist jerk like a piston. And before the blow landed, I closed my eyes. *Whopp!* My body stiffened automatically against the blows; and I said aloud in my heart, that all the world could hear: 'I'll kill you! I'll kill you! I'll kill you!' On and on, as the blows fell, I shouted this vengeance within the secrecy of my heart. His wrist jerked; and the heavy whip fell. *Whopp! whopp! whopp!*

Soon, he was panting for breath. Panting, panting, for he was a man long past middle age. *Whopp-whopp-whopp!*... the jerking wrist and the explosion of the whip on my stiff khaki shirt. I wished he would fall down dead from exhaustion. Each time the heavy, knotted tamarind tree of a whip fell, each time it cut across the bruised landscape of my young tender back, I swore to kill him. The blows fell: twelve... thirteen... fourteen...

I had looked up from my copy book in the tedious afternoon class of penmanship. *Manners maketh man!* We were writing it out twenty times in our best handwriting. And it was then that I saw it, rolling and wobbling like a hub cap disconnected from a motor-car wheel. Rolling and wobbling, it had travelled, as if in two minds, from the passageway between my class and the class beside mine. And it had travelled, still wobbling, under the benches behind my bench; and then it came under my bench itself. All the other boys in my class were still looking into their copy books; and the master up front was mumbling something about making our 't's' slightly shorter than our 'h's'. But I was watching the sixpence roll into my possession. The nearer it rolled to me, the less hungry I felt. It meant a loaf of delicious homemade sweet bread from Miss Haynes, the best sweet-bread maker in the whole world.

There it was! coming slowly, wobblingly slow, and turning and spinning, though still rolling; but rolling in such a way that any minute it would get tired, and its knees would buckle, and it would wobble for the last time, and spin around on its circumference as all coins did when it was time for them to fall flat on their faces. There it was! My foot was moving to reach it, to kill its dull silvery ring before it dived into its final betraying spin.

My foot reached it. I could feel it, a cold piece of metal, on my warm bare foot. I sighed heavily. The boy beside glanced around. A sixpence! *My* sixpence! My mouth began to water. And immediately, I could feel the warm loaf of bread placed into my hand by Miss Haynes, whose hands were still sticky and wet and sweet from the grated coconut and the vanilla essence and the prunes and the currants with which she honeyed her bread. And then!… a large shoe was standing on my foot. And I shouted in disgust, 'Man, move 'way yuh blasted foot, man!' But the heavy leather-heeled shoe remained on my bare foot.

And when I looked up, it was the headmaster looking down at me. The other boys in my class had turned around by this time, to see what was going on. And the assistant master standing up front had stopped talking about making 't's' shorter than 'h's'. Nobody but me saw the headmaster reach down swiftly, scramble up the sixpence, and push it like lightning into his pocket. I wanted to kill him then.

Something on his face, something about the way his heavy eyebrows drooped down, told me that my sentence was going to be heavy, and swift. The loaf of bread vanished from my mind; and my mouth was filled with a tasteless dryness, and a sickness. And my body became chilly and nervous. And I felt very lonely, because nobody but the two of us, and perhaps God, knew what had happened.

The headmaster lifted me by my collar from the bench, and pushed me all the way to the platform at the front of the schoolroom. And the school itself became very quiet. Only the pins and needles of a terrible suspense were falling then.

'You was going to burgler?'

'No, sir.'

'Was you, or was you not intending to burgler, boy?'

'No, sir.'

'You is a burgler!'

'No, sir.'

'But I seen you with my two eyes, with intents 'pon burglering, boy!'

'No, sir.'

'All right, then. Well, what was you intending to do with it, then?'

'Nothing, sir.'

'You calling me a damn liar, boy?'

'*Me*, sir?'

'You calling me a liar, ain't yuh?'

'*No*, sir.'

'You knows what a liar is?'

'Yes, sir.'

'Boy, you begging me to expel you from outta this school, for life?'

'No, sir. Please, sir!'

'You knows what a liar is? What a liar is, boy?'

'A liar, sir, is when one body say something is so, and the next body say it ain't so, sir.'

'Yess! And that is why I affirming that you did, with intents to put your foot 'pon it. With intents to burgler it. So, is it me who is a liar, then? Or is you who is the liar?'

Not even the pins and needles of silence were dropping now. It was quiet and tragic as the moment just before a bride arrives at the bottom of the aisle on her wedding day.

'Is it me? Is me who is the liar, boy? Answer up!'

He had tricked me into answering. But before I could answer, he had walked across to the far corner of the platform. He took three tamarind rods from the top of the cupboard which contained our reading books, bent them backwards and forwards until they were about to break, until they were shaped like U's. But he didn't break them, though. He was only pretending he was going to break them. It seemed so to me. Then he came back for me, with the largest rod, flicking it through the air as if he were killing flies which no one but he could see. And the rod made a terrible, awful sound, as it hummed through the stillness in the schoolroom.

'Boys!' he shouted to the entire school. 'Eight Commandmunt!'

And the boys shouted back: '*Thou shalt not steal, sir! Thou shalt not steal!*'

'Yeah!' A grin of satisfaction came to his face. 'Thou *shalt not* steal!'

And then the room went quiet again.

'You is a thief!'

'No, sir.'

'You is a *thief*!'

'No, sir.'

'You calling me a liar again?'

'No, sir.'

'Well, I says you is a thief, and you is a thief. That is all.'

'Yessir.'

'All right, then! That's all I want to hear. Bend over, you damn crim'nul! You admit it. So, come, bend over and take these licks!'

…fifteen… sixteen. He was almost completely out of breath now. With each lash, he gave off a heavy, laboured exhaust, as if something inside him was going to collapse. Eighteen… nineteen. And then, for a long time, nothing happened. The savagery of the rhythm and the jerking of the wrist and the blows falling, stopped. I waited with my eyes closed; I waited and waited, oh Lord! for years, it seemed, and still the whip did not land again.

I had beaten him. I had defeated him. My youth had conquered. But I wished he was lying on the platform, dead. I had merely defeated him. Not killed him. I opened my eyes, and stared at him with daggers in them. There he was, a large, cruel man. And he was laughing. Laughing at me; and at the beating he had given me. Saliva and remnants of his lunch of soda biscuits and cheese spluttered from the spaces in his mouth where four yellowish teeth were standing guard.

'Open up yuh damn eyes, you, you animul!' He was still chuckling. Little raindrops of biscuits continued to fall out of his mouth, into my face. 'Open up! Open up! you, you… *pig*!'

All the boys in the schoolroom were laughing now. I knew they were laughing, that they had to laugh because they knew he would turn around and flog them, had they not acknowledged the fact that he himself was laughing.

'Boys, what shall I do with this, this… *demon*?' he asked the school. 'Tell me, boys. What should I do with this demon?… this, this *beast*?' And like a flash of lightning, the wrist jerked, and the rod whizzed through the air; and when it landed, *whapp!* it doubled me in two, in pain. 'Heh-heh-heh!' he chuckled. 'Tell me what to do with this, this…'

And a little exasperated, he held me by my ears, and lifted me slightly off the floor, and then he dropped me down. *Whapp!*

And I fled out of his reach.

I was awakened from my plotting by the jingle-tingle of the school bell. The headmaster was standing like Lord Horatio Nelson's statue, on the small platform. In his hand was the little bell with which he always brought the school to attention – whether it was to administer a public flogging; or to administer praise, which he seldom did. He was ringing the bell now, ringing it until the schoolroom became dead, and as silent as the neighbouring graveyard that belonged to St Hastings Church.

'Silunce!' he shrieked; although the schoolroom was already very quiet. And silence was born. 'Scriptures!' he shouted. And in the peace and stillness of the room that was our only world, our entire existence for seven hours from nine in the morning until four in the afternoon, we prepared ourselves, all of us, for the scolding, tight, puritan chilliness of the Scriptures. The Scriptures frightened all of us, and brought the awesome nothingness of death even more realistically near to us; touching us, and rubbing its fingers on us just like the hell of our lives in the island.

'Commandmunts!' he commanded.

The Commandments provided the germ of the lessons in Scripture in our school. The four assistant masters put their little gobs of chalk into their back pockets, and stood ready to drown out our voices with their bigger voices, as all of us rehearsed the Commandments. And we, about two hundred frightened children, launched into the Commandments, with such promptness,

27

as if an electric switch had been flicked on. We began at the First Commandment; and we worked our way, slowly and in pain, right through to the Tenth.

I did not know the Commandments very well. My mother never told me about them. I could not understand how or why they would apply to me; or to my father, or to my mother. And I did not care about learning them. But being in school, being in the headmaster's school, I had to say them. The headmaster told us that if we learned the Commandments well, we would all go to Heaven; and be good boys. Lester, the Little Einstein beside me, was bragging and boasting again. He was saying his Commandments out loud, holding back his head, and sometimes even closing his eyes, he was so sure of himself. *Thou shalt not do this… thou shalt not do that; thou shalt have none other Gods but Me…*

'Lester?' I whispered. 'Pssst!'

'Man, you ain' hear me saying the Things? You want Blackman to cut my arse, or what?'

'Lester, what they mean by having none other Gods?'

'Only *one* God!' And immediately as he had spoken to me out of the corner of his mouth, he went on saying aloud, something about *coveting thy neighbour's horse, nor his ass, nor his wife…*

'But, Lester. How many Gods they is, though?'

'Ask the headmaster!'

'But suppose a man was to feel like having more than one God! Suppose he was a kind o' man like what they have in Africa. A kind o' man what could have more than one wife…'

'A wife is a God? You calling a wife a God?'

'But I don't understand, though…'

'Stop!' yelled the headmaster, in a voice like a plantation overseer's. 'Stop, and lemme hear how this arse saying the Eight Commandmunt.'

He waited very patiently until I was ready. The school was hushed. Something terrible was about to happen. He knew I did not know the Eighth Commandment. But he was giving me a fair chance to prove my ignorance in front of the entire school. Our headmaster was such a democratic man! But it seemed very cruel to me, that he should ask me to stand on the platform and say it for the boys to laugh at me. He waited over me like a plague, all the time caressing the hills and valleys in the whip. And a smile broke out on his face like a plague.

'Come come come! Stan' up and let me and the boys and the teachers see what a real big genius you is.' That moment, the whip cracked, *whapp!* and before I knew it, I was standing on the lonely wide vast platform, looking into a sea of faces, all of them bewildered, all trembling, all of them drenched in the perspiration of fright and terror; and all of them dying with suspense, because they did not know what fate and chance the headmaster and the whip held for them. 'Come! Eight Commandmunt!' His voice was almost hysterical. I tried to shake my feelings out of my body, preparing myself.

I saw the Union Jacks spread out bold, in red, white and blue, over the four doors and six windows of our school; and I looked for help at the old faces of the men and women wearing crowns, as they peeped out of forests and jungles of beards. But the faces of the men and women, so strange and so distant and unknown to me, merely stared back at me. I noticed one face, that of a man – Edward VI was written beneath the large gold-painted frame, in large shaky pencil scribbles. The picture frame held Edward VI enmeshed in his rectangle of a world, with the scorpion dust and the cobwebs with which he had been living since the first day my mother dragged me to school. I noticed that there was just a little ghost of a smile coming from his face to mine. And I began to smile. And the headmaster himself stopped smiling. And he watched my smile. He mistook my smile for something that was not a smile. And again the whip cracked, *whapp!* and then, in a jiffy, Edward VI's face drifted from me, like the view from a window after the first few rain drops hit the pane. And the headmaster laughed. And then for no reason, a little pin-voice of a snigger, somewhere on the horizon of the sea of faces, giggled. And that made the headmaster stiffen.

'Who' that?'

The school was dumb. The assistant masters stiffened. They stood like small men, made out of limestone. I could feel the movement of many consciences; and the shuffling of the feet of uneasiness, as if each one of those boys was searching inside himself, deep deep down, debating whether he should inform on the culprit, as the headmaster called us, or whether he should remain silent, and suffer with the entire school while the headmaster raged and romped on one of his frequent flogging orgies.

'I say who' that laugh-out just now?' And then his body relaxed. 'All right, then…' He had made only a few false steps in the direction of the nearest class when a little voice, similar to the voice that dared to whisper, said, 'Me, sir! Is me who laugh-out, sir.'

Tears were in the small boy's eyes. I felt so sorry for him, although we were in the same predicament. He was a very fragile, effeminate boy, the son of Mister Fuguero, the village shopkeeper. But the headmaster disregarded his size. It seemed, by the cruelty he let loose on this little boy, that there was a deep bitterness in his heart for the fact that the boy had such a rich father. And so, he hurled a tannery of blows on the boy's shoulders and on his buttocks and on his legs and on his hands when he put them up to shield the ubiquitous whip from knocking out his eyes. And all the time, the headmaster was laughing and singing the song:

> 'Ring the bells, merrilee;
> Ring, loud and long…'

and all the time the assistant masters were laughing 'kiff–hiff–kiff!' and some of the boys were laughing too; and the little boy, Mister Fuguero's son, was screeching and shrieking and hollering and calling out for his mother and his father to come and take the headmaster off him. And then his voice disappeared under the tide of his emotion, until all we could hear was the noise of the headmaster's whip, and the kiff–hiff–kiff! of the assistant masters which punctuated the terrible silence of this tragedy.

When it was all over, the headmaster was fagged out; wringing wet like a dish rag. Panting, he retreated from the little boy who had wet himself, and who was peering stupidly at the warm veins of water sliding down his legs from under his short khaki pants.

Satan was in him now. He decided to deal with me. He said I was a crook. That crooks didn't have no damn right to be in school. Crooks should be lock-up in Glendairy Prison-house, he said. And they should be cutting limestone in the prison rock quarry, not learning Scriptures. And after this, he called me by a big word: a delinquent. But I did not know what one looked like, because I had never seen one of them in my life.

His first blow landed on an old wound. I thought I felt blood squirting all over the back of my shirt; and between my tears, I imagined the blood squirting all over the schoolroom, drenching the boys and the assistant masters. And I was glad for this brutality. I was very glad, because now I was showing them how I was suffering; and I was showing them how great was the suffering our headmaster could inflict. The second one: *whapp!* In the same place as the first. Now the blood seemed to be rising like the waves in the sea, near the Hastings Rocks. And they rolled and came and smashed against the concrete walls of the schoolroom; and suddenly, miraculously, they changed from blood into water sprays. And all the boys and all the assistant masters were scampering to the sides of the room, trying to escape from the drowning turbulence of the waves and the sprays of blood. And Edward VI changed his expression from a glimpse of a smile; and he was now choking with laughter; and the other faces in the room, dead faces, faces imprisoned in their old gold-painted picture frames, these faces burst out of their frames, and choked with laughter, and chuckled and opened their mouths wide wide…

I stopped counting at the tenth lash. I would really kill the headmaster. I would have to kill him, because he was a cruel man. Because, too, he seemed to take such a strange delight in beating me. He liked to beat me. Willy-Willy, my mother's friend, told me one night, that the headmaster liked beating boys. He was a 'missy-missy' man, Willy-Willy said. He was a 'she-she' man. Perhaps that was why he expressed this strange affection on me; and I wondered why.

And when the storm abated; and the waves were calm again, and placid; and the faces on the walls, the faces of the assistant masters and the faces of the men and women wearing crowns on their heads, and scorpions and dust on their lips returned to their serious imprisonment within their golden frames; and I had opened my eyes, I could see the boys in front of me, slightly blurred, and looking like many many sea-cobblers floating together in the calm sea. I could see the headmaster's face relax; and a happiness appeared on it. Now he was as pleased as a child. All around me, I could hear the voices of the schoolroom, rambling on in the tone and manner of a funeral, saying the Commandments. And I felt good. Better. Washed out, christened and chastened by the terrible flogging; and so I joined them reciting the Laws of God.

We travelled through the Commandments five times. The headmaster waited until we finished the last Commandment, and then he raised his voice above our voices, and guided us through them once more. When it was all over, finally, he took his little tuning fork from his waistcoat pocket, put it to his ear, removed it from his ear, struck it lightly on the desk nearest him, hummed a note which the tuning fork told him about, and then he encouraged us to join him and the tuning fork.

'Music!' he said.

Dinnnnnnnnnnngggggg!

'Do-re-me-fah-lah!' he sang, in his deep rich baritone voice. All of us, including the assistant masters, echoed 'Do-re-me-fah-lah!' like a crowd of angels with one voice. He struck the fork again, and a louder, higher note came out. It was a very musical instrument. (In my happier moments at school, I would pray to grow up quickly, and get a good job in the rose gardens of the rich people who lived out the Front Road, or get a job fielding tennis balls in the Garrison Savannah Tennis Club for two shillings a week, and with this income, buy myself a tuning fork. But one day, when I told this ambition to Miss Brewster, she slapped me around my ears, and told me, sternly, not to say those things again. Little black boys should not desire to work in those jobs for white people, she said. It was not uplifting, she told me.) *Teeniinnnnnggg!* said the tuning fork again, as if it were laughing at all of us. The headmaster said in a very loud voice, 'Do-re-me-soll!'; and once more his band of angels said, 'Do-re-me-soll!'

Satisfied that we had the correct key, the correct chord, the correct pitch, he announced, 'Rule Britannia!' The Union Jacks in the room with us seemed to swell with pride, and flap and flex their muscles, although no wind, save the wind from our mouths, was blowing in the room. The men and women in the picture frames smiled. And immediately we rushed like horses, wild with the knowledge of this song, and bolted into a startlingly loud harmony:

> '*Rule Britannia, Britannia rules the waves;*
> *Britons, never-never-ne-verr shall be slaves!*'

and singing, I saw the kings and the queens in the room with us, laughing in a funny way, and smiling and happy with us. The headmaster was soaked in glee. And I imagined all the glories of Britannia, our Motherland, Britannia so dear to us all, and so free; Britannia, who, or what or which, had brought us out of the ships crossing over from the terrible seas from Africa, and had placed us on this island, and had given us such good headmasters and assistant masters, and such a nice vicar to teach us how to pray to God – and he had come from England; and such nice white people who lived on the island with us, and who gave us jobs watering their gardens and taking out their garbage, most of which we found delicious enough to eat... all through the ages, all through the years of history; from the Tudors on the wall, down through the Stuarts also on the wall, all through the Elizabethans and including those men and women singing in their hearts with us, hanging dead and distant on our schoolroom walls; Britannia, who, or what or which, had ruled the waves all these hundreds of years, all these thousands and millions of years, and had kept us on the island, happy – the island of Barbados (Britannia the Second), free from all invasions. Not even the mighty Germans; not even the Russians whom our headmaster said were dressed in red, had dared to come within submarine distance of our island! Britannia who saw to it that all Britons (we on the island were, beyond doubt, little black Britons, just like the white big Britons up in Britannialand. The headmaster told us so!) –*never-never-ne-verr, shall be slaves*! On and on we romped and played on the waves of freedom in the song; on the waves of the oceans, our oceans, filled with the sailing ships of Britannialand; and with the men and women wearing crowns who were from Britannialand...

The waves raged and our voices raged like the waves. The headmaster was sweating; but it was a joyful sweat which was pouring down his face. And as he opened his mouth wide wide wide, and the words and pieces of biscuits came out, and some of his perspiration went in… and the assistant masters trying to please him with their loud voices of tenor, alto and bass, everything in that small schoolroom was joy and happiness and strength… the strength of having lived in Britannialand.

But at last it was all finished. Done with. But not the headmaster. He wanted to sweep us on the wings of horses, and he announced, 'Ride On, Ride On, In Majesty'. But before we could muster our courage, and gain our pomp, to ride on to death, a head appeared at the window at the front of the school. Hunger pains came back to me like a rusty nail in my guts.

'Pssssssst!'

Heads turned. Voices lagged. The men and women on the walls shook their heads and their crowns in reproof. The headmaster frowned; and a cloud of darkness settled like an all-day rain on his face. But when he saw who it was who had dared to interrupt him, the cloud disappeared, and the sun came out again on his face. It was Shortie, the school messenger.

Shortie was about forty-five years old. And he was the only man living, who could, and did, dare to whisper to the headmaster while he was conducting. The headmaster held his hand in the air, giving us the signal to stop. He went to the window to talk to Shortie. Shortie removed his hat and rested it on his chest. And he said in a conspirator's voice that was so low that we could not hear nor understand, 'Whizzzzy-whizzy-whizzzzy…'

The headmaster smiled: a soundless laugh. He wiped the sweat of the song from his face and from the top of his head with a dirty handkerchief, which I remembered had been white when he brought it to school on Monday morning.

'School lay-by!'

Boys and benches and desks and slates on which we wrote our lessons (there were few exercise books in our village) and feet and assistant masters were scrambling out. The headmaster called us all back, and made us walk out slowly, like soldiers on a parade square. But I walked slowly, insolently slow.

Shortie was still talking to the headmaster when I got outside. They were standing beside the outdoor closet which we boys used. I entered the closet, closed the door, put my ears close to the door to listen, and my eyeballs to the keyhole. Shortie was talking.

'Man, be-Christ! Looka, Blackman, man, I thought you wasn't going stop that damn Britannia-thing! All you teaching them boys is singing, singing, be-Christ! Every afternoon, all you doing is singing, singing…'

'Ease me up, Shortie! That is eddication, too!' And he laughed. 'But how you make-out with the roses and the fruits?'

Shortie hawked up a mouthful of spittle and spat it on the ground two inches from the headmaster's feet. 'Well, let we look at the transaction this way. I went 'round by the Marine Hotel after spending the whole blasted forenoon and afternoon walking up to every white lady' door, without success. Because, as you know, Blackman, man, the tourisses not coming in in droves this time o' year. Also, so knowing that provisions like roses and fruits don't keep long in this kind o' bad hot weather, I had was to get rid o' them real fast to the nearest bidder. And that happen to be the white lady what gives out her clothes to Mistress Sobers to wash, Mistress Sobers who have a little boy coming to school to you school; and then…'

'But, Jesus! Shortie, that lady have her own-own rose gardens!'

'That ain't nothing, Blackman, man. That ain't no problem! It don't matter if I happen to carry coals to Newcastle this time. She buy them. And that is what count. And I treating you like a real man, now. I treating you real nice, man. Fifty-fifty! Look, Blackman, I have seven shilling' to put inside your hand right now.'

'How much you get for the things?'

'Fourteen shilling' 'pon account, and a 'nother…'

'But oh Jesus Christ, Shortie! To *them*, it worth two-times that amount!'

Shortie ignored him. He felt inside his hip pocket for the money. He dropped the coins noisily into the headmaster's hand. And without counting them, the headmaster pushed them into his waistcoat pocket. 'And when next week come, when the end-o'-the-week come round next time, Blackman, I have a 'nother seven bob to hand over to you. Heh-heh!'

'You not two-timing me, eh, Shortie?'

'Two-timing you, Blackman? Blackman, look at me! Look in my face! Tell me, *iffing* you ever had the occasion to have suspicions 'bout my transactions with you? No, no, oh Christ, man! Don't laugh in my face, and say a thing like that, man! Don't give me no damn hee-hee-laugh, Blackman. Tell me right now, in front o' my face, *iffing*...'

'Hold yuh horses, Shortie! I tired as arse from teaching Scriptures and Music this afternoon, man... but, don't tie-me-up, eh?'

'Blackman, look at me! Good Jesus Christ, man, you like forgetting that I stand up 'pon more than one or two occasion and face your madam, and tell she you wasn't in a certain woman house, when you *know*...'

'Bygones be bygones, Shortie. I trusts you. You in my confidences.'

They went on talking about the roses. Our school gardens contained the most beautiful roses in the island. We never won any prizes for learning to write; but we won all the prizes for gardening. The number of rich white people who lived near our school must have had something to do with this. But the headmaster never told us the reason. He made us plant and weed and water and prune and cut the roses. Red roses, pink roses, white roses, blue roses!... All kinds of roses! But the headmaster and Shortie reaped them and sold them to the white people and the tourists at the hotel. Shortie spent most of his share in Mister Fuguero's Rum Shop; but nobody knew what the headmaster did with his. And sometimes, when Shortie got blind stinking drunk, he would scream and yell and say that Blackman was an arse, that all he did was to bathe his wife with blows, breed her twice a year, and keep her busy with children. And Mistress Blackman, a very thin woman with lines of grief and matrimony on her face, would come down to the school the afternoon when the teachers got their small brown pay envelopes, and complain aloud in the hearing of the assistant masters and in the ear-sight of the boys, that she didn't know what the bloody hell the headmaster did with the money he got from the Government for being headmaster; that she had seven half-starved children running around naked at home, and so on, and so on...

'Gorblummuh!' the headmaster was saying, as if he was a gramophone record stuck in its tracks. 'Gorblummuh! Look, Shortie, don't two-time me with that next seven bob, eh?'

Something thick came up in my throat, and I had to cough. The headmaster looked around with a jerk of his head. He came to the closet door, and flung it open. My trousers were in my hands, and I was pulling them up. He laughed, and closed the door. But I was coming out anyhow.

'Oh! is you, eh, Sobers?'

'Yessir, I was just going to the closet to number-two, sir.'

'Number-two, eh, Sobers?' There was a strange, great kindness in his voice.

'Yessir, Mister Blackman, sir.'

'Shortie, this boy Sobers is a damn fine student. Onliest thing he ain't have much manners. Eh, Sobers? But, Shortie, Sobers here is one of my finest gardeners. Say how'd to your mother please, Sobers, when you get home. And tell Mistress Sobers she hads better put some coconut oil and things on them scratches you happen' to get this afternoon.'

'Yessir, Mister Blackman, sir.'

'Cause, if not, they might turn-out and get information in them, and turn into a real bad sore, or something. Eh, Sobers?'

'Yessir, Mister Blackman, sir.'

'Good boy! Well, good evening, Sobers.'

'Good evening, sir, Mister Blackman, sir. Good evening, Mister Shortie.'

'Ain't that boy a damn mannerly boy?'

'All right, boy!' Shortie said.

'Something good in that boy. But it pain me to had to give him a real stiff cut-arse this afternoon for stealing a six-cent piece…'

'But, Blackman, as I was telling you, you ain' have no damn business suspecting me, man, 'cause I is a man, and you is a man. And I stand up and argue strong strong in your favours, and more than… What you say just now?'

''Bout the money?'

'You say something just now 'bout beating that boy?'

'Cut his arse going and coming! Give him the best cut-arse I ever administer in my forty years' teaching school. Heh-heh-heh!'

'Gorblummuh, Blackman, you know what you do?'

'Jesus, Shortie! When that tam'rind whip crash-in in his backside, he fly-up in the air like a piece o' lightning! Heh-heh-heh!'

'Blackman? Blackman? Stop laughing, 'cause this ain't no blasted laughing matter! Stop laughing and lis'en to me, man.'

'Uh-huh?'

'You remember some time back, two or three years gone by, that one dark night three policemens run back down to the Main Guard with their hand break in two places?'

'You talking 'bout the Bulldozer!... a fellar name' Nathan!'

'Be-Christ! that is who I talking 'bout!'

'Yeah, the Bulldozer was a terrible man. He beat them three policemens, and then he turn' 'round and beat up the inspector what came up...'

'Well, you know who Nathan is?'

'Who Nathan the Bulldozer is?'

'That boy... that boy Sobers what just went down through that school gate is to call Nathan father...'

'Jesus Christ Almighty!'

'You just make a mistake, Blackman! You make a sad little mistake when you touch' that man' son...'

'But I been under the impression that the short fellar Willy-Willy was Sobers' father. 'Cause once or twice, I have see' Willy-Willy with the boy' mother.'

'You been under the wrong impressions, Blackman.'

'But I thought...'

'You has thought *wrong*!'

Drifting away from Shortie, who was still talking to the headmaster, I carried a deep hatred in my heart, deep deep down. There was no one in sight when I left the school. The church, as usual at this time of afternoon, was deserted. The sexton was watering the graves of the dead. He was wearing his old black-and-mauve cassock. The tall headstones and gravestones in the burying ground were shining in the sun. And the mayflower trees were talking to the two conceited palm trees – (my mother was going to scream like hell the moment she found out about my cuts. And my father was going to curse Blackman and the Education Board and the Government for making Blackman a headmaster. But I was not sure I would find him. He did not live with my mother and me in the small shack. And if I did find him, under the tree in the Pasture where he gambled and lived from one playing card to the next, he might be too dead drunk even to talk to me) – which looked like two gigantic boa constrictors; and the shining barks of the mayflower trees crawling with the sunlight, and sprinkled with flowers of yellow and red, were shaking ever so gently, just like the old woman who came to church and sat in the seat at the rear and fell asleep just as the vicar was going into the pulpit. It was peaceful; and it was quiet. Quiet quiet quiet, so soon after the sadness of school.

Above my head where the sexton was watering the dead, on the side of the road on which I was walking home, the tall grey church wall walked silently along with me. I felt like a man, like that man the headmaster told us about, walking walking walking over the desert, the Arabian Desert; and he did not even have a stone in sight, so that he might kick his foot on it, and break up the monotony of his long, unchanging sad journey home. Alone, and without the voices of my friends…

Over the church wall, suddenly, hopped a crowd of boys. They formed themselves on either side of the road. And I had to walk through their ranks; through this boisterous, jeering, laughing guard of honour, led by Lester. I got near the end of their ranks; and the ranks closed about me. And the jeers turned me back. And when I turned to run, that end was shut tight by their jeers. I was in the middle, and they were closing in on me; and backing away as I held up both fists in fear, and challenged them out of fright to fight. But they did not fight. They did not want to fight. They only wanted to jeer. They were not interested in fighting. They pressed in on me and jeered; and they backed away and jeered: opening and closing their ranks like the bellows of a horrible concertina playing a horrible tune. 'Thief! thief! thief!' they shouted.

'Come and fight! Fight! fight! fight!' I heard my voice shrieking back at them.

'Thief! thief!' They pressed in, and when I thought I could

smash my fist into them, they backed away and laughed. 'His father is a jailbird! And he is a damn thief! Thief! thief! His father is a jailbird! Thief! thief! thief!'

But they would not fight. I wanted to spill blood. I wanted to make contact with something, even the church wall, or with the hard bony faces that pressed in on me. I wanted to pour out my feelings for the headmaster on something hard, to fight, fight, fight… But they only jeered.

'Thief! thief! thief!…'

I dashed to the gutter for some stones; and I raised my head to take aim. Tears in my eyes, I got up, aimed, and holding over me was a woman, Miss Brewster, the headmistress of the girls' school. My enemies ran. And I was left behind, alone with their jeers in my ears, and my own tears in my eyes – and with Miss Brewster.

'Thief! thief! thief!'

2

And when I could see again, clearly, and when I opened my eyes and lifted myself out of the gutter with the dust and the bits of old dried cane peelings and the horse droppings, Miss Brewster dusted off my clothes, and she ran her second finger over her tongue and wiped the saliva that was there on the bruises on my knees. And it felt good.

'They won't fight. They won't fight.'

'Never mind. Never mind, son.'

She pressed me against her skirts; and she ran her fat warm hands around my neck. And like this, we walked the remaining quarter mile to my home. No one, not even the headmaster, would dare to call me names, now that Miss Brewster was walking beside me, as my guardian angel.

We drew near the girls' school, Miss Brewster's School, as we called it. She dropped her hand from around my neck and told me to wait at the gate. This school belonged to Miss Brewster; and Miss Brewster to the school. She had dared two world wars, and a riot in the island plus an epidemic of yellow fever touched with typhoid fever, and still she refused to die, refused to resign as headmistress of *her* school. Now, she was as old as the hills. But no one dared say aloud how old she was. And she would tell no one. Miss Brewster was strong. Age could not come near to her, could not touch her, except to rub its fingers through her hair, and leave it white and silvery. My mother attended this school, Miss Brewster's School. She went to school until she was fifteen years old. But one month after her birthday, one October day, she found her stomach gradually getting bigger, although she might be eating less; and then Miss Brewster, and all the older women in the village, discovered the reason: I was hiding somewhere inside her womb.

The dying clammy-cherry tree in front of the school was standing up like a watchman, tired of watching, and tired of standing. I was watching it, when Miss Brewster came out with a large paper bag in her hand. She opened it, and I saw she had biscuits in it. The biscuits were the biscuits the Government gave us poor children to help nourish our little bones while we sat in school and learned. She gave me one biscuit; and she put the bag into her lunch basket. And she gave me a look which told me that I was not to mention that I saw her taking home the school biscuits. She then locked the school door, unlocked it, locked it again, and shook it many times, with great force – as if she were trying to break the door down. She mumbled to me about the great loss of biscuits and Carnation milk, and having to call the police every morning to take fingerprints from the biscuits that remained.

'Every morning, every morning,' she was mumbling. 'Every blessid morning. Biscuits gone! Carnation milk gone! Lord have His Mercy! Every blessid morning I open this school door, and I *know* I going to face some sort o' larcenies or thefts. Mondee morning, two glass windows breaken… broken. Tuesday morning, they come again, and they not satisfied with thiefing the biscuits and milk, but Lord have mercy! they break another window in the mistresses lunch room. Thiefing thiefing thiefing! This village is a village o' thiefs!'

She walked around the school, checked every window and door, and then came back to the main entrance. She took the key out of her handbag, unlocked the door, slammed it shut with a great bang, and then locked it again.

'Take that! Lemme see if a thief going break down that tonight!' And she looked at me, and winked her left eye, and then her right eye, as if she and I were two thieves conspiring to break down the door ourselves. She pocketed the key as if it were the key to her own door; looked around the playing field again; and then, slowly, proudly, with dignity and with care, descended the broken concrete steps like a queen of Sheba.

'You find that father o' yourn yet?' she asked me, when we reached the road. 'You mustn' grow up to be like your father, eh, son?'

'No, ma'am, Mistress Brewster.'

'Good!'

'Yes, ma'am.'

''Cause you know what happen' to *him*!'

'Yes, ma'am.'

'Sometime tomorrow, I want you to come 'cross by me and clean out the pig pen, hear?'

'Yes, ma'am, Mistress Brewster.'

'And I have a nice little book with pictures in it, to give to you… 'bout a nice little boy, name' Jesus. You know who I talking 'bout?'

'Yes, ma'am. Jesus.'

'Yes. You read that book and you will be a more better boy. And nobody wouldn't be able to look at you and say that you take after your father, and that you is no thief. You hear me, son?'

'Yes, ma'am.'

'Right! You learn good in school. Get yuh eddication. Yes, son. Get eddication and move outta this place. Don't set your affections 'pon nothing on the ground! Set your affections 'pon things above! You lis'ning to me? Good! Don't you set your affections 'pon no gard'ner-job, nor no job fielding tennis balls down at the Garrison Savannah where those gentlemens and ladies from Away does play tennis. Them is backwards things. I wants you to set your affections 'pon something more higher than running 'bout the place in a blue suit picking up tennis balls when somebody hit it outta the tennis court, you hear me? And furthermore, I wants you to come 'cross by me every afternoon after you done doing your duties for that mother o' yourn, and let me and you sit down with a book in our hand, and learn some eddication. You take a' example from Franklin. You know what progress and headways Franklin make?'

'Yes, ma'am. Franklin gone 'way to England to learn at a school name' Oxford and Cambridge University.'

'Yes. That is progress! Franklin didn' spend his time fielding tennis balls. Franklin spend his time reading books. You take the thing from my Godson, Franklin, and you learn. Learn! Hear?'

'Yes, Mistress Brewster, ma'am.'

'But I can't take you this afternoon, though. 'Cause I have a

Mothers' Union meeting to attend at the church.' We were coming near my house now. Miss Brewster slackened her pace, and put her warm hand around my neck again. 'Yes! That's good, son... learning! Learning! All the little boys in this village running outta the schoolroom 'pon a' afternoon, and they running into the rich people' rose garden, watering garden, fielding tennis balls, going for milk, Lord, I don't know how we old mens and womens could call weselves teachers o' youths, and we can't place more goodness and ambitions in them children's heart! But anyhow. Son, learning is your only escape. And try hard not to take after that father o' yourn. He ain' no example.'

'Yes, ma'am.'

'Your mother still killing sheself washing clothes for that white lady out the Front Road?'

'Yes, ma'am. Mammy still does washing.'

'She going break her back if she ain't careful! But, poor soul! She have her troubles, poor soul!'

'Mammy had all the lady' clothes done wash' and starched last Thursdee when the rain come down, and...'

'Oh loss!' Miss Brewster rolled her eyes around and around in her head, and looked up at the skies, and sighed as if she were in pain. 'But how old you is now, son? You must be reach high-school age.'

'I is nine, ma'am.'

'Nine? And... and you still is in First Standard? Boy, you is in great great need o' learning and eddication. We have to do something 'bout that, anyhow. Well, look, son, you better run 'long now, and help your mother...'

Smoke, the fortune-teller of food cooking, was pumping itself through the tall weeds and tomato vines around our house; and through the small window of the detached kitchen shack and through the countless cracks and crevices of the paling that kept my mother's business from the eyes of the village.

My mother and I lived here. Apart from Willy-Willy, no other man came to our house. My father fell by the wayside from her love. And she never looked at another man – except to sit in the darkened front room with Willy-Willy and me, and talk ghost stories and tell tales far far into the night, until I could see goblins and spirits and duppies and vampires oozing through every crack in the old house. But I was her only man.

Fish were sizzling in the frying pan, and crying out with loud hisses as she added water, or more oil, or something in the pan. Apart from the thoroughness with which she flogged me, nothing could she do better than cook. A man's voice was coming through the paling. When I opened the gate, Willy-Willy's voice was loud, straining to be heard above the rebellion of the fish and the water and the oil in the pan, and my mother's own shouts, 'Jesus God! this frying pan hot as hell! Hot, hot, hot!'

'Don't burn down the blasted house, darling love,' Willy-Willy shouted, above the hiss of the pan. 'Don't burn it down, man! In any case, though, I don't mind if you burn down the house, once you don't burn down the fish, too! Heh-heh-heh!'

'Heh-heh-haiii! You laugh! Laugh, Willy-Willy.'

'But as I was saying. Gorblummuh, man! I travel up and down this damn world… I travel 'pon the high seas and the low seas, and I still insist and maintain that the 'Mericans is more better people than the English people. Them English people too damn *tight*! Take for instance, the sailors what comes in 'pon them man-o'-wars. Them whores down in Settle Street does have the time o' their lifes trying to make breakfast outta them limey-bastards. But take the 'Mericans, now. Gorblummuh, darling love, is dollars and cents what them boys does throw 'bout Bridgetown when a 'Merican ship come in! And you know what else? You know what…'

'I is not a whore, Willy-Willy. So, I won't know.'

'I not referring to you as a whore, man. I not so low as to do that. 'Cause, I inside your house now waiting for something to eat. And I won't do a thing like that. I just drawing a reference base' on certain facts and figures what I come to a' understanding with, due to the fact that as I said just now, I is a man what travel this world upside-down, and downside-up.'

'I know. I know, Willy-Willy. I just making jokes.'

'Them is damn funny jokes!'

'Behave yuhself, man.'

'Mammy, Mistress Brewster say how-d.'

'And I stating and affirming, furthermore, darling love, that all this kiss-me-arse noise you hears 'bout this island 'bout how Brit'n is this, and Brit'n is that… Where the hell you come from, boy? You is a ghost? That you appearing and nobody ain't seeing how and when you appearing?'

'Who' that, Willy?'

'Your boy-child come in here like if he is something rising up outta a grave!'

'You boy! You ain't have no damn manners? Lis'ning to big people talk? Boy, where your damn manners? You intends growing up like a damn animul, like your father? Say good evening to Willy-Willy.'

'I say good evening already, Mammy.'

'Say good evening again! Say good evening again!'

'Good evening, Mister Willy-Willy.'

'All right, boy!'

'Looka, boy! Go an take off my good clothes offa your backside, and dress yourself in yuh home-clothes, do! And don't sit down in there whilst big people talking. Come come! Get out here and find something to do. Yuh left for school this morning without cleaning out the fowl pen. And be-Christ! don't let me catch you like last night sitting down in there burning out all my kerosene oil outta the lamp, saying you reading books, you hear! Oil too blasted dear these days for you to sit down and waste-out all my oil! Go on, Willy-Willy, dear. I lis'ning to you.'

'What I was talking 'bout?'

'You was saying something 'bout them cheap bastards from up in England.'

'Oh, yes! Darling love, as I affirming to you, I am a man who have travel round this globe what Christopher Columbus discover' in 1492…'

'Who? Who dis-what in 1492?'

'Them is advance' thoughts, darling love. You won't understand them. So forget it. But I telling you…'

'Beg pardon, Willy-Willy. But could you lend me a shilling. I have to buy starch to put in that white lady' clothes this evening.'

'Oh Christ, man! I just spend the last six-cents piece I own and possess. I sorry sorry, man. But I just come from out by Fuguero, and be-Christ! it is a damn good thing Fuguero know I is a reliable customer, 'cause he had to trust me with...'

'All right, all right. Look, you boy, come here!'

'Yes, Mammy?'

'Blow you! You ain' take off them clothes yet? I not send you inside half hour ago to take off them clothes?'

'Yes, Mammy.'

'And why the hell you ain' take them off?'

'I was taking them off when you call' just now, Mammy.'

'Well, anyhow, keep them on!' She did something to the frying pan, and immediately she disappeared from me in a volcano of smoke. I began to wish that when the smoke cleared she would not be there. But when the smoke cleared, she was there anyhow. And I was frightened that she might not have been there; and I asked God for forgiveness in my heart; and I felt very shaky. 'I just put these two-three fish head in the pan, and they ain't done-ing for some time yet... Willy-Willy, beg pardon, boy! I here talking to this ram-goat what I gave birth to.'

'I understand, darling love.'

'...So, you run back out, up by the Marine Hotel, and wait till you see Girlie come to work. And when you see Girlie come to work, tell 'er please to lend me a shilling. If she say she can't spare a shilling, tell 'er to make it twelve cents, then. 'Cause I flat-*broke* as the devil in hell!'

She said nothing more. The volcano erupted again, this time silently, and again she was lost from my sight. And I did not wish any evil thoughts. Willy-Willy went on talking. But I was eating the smells of the fish heads; and I was waiting until the smoke cleared to see if she would say something else; or if she would notice me standing there, and offer me a half-done fish head.

'...And talking 'bout 'Merican mens bring' me to talk 'bout 'Merican womens. Darling love, them 'Mericans is the sweetest sons-uh-bitches in this Christ's world...'

'What you standing up there for, like a overgrown billy-goat? You not heard me just send you on a' errand? I need that money to buy starch with to starch that white lady' clothes with. Today is Thursdee. Willy-Willy just say he broke. And I still have to get that damn bundle o' clothes back in that whore's house before twelve o'clock noon on Sa'rday.'

But it seemed so cruel for her to send me just then on an errand, when the hot fish heads were wriggling in the hot oil, until they seemed so brown and crisp as if stricken by a delicious bout of palsy... and all this was making my stomach ache. I moved away just as she was about to swing a fist at me. She didn't even think of putting a handful of steaming rice in my hand, to send me warm and rejoicing on my way. All she was interested in was listening to Willy-Willy's dirty stories; and laughing with him, as if the two of them had won the Grand Prize. But perhaps she, too, had had a rough day. Perhaps she was only laughing because she had already cried the whole day; and since nothing had happened to cheer her up, she had decided to laugh on the outside, and cry on the inside. Perhaps it was that. The smokescreen went up again; but she was still visible. She grumbled something, and said, 'Heh, take this!' And the warm fish head slipped and skated about in the grease in my left palm...

I was to borrow a shilling, or a sixpence, from Girlie. Girlie lived next door to us. She worked at the hotel, doing something – not working in the kitchen. She used to work in the kitchen years before; but when they found out that the stores were disappearing faster than they were eaten up by the tourists, the manager of the hotel set Macdonald, the night watchman, on guard; and one night, after a great hassle, he made Girlie take down her panties, and two chicken legs dropped out, with four hard-boiled eggs. From that night, Girlie was employed doing something else – but not in the kitchen. And it was through the persistence of Girlie that I first tasted the taste of turkey, when I was nine years old. She had brought it out late, and cold, and crumpled, in a paper bag which was wet and leaking from the cold rice she buried the turkey in.

The money I was to get from Girlie, my mother would have to buy starch with; and with the starch she would starch the clothes she washed and ironed for the tall foreign white woman who lived alone in a large stone mansion, ten times the size of our house, out the Front Road. This woman was very mysterious to me. She never went to work like the other women in my village.

48

She never left the house. And I wondered how she got so much money to buy all the things she had in her house: a large white thing which kept food and things cold and fresh, and which made them last three or four or five times longer than the salted pig's head which we corned in a jar; a radiogram which brought foreign voices speaking foreign tongues right into her living-room cluttered with beautiful furniture; and a chandelier which told the time of day and the time of night by its musical clinkings when her head touched it. And whenever I knocked at her back door – because my mother told me never, never, never knock at the front door of this powerful white lady – and she would come to answer it, her eyes red as fire, as if she was sleeping for days and days, with a drink in her hand, rattling the ice cubes around and around in her glass. And once, she gave me an ice cube: the first ice cube that ever played its chilly spine-tingling games in the palms of my hands.

My mother received from this wealthy white lady, every Saturday at exactly seven minutes past twelve noon, exactly five shillings for washing a large bundle of clothes, which took my mother five days to complete. The clothes consisted of innumerable dresses of expensive sea island cotton; silk and linen handkerchiefs; countless panties; slips and brassières which looked as if the white lady's breasts were still in them, although invisible. And there would be many many pillowcases and many many sheets with a strange mark in the centre of the sheets. My mother scrubbed out the marks; but she never commented on them.

One time, my mother decided to steal one of these countless pillowcases. Our two pillowcases were beginning to look like fishing nets. But when she took the clothes to the lady that Saturday afternoon; and the lady counted them, and realized that two pillowcases were missing, she made such a stinking fuss, and threatened to throw my mother in jail for petty larceny, that my mother, drenched in shame and in tears, ran home and dragged the pillowcases off our bed, and spent the whole night that night washing, rinsing, starching and ironing the white lady's pillowcases. Nobody in our circle of friends in the village ever understood why one woman could possess so many clothes and so much laundry.

And once, out of girlish wickedness, my mother leaned over her paling, and called out next door for Girlie to come and see how many 'panties one woman could own and possess'. And Girlie came with her eyes staring wild.

'Girlie! Girlie! Drop whatever the hell you doing, and come in here now, this very minute! I have something special to show to you. Come and see how *people*, how *decent people* does live.' And Girlie, always malicious, always waiting for some gossip on which to chew her cud, appeared like a spectre in our gateway.

'Lord Jesus Jesus Jesus!' Her breath left her, when she saw my mother hold up twenty-four pairs of panties in her hands – all white! 'Jesus God! Mistress Sobers, you mean to tell me that one woman... one *person*... Mistress Sobers, one human being does wear *all* them things? Lord Lord have His mercy!'

And my mother said, superiorly, with a certain inside knowledge of white people that Girlie could never boast of, 'Darling, sugar, you wait till you see *these*!' She brought out more panties. Girlie rolled her eyes around and around in her eyeballs in amazement. 'You just wait till I get my hand 'pon a piece o' change. Just wait! I going to go down in that Cave Shepherd Store in Broad Street, and buy-up ever' blasted pink trousers they have in my size!'

The two of them shook their heads from side to side in wonder, pondering and puzzling over the strange fact in front of them: that one woman could ever think of purchasing so many underclothes.

'You think she does wear all these?' Girlie asked. 'Be-Christ, if she wear' one for breakfast, one for lunch, one for dinner, and then turn 'round and put on one to go to bed in, gorblummuh! Mistress Sobers, she could still rent out half-dozen every day! Lord Lord Jesus!'

'But notice something. Notice something basic,' my mother pointed out. 'Notice what is so damn important 'bout this case we examining. Child, look! You have to observe the ways o' white people with both your damn eye' wide wide wide open! Notice how these people does operate. Child, I telling you...' She went on to shake her head from side to side, with the ponderousness of the opinion she was about to express. 'Them white people, them blasted white people is some funny funny, smart bitches. Now, tell me… a black person… *iffing* she was in possession, if she was in a position, money-wise, to own and possess all these underwears… you think they would buy *all* in *one* colour? You think that any black person you know, or I know, in their right senses, would go down in Town… *catch a bus to go down in Town*… and come back with twenty-*fourrrr*… twenty-sev'n pair' o' underwears, all in one blasted colour? And white ones at that?'

And Girlie shook her head, saying no.

'No!' my mother agreed. 'No! Them would have to buy up all the colours in the rainbow! Black, pink, purple, blue, red, cream, and then, *maybe*, when they run outta colours, maybe, *maybe* – white! *Maybe*.'

'But look how these white sons-uh-guns does do things, eh, Mistress Sobers?'

'Learning, darling! Eddication! They have it all up here!' My mother touched her head to show Girlie. 'They have all what we wants, bad bad bad, right up here. Up here!'

And these two women, mystified that any sane person, white or black, would buy so many pieces of underclothing, all the same colour, stood for a long time, in silence, and pondered on the motive for this abnormal behaviour. The motive was beyond them. The lines and knots in their faces, and the worry in their eyes, said so. But most of all, perhaps, they were worried by the behaviour of white people in general – the same white people whom they saw only at intervals, and knew only through the back door, or from the garden, or from the steaming kitchen.

With my mother, everything was routine. The routine of steel. On Mondays, she soaked the dirty clothes from the white lady in a large wooden tub (in which she gave me my weekly baths), and threw washing soda and Glauber's salts in the water. On Tuesdays, she rinsed the clothes through five sets of water, and threw blueing in the water. And then she hung them on the clothes lines which ran like the arteries of an old woman's hand throughout our backyard. On Wednesdays, she rinsed them again; and again she added blueing. Then came Thursday. Thursday was the most trying day in her life of washing clothes for white people. And Thursday became, in my life, a terrible Remembrance Day. For if on Thursday afternoon the clothes had been given their doses of starch, and the rain had come and had found the clothes and my mother napping, then the whole process would have to be suffered through once more, right from the beginning. So, on Thursdays, I kept, through my instinct of self-preservation, very very far from my mother. Beginning soon after I left for school in the morning, she would hold her two hundred pounds over that huge wooden tub; and she would rub the clothes until her fat melted into drops of perspiration into the tub of clothes and water; and she would soak the clothes in certain apportioned doses of starch (and the starch would have to be boiled and boiled properly, not too tightly but with the required, proper thickness); and she 'would drown ever' blasted piece o' shift, saving that woman' silk trousers'; and then she would hang them up to dry on the lines. And then, fagged from her heart to her bones, she would drink a tin cup of green tea, eat a stale bake from the morning's breakfast, and sit by the window on her rocking-chair that rocked no longer; and watch the clothes with one eye, and the rain with the other, and all the time talk to the people passing in front of the house, while her stubby fingers with half-moons of dirt under the nails ploughed blindly, but expertly, through the tin pan of rice for dinner.

Thursday was such a dramatic day in her life. Thursday was such a tragic day in my life: and looking back I think I received most of my brutal beatings from her on this day. It seemed that the anxiety of not wishing the rain to catch her off guard had installed a feeling of crawling tension in her guts, and a quick-tempered nervousness in her hand. And the only way she knew of relieving herself of this rain cloud of tension was to express it on my backside. But then would come Friday! All the clothes would be taken into the house; and she would put them in the best, cleanest chair, and wrap them in a large clean white sheet. If her good mood endured throughout Friday, she would begin her ironing on this day. But usually she did her ironing on Saturday morning. And she would time her work in such a way that she would be finished just before eleven o'clock. I would be sent off to the public stand-pipe for a fresh bucket of cool water. And she would take her bath, standing on the time-beaten, sun-beaten, water-beaten polished shining rocks in the backyard, panting, and spluttering and splushing and giggling like a young water animal. And she would make sure that I was secure, and out of peeping distance, in the bedroom. The windows that looked out into the backyard would be shut. After the bath, she would comb her thick hair, and plait it into many shiny black icicles that dripped down all around her head; put on a clean nice dress, washed out many times in blueing and washing soda, with only a ghost of the original pattern on it – a dress that fitted her like a glove; and she would walk across the dusty road, like a queen, with the bundle of white sparkling clothes on her head, for the white lady who gave her five shillings and thought it a fortune. That reward, that five shillings, kept us living from one Saturday afternoon to the next.

Usually, the white woman would quarrel with my mother: this dress has too much starch; that dress has a wrinkle and a blemish; the iron touched this handkerchief the wrong way; the Coke stain is still visible; you did not crease this hankie the correct way! And my mother, never able or brave enough to raise her head from under the years of subjection by these people, to look at this powerful strange white woman; and making certain, no doubt, that she and her 'little boy-child going eat bittle next week', would not dare to raise her voice in this woman's presence. But she would bring the recalcitrant piece of clothing back home with her, toss it in a corner of the yard, on the ground, curse me, curse the white woman, suck on her teeth in an awful silent comment on her situation, curse God for not helping us out of the hands of white people, and then, straightway, take the clothing up, brush it off, roll it into a nice ball, and later that same day, she would set about correcting her mistake. Nobody knew how great was the connection between my happiness and the whims of that distant, mysterious white world out the Front Road.

3

I had been sitting on the concrete wall in front of the Marine Hotel for almost an hour, waiting for Girlie. I had counted all the motor cars that had come and gone; and I had wished myself far and away from the island, on the wings of the blackbirds which sailed by. Two dogs, a white dog and a black dog, came from opposite ends of the road, smelled one another, jumped on one another, and then were stuck together in a frantic whimpering game. But suddenly, one dog, the white one, wanted to leave. But he could not, because he was still stuck to the black dog. The white dog was pointing in the direction from which the black dog came; and the black dog was looking in the direction from which the white dog came. And except for the thing which joined them, they were free of each other. In the whimpering tug-of-war which followed, neither one was winning. But suddenly, as suddenly as they appeared, the contest was over, and they ran off. The white dog ran as if it were still joined to the black dog by the thing. And then a little white boy came out of a driveway, leading a large animal-looking, animal-eating Alsatian dog on a piece of leather string. Dogs never liked me. I never liked dogs. Our village, a clutter of poverty and shacks, was filled with dogs, black dogs, white dogs, brown dogs, speckled dogs, all hungry dogs, and none of them pedigree dogs. I did not like this Alsatian dog; and I was not sure whether I should like the owner of this dog. (On Monday morning, the headmaster sped up the school yard on his ticking bicycle, jumped off and left the bicycle running in the direction of Shortie who caught it by the front wheel; and then he rushed into the school, pulled a long fat tamarind rod from the top of the cupboard, yelled out for Lester and when Lester came up on the platform, he rang the little bell.

'I have teach you boys manners. I have teach you boys that the onliest thing in the world what going make you into mens, mens worthy of respect from *people*, is manners. Manners maketh man. Manners maketh man. It don't matter if you come to school barefoot. It don't matter if you come to school in tear-up clothes. What matter is that you got manners. And that is what I here for.'

And he proceeded to throw all the power and brimstone and ashes of his cruelty into Lester's back. Whiff-whiff-whiff! the whip cried out in Lester's back. Whopp-whopp-whopp! the whip shouted when its force had ripped his shirt tail out of his trousers. And we boys, and the assistant masters, watched in silence, in awe, in the doubtful pleasure that it was not one of us, while the headmaster delivered the justice which left many marks of blood oozing through Lester's clean starched-and-ironed white flour-bag shirt. The shirt changed to pink. Whopp-whopp-whopp! And a devil inside Lester closed his mouth shut in insolent defiance, and the headmaster jumped up in the air, and brought down the tamarind whip with a marvellous delight.

'I going beat you till you have the decency to cry! I going beat your arse till it turn black-and-blue!'

But Lester had lost his tongue by this time: the whipping had put him under a chloroform of the deaf mute. The only way we knew he was being beaten was the sight of the blood rising from out of his white shirt, like water out of damp ground when you press on it with your feet.

'I going beat you till you cry, you worthliss black brute!'

And he would have gone on beating him until Doomsday, until night came and hid his prey from him. But in a brief interval of the din of slaughter, a small Prefect Ford, bringing the white inspector of schools to our school, blew its horn, and the whip stopped in mid-air, like a piece of granite, like the statue of the English general in the Garrison Savannah, with his sword held high against the enemies of Britannia.

And late that afternoon, when the inspector inspected our headmaster about the deportment and carriage of his boys, only then did we learn why Lester was beaten.

'They is some boys here, sir, one boy in partic'ler, what don't obey too good,' he told the inspector. The inspector grunted something. 'And I had to give him a lash or two this morning, 'cause, yesterday, Sundee, he pass a lady's house near by the Marine Hotel, and didn' have the manners to speak to the lady, or the lady' son.'

'Good!' said the inspector, not knowing that he had signed our fate for the next lifetime of school.) It was this little boy, Lester's friend, coming towards me with his dog.

I edged my way higher up on the wall. The dog and the boy came slowly along, taking their time, not minding my business. They were a few yards from me. But I was above them. And they were beneath me. And then, for no reason at all, the little boy said, 'Ssssick!' The dog made a leap. The boy dropped the leather string. The dog rushed up on to the wall and pulled me down. Tearing and biting and shaking its head at the same time, the dog had me rolled into the dust in the gutter. I did not hear anything from the little boy. He was standing, like a little man, his hands in his pockets, and a large red lollipop stuck in his mouth. And that moment, Chandler, the hotel watchman, appeared from somewhere.

'You black boy! Get up to-arse offa the white man' dog!' Chandler took the dog off me; and he patted the dog and gave it back to its owner. 'You little black fool, what the hell right you have hanging 'round the white man' hotel? You ain' belongst *up* here! You belongst down there!'

The little white boy stood, patting his dog. And the dog was panting.

'It serve' yuh damn-well right! Ain't it serve him damn right, mastuh? I going call the S.P.C.A. for you now, you blasted idiot! Mastuh, call the S.P.C.A. for he!'

But the little white gentleman only walked on, without answering Chandler. And Chandler, feeling a little insulted in my presence, continued to abuse me, calling me all the names to which I was already accustomed – both from my mother, and from my headmaster.

'Gorblummuh! If I was to ever catch your arse up in here again, boy, be-Jesus Christ! you mark my word, I going tear it up with a lash from this bull-pistle whip o' mine. Now, get to-arse outta the white man' place!' And he made a feint with the bull-pistle, and it whizzed cruelly through the air. I was gone. My trousers were torn in the shape of an upside-down L. My mother was going to rip hell. These were my only other pair of trousers. The better pair I wore to town, to church, and when I went once a month to visit my dead grandmother, lying in Westbury Cemetery. Chandler disappeared, twirling his bull-pistle, and a moment later Girlie came out.

'What the hell happen' to you, boy? You was in the Boer War, or something?'

I tried to explain to Girlie, but Girlie called me a little vagabond; and she reminded me that my mother would be disappointed at seeing my condition. 'Boy, wait till Mistress Sobers rest' she eyes 'pon them trousers. Christ, you behaves just like a damn heathen!'

'But, Miss Girlie, you think that maybe you could fix-up my trousers for me, please, so my mother wouldn'…'

'You don't come putting me in trouble with that so-warrior mother o' yours, nuh! Don't come mashing-up my peace this blessid afternoon. You want to put me and your mother in the ropes, this peaceabul evening, or what? *Me*? Meddling with them trousers o' yourn? Leave me out, boy! Leave me out o' that!'

But she led me inside the servants' quarters; and made me take off my trousers in front of her, while she darned the L-shaped tear. I could never understand why my trousers and shirts always were torn in the shape of an L. No matter what had torn them: a nail in the paling in our backyard; or a piece of broken bottle; or a stone; or a dog. Always an L-shape.

I sat quietly, drawing my legs up, close together, hiding my manhood, watching Girlie as she wet the thread twice with her wet lips, blink her eyes to make them see better, hold the needle up in the air as if she was about to pierce a balloon which I could not see, but which she could see, and then *touche!*… she missed the needle eye! 'These blasted needles they making these days! Christ! I don't know who does make these damn needles, these days!' She tried again, and missed. But she only sighed. She got it at the third try. And I watched her beautiful hands, moving fast and expertly, like some fantastically fast dance, except that instead of hands, there would be feet, skipping, moving, twisting. And then, she was finished. She ordered me to stand in front of her. And as I stood up, she held the trousers out to me; but as I reached out, still trying to hold my manhood betwixt my legs, she withdrew the trousers out of my reach. Then she came nearer to me; holding out the trousers with her left hand; a wicked smile on her face; and with her right hand, she tugged at my testicles. And she screamed, 'Aieeeee!' I was too stunned to do anything, or to say anything. I did not know why she would play this joke on me. (Willy-Willy was talking one night to my mother; and I was lying in bed, on my bed on the floor. But they thought I was sleeping. But I was not sleeping. And I heard Willy-Willy say, 'Darling, love, gorblummuh! they is some real worthliss bitches living next door to you, though! Gorblummuh, though!'

'Next door to me? You could mean Girlie?'

'Be-Christ! she now robbing the cradle! Girlie, be-Christ! ain't satisfy with hard-stone mens, but she running after school children. Man, Ruby, that bitch living next door, man, she hold on 'pon...'

'But, Willy-Willy, what the arse you telling me?'

'That hard-back woman love *boys*!'

The horror Willy-Willy put in his assertion, warned me never to get too close to Girlie. But it was a confusing statement. For Willy-Willy himself had seen me passing water behind the paling one day, and he exclaimed, 'Christ! that water foaming! Boy, you is a man!' And the realization shocked me, and made me proud. A few days later, he took me aside, when he was visiting my mother, and he said, 'Boy, I have notice' that your piss foaming. That mean and connote one thing. You is a man. You ain't no more little boy. And you could come outta school now, and help populate this village. How old you is, Milton?'

'I is nine, Willy-Willy.'

'Be-Christ what I tol' you? You is a hard-back man. Come outta Blackman' school, and help me breed the womens in this village. That is the only mission a man have in life, Milton. And I going tell you something now, 'cause something in you click in me. We is friends. Milton, there ain't nothing under the sun, nothing on this earth, or in the next one to come, that is more sweeter than a piece o' woman. Be-Christ!... and you is no longer a baby that I can't talk to you in man-terms. You is a man, the same blasted man as me. 'Cause you does foam when you piss, and I foams too. A piece o' woman, regular, and gorblummuh! mark my words, boy, you throw 'way them school books real fast. But one thing, though. One thing. Never... *never* let a piece o' woman go to yuh head. Never. A piece o' woman, regular every night, could put a man in great health. But when it go to yuh head, *bram!* out goes you!' And I had held my head down, in shame, in oppression of the heaviness of this advice. And the fact that it was given to me, in our house, in the absence of my mother, by my mother's friend, made me feel like a kind of spy. Willy-Willy ended his advice with the possibility, 'I going make Girlie give you piece! Girlie slightly more older than you... she is thirty-five year old last Christmas... but she sweet. And she would give.') And now, I was face to face with Girlie. But still I had no desire. The desire was still embryonic. And because of this, I could not understand why she would want to do this to me. I could not understand why a big woman like she, a big adult, would think of doing a thing like this. And although many times I did sit in my mother's rocking-chair and peep at Girlie; and watch Girlie hold down low low to the ground without bending her knees; and watched the exposure of her sweetness above her thighs; and although I had followed the soft blue veins of honey right up her legs, until her legs were out of sight, and they faded into her thighs, my eyes were only the eyes of the explorer, never the eyes of the covetor. And those thoughts born out of my exploration never were fostered into a wish.

I received my trousers from her. She looked very annoyed, as if I had done something wrong. And for the first time since I left home, I remembered my mother's message to her.

'Miss Girlie... Miss Girlie, my mother ask' me to ask you if you could see... if you would mind lending her a sixpence, 'cause the missis' clothes still needs starch, and she don't have not even one cent to buy starch with.'

'Gimme some o' them!' she said, and laughed and reached out for my testicles again. 'Aieeeeee! Gimme some o' them, nuh!' Girlie knew; and I knew that she knew that my mother would never believe me should I complain about her teasing; and this is what made my humiliation the more unbearable. 'All right, you little man!' she said. And no more. She took six black coins, pennies, old and worn flat without even a trace of the white woman sitting on the horse which swam, holding the three-pronged spear in her hand; and these coins she took from her purse which she kept under her dress. And she dropped them, one by one, like six insults, into my outstretched hand. I folded my fist over them. And I ran out through the half-open door. Girlie tried to trip me; but I was gone. 'Aieeeee!' she screamed playfully. But I did not look back.

Outside, it was gathering dusk. The church steeple looked cruel and godly and cold in the evening of dark green, of trees, of dogs barking, and mosquitoes flying about. The church bells were ringing for some reason. And a few blackbirds and sparrows were rambling home in this bad light to their nests. I walked on the right side of the road, the side far away from the gate through which, earlier, my little white friend and his dog had come. I was approaching the gate, and I had to be careful. No one in our village had ever had the guts to complain, to walk up to a white man's house, and complain to him that his dog had bitten him. But in my hand I carried a fortune; and I had to be doubly careful. If I was to be frightened by the dog; if I was to be mauled by the dog, I was going to make certain that I died with the six black pennies in my hand. That way, my mother would know that I did not 'play the fool' with her money.

When I drew alongside of the gate, the boy and the dog were sitting on the large red-painted boulder which prevented the gate from buckling back to the posts. I watched the road through one eye, the dog through the other, and I held the boy's movements steadfastly in my consciousness. Slowly, I was opposite my enemies. And nothing happened. I was about to pass them. Nothing happened. I relaxed, and began to think about the rice and fish heads waiting for me at home. And then I heard the boy make the hissing sound, 'Sssick!' I looked back. The dog with hundreds of white snarling teeth in his mouth was coming at me. But I was too fast for the dog. The terror of a beating from my mother sped me to reach her, safely, this time. 'Kiss my arse, dog!

Not this time, dog!' I was mumbling to myself. The white boy called the dog back, and the dog gave up the chase. And I looked back, a conqueror, at my vanquished foe. And when I looked in front again, Lester was coming towards me, with a loaf of bread as large as his head, eating it and smiling at me.

'That willow was flying like lightning, though! Like lightning, though!' And he ran off, crying out at the top of his voice, 'Thief! thief! thief!' And for some reason, I ran too; and when I stopped running, I was in front of our house.

The smoke had died. And the smells had died. But I could still hear a man's voice inside. And my mother was laughing at the top of her voice, in that high, cackling manner, 'Ah-heh-heh-hehhh! Ah-heh-heh-hehh! Oh, Jesus Gawwwd!' And her voice would rise again, high high high, and then disappear, and then when you were not expecting to hear it again, it would come up at you like sprays climbing the pier down by the wharf. 'Ah-heh-heh-hehh! Oh Christ, man, Willy-Willy you going make me shit myself with the laughings!'

'Yeah, man! During them days, I was a big man, a working man. I was up in Amer'ca working with fellars what went abroad 'pon the orange-picking scheme. Gorblummuh, Ruby, we corned money like water! Eighty cents a hour, and I working like I is a real slave, and I pulling in them Uncle Sam greenbacks, and slamming every blasted nickle…'

'What a nickle is?'

'A nickle is a piece o' change!… I banking every blasted nickle 'pon the bank. And then one morning, I get up on the wrong side. And I look 'round, and be-Christ all I seeing is black people working from sun-up to sun-down, and all the brown-skin boys and the white boys sitting down in the shade. And bram! I run 'way. I catch a plane. I don't know where the hell the plane taking me. But I on it! Swoosh! I land up in Harlem, be-Christ! and I *done* working. I living a real hep-cat life. You should 'ave see' the diff'rent kinds o' clothes I had! Gorblummuh! when Willy-Willy walk down that main street up in Harlem, Fif' Avenue and One-twenty-fif' Street, gorblummuh! is womens what watching the old man!'

'Them was real good days!' my mother said. I felt she had taken a part in those days; and since she had never told me, I felt very left out. I waited outside in the yard, hoping to hear more of what they were saying. 'Them was the days when you was sending me money like if I was a real lady! Every other mont' a money order in the postman' hand, a postal order... something! Yes! Them was the days! And now, I poor as a bird's arse!'

'Gorblummuh, in them days, I spend money like water! 'Cause I had money in them days.' He coughed. It was as if stones were inside his chest and his chest was made of tin. The rackling went on, and he coughed, and I heard a pounding on his chest. Perhaps it was my mother pounding the cough out of his constitution.

'That cough sound nasty, man. It ain't sound nice. That cough need' some strong mirac'lous bush-tea, Willy-Willy.'

'I all right now, though.' And for some time, nothing was said.

Then my mother said, as if she really cared, 'But what the hell that boy o' mine could be doing up by that hotel, all this time?'

'P'raps, Girlie hold on 'pon he, and got he strapp' down in bed! Heh-heh-heh!'

'Christ, Willy-Willy, that ain't no laughing matter, 'cause it involve' my child now! I will tear Girlie to threads if I just think she bringing any damn freshness to my boy-child!'

'Gorblummuh! and if you don't rescue that boy, Girlie make you into a grandmother!'

'Willy-Willy, what worthlissness you bringing to me?'

And at this point I entered the room, noisily. When Willy-Willy saw me, he laughed out loudly; and my mother had to tell him to shut up.

'Gimme that money outta your hand, boy!' And when she saw it was only a sixpence, she sighed and abused Girlie. Willy-Willy laughed again.

'Ruby, darling, I broke as arse, man. You couldn' lend me a penny? I need cigs, man.'

'Lend *you* a penny? Christ, man, you should be bringing silver and gold and dropping it inside my lap! And now you asking me to lend you money?' But she gave him the money anyhow; and he put it into his pocket, belched aloud and then said, 'Excuse,' and straightway left. My mother put the five black pennies under the tablecloth in the front house, and she went for my dinner. Willy-Willy was hungry, she said, and he had eaten a little too much. There was only a fish head for me, and some rice. The rice was steamed and it was soggy; and there was no sauce. But we never had sauce with our food, except on Sundays when my mother would prepare a meal that would make you endure the other six days of near-starvation, just because you wanted to live for that next Sunday meal. As I ate my dinner, she grumbled; she grumbled about the washing; she grumbled about the money she borrowed from Girlie; she grumbled about the little wages she got from the white woman; and she grumbled about life itself. 'Boy, I didn' know how the hell I was going to get through with them clothes for her, if Girlie didn't, out of the kindness of her heart, have pity on me, and lend me this piece o' change!' And I listened to her droning, and felt so sorry for her; and so sorry for myself, because neither she nor me could do anything about it. 'Girlie lend me that piece o' change, and I have to thank one person for that. I have to sing my praises 'fore God. I raises up my head and my heart to the heavens, and thanks Christ! and praises Him, that He, and He alone, is so damn good to me... Get up! get up offa your behind boy, 'cause you don't have the whole night to eat that little food! You have to go to the stand-pipe for water, and you have to clean that lamp chimbley, 'cause it black as hell with sutt, and you have to clean-up the yard! Now, who the hell I saying I giving thanks to, if not to God? I opens my eyes every morning, and not one blind cent I own or possess to my name! Not one cent! This morning. Yesterdee morning! Lord Lord Lord!' I finished my dinner, and I went out into the yard to sweep it up with the broom made of pieces of dried sticks. Out in the yard, my mother's pleadings for help came to me.

'...and no damn starch neither! I can't even complete my chores. No starch mean' no ironing. And, Lord today is Thursdee already! No ironing mean' no clothes. No clothes mean' no money. No money... hey, you boy! Get 'cross the road for that bucket o' water, fast! And stop yuh dreaming!... and no money mean' no food. I can't pay thiefing Mister Fuguero for renting this rat-nest he charging me two shilling a week for! I can't do *nothing*. Can't do nothing, nothing. I living it is true… Milton? You hear me send you for that bucket o' water?… living, but I done *dead*, already. Nothing, nothing, nothing. Lord, this world o' Yourn gone 'stray bad bad bad. This world that You put we in, to live with one another in, and love one another in, Lord, it turning 'round 'pon pounds, shillings and pence, every blasted twenty-four hours! It not spinning 'round 'pon love and charity as You say it ought to spin 'round 'pon, at all! This whole blasted world that I live in going backwards like them days during the war when a person was a lucky bitch if he had a grain o' rice to put inside his child' mouth, once a week. Christ Christ Christ! It taking everything outta me, just to live!'

There she was, a lonely, lonely, defeated woman. She seemed lost, left alone, now that her friend Willy-Willy had left. When he was there, she was laughing, cackling out loudly, expressing the feelings she had inside her, the feelings which were coming out now like teardrops of grief. So much grief! My whole life; her whole life: grief, grief, grief! She was standing in the doorway, looking at me fumbling with the galvanized bucket. I could smell the perfume of her labour, for which she was paid so little. She was a big woman. A beautiful woman, in a sense. There was great power in her forearms, which were no longer the forearms of a woman, since she had to do the work of two men to keep me alive. And the size of her hips told you that she was a child-bearing kind of woman. Her nose was broad and long and flat. And her eyeballs came right out of her head at you. They were sad, filmy eyes, eyes almost always red from the grief they expressed. But they were not really cruel eyes. My mother was not really a cruel woman. Perhaps what looked like cruelty to me must have been her disgust, her inability to provide a simple living for her child; and the exasperation and the frustration she must have felt every day of her life when rudeness and the smell of man pulled her from her course; this failure must have got accustomed to coming out of her, at the wrong moments, and in a strange, uncontrollable nervousness.

Her eyes again. Watching me; always watching me. Kind, soft, frightened eyes. Eyes made for crying and weeping. My mother looked always tired and haggard, like a woman who had one child every year for twelve years. But the evil smell of her earlier womanhood had kept her from being involved with men all these years. And so, she appeared to me to be very different from the other women in our village. They had men like a sow has pigs. She was not like Girlie. Girlie had long, large, pointed breasts which she deliberately made shake, every step she took. My mother's breasts were solid, like two mounds of stiffly kneaded dough which refused to shake; but which looked as if they were always shrugging their disgust at men. And this is why I could not understand what went on between her and Willy-Willy. Her complexion was dark. Black. A soft, smooth black, like silk, which changed its blackness into shades of brown and purple, or blue, or very dark crimson, whenever she passed in front of our kerosene lamp.

She never told me her age. I never dared to ask. She never told me anything about herself. She never mentioned her mother, her father; and I never even wondered whether she had any brothers or sisters. These things, these thoughts about family seemed so foreign to us. She was just a woman, living in a world. And I had come from somewhere to help make her life more miserable. And it was in this sense that she appeared to me to be not quite a woman. I found out nothing about my mother. The wall of silence between us was broken only when she summoned me to her presence to remind me that she was my mother by flogging the life out of me; or when I was to go on one of the countless little errands for her, always running across the Front Road to see if the white lady would mind advancing her a shilling to help with the washing – which the white lady never could bring herself to do; or to borrow a sixpence or a penny from Girlie 'till next Sa'rday, please God!'

'You must be damn tired, son,' she said to me. She must have realized just that moment the terrible weight of life. 'Walk 'cross the road for the bucket o' water, and come back and siddown, then.'

'Yes, Ma.'

'And look! Come, take this penny, and go to the doctor shop, and buy yuhself a cent in sweeties.' She left for the money. When she returned, her face was the face of kindness. My mother was capable of such kindness! 'If I have give' Willy-Willy, that worthless man, a penny, well, I could give my own-own child a cent.' She placed the penny in my hand, and closed my hand into a ball with her own hand on top of it. 'Let that whore out there in the Front Road wait till I feel like finishing her clothes! Buy yuhself a penny in sweeties from the doctor shop, boy.'

And I went my way rejoicing. Sweeties, sweeties, sweeties! Something must have been wrong with my mother. It was not often that she gave me money to spend on myself; and to give me a whole penny now – some terrible magic must be at work in her heart. But I kept the penny, anyhow. I did not stop until I reached the doctor shop which was in the Front Road, facing the back road that led to the village. Like most things in our village, the doctor shop was in the white people's district. I do not know whether the owner of the shop, Mister Smith, a white man, did not like the people of the village or not; but he always took our money, and sometimes he would let you bleed to death before he would give you an aspirin. The doctor shop was where they sold drugs and coconut oil and pills for different things; and toffees and sweets that cost a cent each; and where the white people used to come dressed as if they were always going to church, in their best, and hand Mister Smith a long list, and Mister Smith would place a pile of things which I had never seen before in my life: Elastoplast, Eno's, Dodd's Kidney and Liver Pills, headache pills, bladder pills, digestion pills, anti-digestion pills, and other things which we in the village never knew how to use. This was one other thing about the white world that lived in the Front Road – they used so many different things, while we would drink a glass of rum for a pain in the belly; or put some oil leaves on our heads if we had a headache; and things like indigestion never troubled us. We didn't have anything to digest. But I liked to go to the doctor shop, although I never had anything to buy from Mister Smith. But I liked to see those large beautiful bottles, that looked like soap bubbles blown up big big big, and filled with pretty liquids, red, green, blue, mauve – things I thought should be drunk. Mister Smith never told me what they were used for. But one day, when I was jumping on and off the large scale in the middle of the shop, he hollered at me and called me a heathen. And I called him a big white idiot. And he held me and took me around in the back of the shop and made me sit down in the smelly smelling sickness in the back of the shop, and he took a very beautiful bottle from the shelf and uncorked it – the cork was not a cork made out of cork, but out of glass, like the bottle – and he put the bottle to my nose and immediately I felt as if I was a bird, flying flying high up in the clouds. And when he let me go, I ran out of the shop thinking I was a bird and I fell in the middle of the Front Road, and many people stopped, wondering what had happened to 'this little coloured boy'. I threw away my wings; I got to my feet, and ran straight home to my mother. And my mother flogged me for going out 'there, in the white people district'. From that time, I never ventured near Mister Smith, or his doctor shop, unless I had real money in my hand.

'And what the hell you want now, *boy*?' Mister Smith used to say the word 'boy' as if he meant 'animal'. He came from behind the fence of bottles. 'What the hell you want?'

'Sweeties, sir.'

'Money! Money! Gimme the money first!'

'I got money. I got money.'

He threw the two red drops of stiff blood-like things on the glass counter, and he snatched the money from my hand. 'Get out, now!' I had my sweets and I didn't care; and so I ran out of the white district and into my own district, the boundary of which was the church wall. And then I went home for the bucket to go to the stand-pipe.

Dogs were playing in the road; and women were sitting in doorways, their frocks tucked tightly betwixt their legs; and some of them had little children biting their breasts; and when I saw the babies at their mothers' breasts, I felt very ashamed, and I looked the other way. Suddenly, everybody started to run ahead of me, in the direction of the stand-pipe. Screaming and hollering was coming from the pipe. But I had my sweeties in my mouth, and I continued to walk.

'I going kill you, you hear? I going kill you!' a woman was screaming. 'I going kill you, as good as a blasted cent!'

'Well, kill muh! Kill muh! You say you going kill me, well, kill muh! Kill muh, stinking Blanche!'

And they rushed to each other, and were stuck there. Blood was coming down Blanche's face, and most of the other woman's dress was ripped off. Little boys and girls were hovering around, laughing at the woman's behind exposed. And there were some men there too, encouraging the women to kill each other.

'God blind you in hell, Blanche! You live with ever' white man you could get your nasty hand 'pon, but be-Christ take off your hand offa my man, hear? Gorblummuh! or the judge heng me for you.'

'You hear she? You hear she?' the other woman said, tears in her eyes, appealing to the cruel crowd. 'But look my crosses for me, though, nuh! This, this… whore say I sleeping with *her* man? Looka, woman, even iffing I had eyes 'pon that man, I still won't…'

'Kill she! Kill she!' the crowd cried. 'Beat she! Beat she!'

'…You don't know that man o' yourn have lice in his head?'

And the people bawled. They threw their caps up in the air and they bawled. 'He have lice, oh God! Lice! Oh Jesus Christ, Lonnie have lice in he head!' And they laughed again.

The women had each other on the ground, in the road, and marl was in their hair, and dust on their faces. But they kept on fighting and rolling and shouting and cursing. And the men stood up, close close to the women and wouldn't pull them apart. Lester was there too, shouting and saying, 'Kill she! Kill she!'

And when it was all over, and the women had ripped off most of the clothes from each other's bodies; and their breasts and large hefty hips were flabbing and sagging and exposed; and their trousers were ripped in threads, I went into the pipe and turned on the tap. The cool water ran over the lakes of blood, and the blood poured down into the drain-pipe in the middle of the pipe. Blanche went away screaming for her husband to come. And the other woman – Blanche had called her 'this stinking foreigner whore from Sin Lucia' – remained in a knot of women, talking about why she should have killed Blanche 'dead dead dead as bloody-hell!' Blood was streaming down the woman's face, like perspiration; and the women were talking, all at the same time: telling this woman she should kill Blanche; that Blanche thought that because she was living with a white man, she could take away the men from the other women in the village; that Blanche was what the Bible called 'a woman of easy virtues'; that it was women like Blanche who 'were no blasted good, neither in this world, nor in the next two to come'; that Blanche was no good... 'And be-Christ! nobody can't find out yet how one woman could be more rotten than Blanche. Blanche' belly does be big big for six months outta the year, and when you look round, bram! Blanche' belly gone back down flat flat as a bake, and no baby ain't come! Blanche was in the fambly-way three times since I first know Blanche! Three times a baby was inside Blanche' womb, and three times nothing ain't come out, at birf'... 'You hear me? Blanche not good. Blanche not good. She not even fit for the dump heap up in the back o' the Marine Hotel'... 'And you know they is so much mens, men all colours, coming when the sun set, knocking down Blanche' window, like if she is some dog in the midst o' heat. And the stupid man she live with, he in there, grinning, like some'... One o' these good mornings, we going find Blanche... not Blanche, but Blanche' body with her insides tear-out, laying-down sprawl-out in some back-alley. And she going be dead dead dead *dead*...'

And all this talk frightened me; and I ran all the way home, with the bucket of water on my head. And when I turned the paling into the backyard, the bucket was half empty. But my mother was not at home; and so I took my time with my chores, and dillied and dallied and thought of growing up and fleeing to sea away from the headmaster and my mother and the village.

My chores were divided into two departments. The outside chores. And the inside chores. The outside chores were nasty chores: like cleaning out the pig pens (we had a pig once; but one night late late late, so late that it was night turning into morning, a man came and brought a knife with him. I had passed his house earlier that week – Thursday and Friday afternoons after school – and I had seen him, always on his front steps, sharpening the knife, until the blade of the knife disappeared into a pin. This same man came and brought his knife and a large piece of iron. And my mother woke me up and sent me to the pipe for many buckets of water. And I thought my back would have been broken from carrying so many buckets of water. But my mother said I had to get the water, because she needed it to kill the pig. And after the water was thrown into a large drum which we borrowed from another neighbour; and the water was erupting inside the drum like a geyser; and the man approached the pig in his castle; the pig slipped through his hands like a gobble of vaseline, and we spent all that morning chasing piggy-come-piggy! piggy-piggy-piggy-piggy! all through the village, until just as we found him, the sun came up and caught the tops of the sugar canes on fire. And when we got him, the man slapped him two times on his behind, and said, as if the pig were his own child, 'Take that!' And we brought piggy back home; and the fire was ashes under the drum of geysers. But the man did not mind this. My mother held the hind legs and the man held the front legs; and I remained in a corner of the backyard vomiting up last night's tea. The man took out his knife, and measured something on the knife against something on the pig's throat, and then, tssssss! and the blood squirted right into my mother's mouth and face. And she said, 'Jesus Christ!' And she released the pig's legs, and the pig jumped around. But the man caught it this time. And she shouted, 'Gorblimey! This pig have devils in him!' And slit! off went the pig's head, clean clean from his body. 'You is a murdrer! You is a murdrer!' my mother shouted to the man. 'You is a born murdrer. You just cut off that pig head like if you born doing that!' 'Ruby, shut your arse-hole mout', do!' the man said, laughing. 'You don't like pork chops?' And that was the end of the pig, the pig; that was the end of Piggy) and cleaning out goat pens, and sweeping the yard, and putting your fingers into little ant-hills of droppings from the fowls and the ducks. The inside chores (you had to wash your hands after the outside chores before you dared to enter the house: 'Cleansiness, boy, is the next thing side-by-side o' godliness!') were cleaner chores; chores which a girl would normally do, but which fell to me, a boy, because there were no girls in my family. There were two chores which fell to me: making up the bed; and cleaning the lampshade of the kerosene lamp.

Our bed was made of straw, dried grass. The grass was stuffed into a large mattress which looked like an oversized pillowcase. The grass was cut in the green, luscious season of the growing guinea grass. When cut, it was spread thinly on the ground to dry.

On the mornings of those nights when I could not sleep because I had dreamed I was outside in the romping streets playing with Lester, and I had wet my bed, the straw would smell like burnt refuse. And one sad night I had dreamed I was drinking gallons and gallons of molasses water with big chunks of ice in it; and Lester and I were engaged in a urinating contest to see who could pass water the longest. And I was winning. Lester had stopped. And he was counting for me, up to one hundred and ten... *'one hurn' and 'leven, one hurn' and twelve, one hurn' and thirteen, one hurn' and fourteen...'*; and I could not stop; and I was laughing and shouting my victory into his ears. And when my mother screamed, I realized that the molasses part of the dream was a dream. And the counting part was a dream too. But not the urinating part. That was no dream. For the rivers of water had dripped right through the straw, like raindrops travelling through the leaves of a tree. And my mother had jumped up, 'You! A big man like you, still wetting your bed?' It was a question and a condemning statement. That night, when the heaviness of her hand on my body had subsided, I vowed that I would never, never urinate again – neither inside nor outside. But the same thing happened again the next night.

After the bed, I cleaned the lampshade. Every evening, from that day when boastingly I held a glass of water at the age of five without drowning myself, she gave me this honour of cleaning our lampshade. I was in love with glass. I would put the shade to my eye like a captain, and sing the song, 'The Captain has a spying-glass, the captain has a...'

'Come come come! Take off your damn shirt and lemme see how that man brutalize' your body!' She was screaming. Her eyes were red. And before I could unbutton one button, she had dragged the shirt off my back; and she had ripped off the trousers too. 'Christ! Oh Lord Almighty!' And an avalanche of emotion poured out of her in meaningless mutterings, as she saw the system of dried red rivers across my back. And spinning around, and spinning me with her, she took me to the light from the open window to inspect the wounds on my back.

'Come come! We going up at Blackman!' She dragged me out through the back door, and across the road, naked. 'I can't believe that my two eyes has discern' this brutalization of my child!' Tears were coming down her cheeks. 'Wait. We can't go 'cross the Front Road like this. You naked... let we go back.' She took me back home. And when I was dressed, with my only pair of shoes on my feet, and she had wet her fingers in her mouth with saliva, and had passed them around the ashes on my ankles; and when she had put on her own canvas shoes, she took me back up the road.

The anger in her body was quivering through her hand that grasped mine like a vice. There was sweat in her hand, too. But she dragged me along across the road to the corner of the Front Road; we passed the doctor shop with the bright lights shining on its marble floor, and the large rainbow bottles of medicine and death and sickness and health reflecting the light like the stars in the sky. There were a few women, dressed in black, walking along the side of the Front Road, and you could not see them too well, because they too were black. And then we came to the Hastings Rocks, empty now, except for the lonely sea calling out for someone to keep it company. But there was no one, except a few scratching crabs walking around like small garbage carts.

We were drawing near now. The headmaster's house was off the Front Road. On this side road, all the rich black and the poor white lived. His house was the largest of the small unpainted houses. A brilliant gas lamp greeted us. It was hanging from the open front door, like a light from a tree to warn fishermen and fishing boats that they were coming into a harbour. And when the power of the light struck my mother in her face, she slackened her pace.

'Hold on,' she said, not in a very strong voice. She wiped the fringe of her hairline with the back of her hand. Sweat came off in her hand. 'Hold on a sec, boy. We have to appear proper and respectable before this gentleman. We have to appear proper before we could present our case to him.' She wiped the sweat from around my face with the back of her hand. And then she stooped down, wet her fingers in her mouth with saliva, and wiped the scales of ashes and the grey film that lingered around my ankles and on my legs. 'This bitch! Look what he done to you! Wait till he come out here, oh Christ, you just wait! I going to tear-

72

loose in his tail so rotten that he going to mistake me for a...' She pushed my shirt evenly into my trousers; and she passed her hand, twice, roughly, through my hair. Then she dragged her index finger along the corner of each of my eyes. But still unsatisfied that I was presentable, she dabbed her finger on her tongue and ran it all around inside my ears. 'Stand up proper! Stand up! Wet your lips, boy!' I swallowed my top lip, and then my bottom lip, and brought them back up, wet and thick and purple and luscious. 'Yes, wet your lips and make them look nice. Your lips always peeling like cane, like if they always need water. We can't approach that gentleman in no half-way manner. 'Cause I intends telling him a thing or two.'

She fussed and she fussed, trying to gather up courage to face the headmaster. The brilliance of the gas lamp in the open front door must have been too much for her. Or perhaps she had just remembered that, after all, she was only a poor black washer-woman in the village, and he was the headmaster. Or perhaps she must have needed time, more time in which to rehearse the speech she intended to give the headmaster. But something was happening to her: she was not as angry as when she left home. And strangely, the wilts and wemms on my back stopped stinging as we reached the headmaster's house.

We continued to stand in front of the house, wondering whether to knock on the front door, or on the back door, or return home. My mother did not know what to do. And I think she was about to turn back, when the headmaster appeared from the side of his house. He recognized me first, and he called out at me:

'Hello there, Sobers?'

'Good evening, Mister Blackman, sir.'

''Evening, Sobers. Is that lady Mistress Sobers with you, Sobers?'

'Oh, yessir, Mister Blackman,' she said; although she was really *Miss* Sobers. The village had reserved the right to give certain women who had children, and who were unmarried, the title of respectability. And my mother had been given it. 'Heh-heh! We was just passing, and when this boy tell me that you lives here, I had was to stand up and admire these lovely gardens, and...'

'A fine son, Mistress Sobers, a fine son you have there!'

'Yessir, Mister Blackman. I tries my best with Milton.' Pride dawned on her face. 'But I have to confess, Mister Blackman, sir, that sometimes it is a uphill battle I does be fighting with this boy-child.'

'Mistress Sobers, I telling you, bringing up a' offspring, particular a boy-child, is like rearing a prize rose.' He rested his hand, his right hand, ever so lightly on my mother's hand, and led her through the gate and into the thick jungle of rose beds. 'You see this rose, here… no use calling it by the Latin name, *herbibus reddus armarillus*… Heh-heh! Well, anyhow. But taking a look at that rose there. For nine months I been coming home after school trying to see what I could do with it… Plant it, water it four times a day, prune it, caress it… Mistress Sobers, I telling you, this rose tree was just like some o' them boys I have to contend with down at that elementary school down in the village. But, perseverance. *Perseverance.* Mistress Sobers, I persevered! And one morning, I open my bedroom window, and bram! a new red beautiful rose appear'. That is what I call perseverance. And we have to go back to the ants to learn what wisdom is.'

'Oh Christ, if that is not the selfsame thing, the very words I utters to this boy o' mine here, Mister Blackman. Day in and day out, Mister Headmaster, I warns him 'gainst the evilness and the example what his no-good father give him. And if he do not take my advice, Mister Headmaster, he going to be a more worser crim'nal than his father.'

'Heh-heh! Mistress Sobers, a fine son you have here.' He patted my mother on the softness of her shoulder; and then he removed his hand and dropped it heavily on my neck. 'Now, Mistress Sobers, as a' illustration. Take the name you have give' this boy. Milton. You was a thoughtful parent. Now, let we look into the background and the hist'ry of the name, Milton. Now, I don't know if you know it, but, Mistress Sobers, you have pick' a damn fine name for this boy. You have call' this boy after a great great man. A *great* man. Milton was the name of the most greatest man-o'-letters what ever walk the shores o' Englant. In fact, if you ask me, Mistress Sobers, Milton was not only the best man-o'-letters, but he was the best man in his time. And though he was borned blind, blind, mind you… not even with as much eyesight as a night-bat in the daytime, but *blind*. Oh dear me! Has you ever read a piece of po'try by the name of *Samsun Agonies*? To take up a book, and look at that poem, you will see how Milton the man and the man-o'-letters, after who you have had the wisdom and the foresight to name your son, you will observe how that great man complain' to God that God was not fair in turning him inna a man without eyesight, and still turn round and expect him, Milton that is, to get up outta bed at sunrise, put on his clothes, and go out into the cold of Englant mist and fog and earn a living for himself, like we normal human beings. No, Mistress Sobers. It was not true, Milton told God. And Milton argue strong strong with God on this argument. And if you ask me, I have to confess that it take' a damn strong man and individual to stand up 'gainst God with them arguments. And what make the thing so damn funny, too, Mistress Sobers, was that Milton deliver' his arguments and counter-arguments in the Latin language!'

'But, no no no!' my mother cried, moved by the great insult which Milton had given God. 'No no no! Sir, rightly and truly I do not see eye-to-eye with you in this thing. That was rudeness on the part o' Mister Milton. And mayhaps, Mister Milton could have get away with it, being that he is a residunt in the Mother Country o' Englant… 'cause as you rightly know, Mister Head-master, they is things what them could do and escape with, that we can't do saving we suffer for it. But, basic', he was wrong. He was wrong wrong wrong!' And she shook her head many many times, dramatically, to emphasize how wrong Mister Milton was.

The headmaster looked at her, and he did not know what to do, or say. And then, his hands moved. His wrists jerked. He was thinking. Hastily, he cut a half-withered red rose with his pruning knife, and he held it just an inch above the heavy left breast of my mother.

'Mistress Sobers, you is a' individual. You is a' individual and a half! And a person who is also a' individual, is a person what deserve' respect. And to illustrate to you the deepness of the respects I have in my heart for you, I intends to give you one of my prize roses.' He rested the rose against my mother's breast. And my mother blushed. 'Lend me a pin, Mistress Sobers, and with my own two hand, I going to pin this on you, as a symbull, as a first prize to you from me, for being a' individual.' And again my mother blushed. Sweetness and the honey of beauty bathed her face.

She turned her back on him, and fumbled inside the hope-chest of her brassière for a pin. I closed my eyes anticipating any time the waterfall of breasts that would tumble down into her dress, and hang like full, ripe, overgrown mangoes on a slender strap of a branch. But nothing happened. She turned around, and handed the headmaster the safety pin. And he pinned the rose to her dress, just above her left breast, and patted her again, affectionately, on her shoulder.

'*Honour thy father and thy mother, Milton, that thy days may be long in the land which…*' He waited for me to complete it.

'…*the Lord thy God giveth thee!*'

'A first-class mother you have, Milton!… And a fine son, Mistress Sobers!'

A woman's head appeared at the front window; and she shouted, 'Joshua, your food on the table five minutes ago.'

The headmaster looked around, slightly worried, and slightly embarrassed. But he turned and faced my mother and me; and he took my mother's hands in his hands, and left them there for a long, warm, affectionate minute, and he smiled.

'Well, Mistress Sobers, repast. Time for repast!' My mother smiled.

'I understands, sir.'

'Goodnight, Mistress Sobers.'

'I thank you for letting we take up so much o' your precious time, Mister Headmaster. A man in your position, is a man with difficulties, the difficulties o' bringing up all them children in the schoolhouse.'

'Come again, Mistress Sobers! And, Sobers, see you in school, bright and early in the morning.' Something in his voice told me something. 'Well, Mistress Sobers, repast. Time for repast.'

'Goodnight, sir! and God bless you, sir!' My mother grumbled on and on, although the headmaster was already inside his house, and we were trudging back across the side road. 'May the Lord bless yuh, son,' she said, meaning the headmaster. 'Bless your dear heart, sir. You is a man put by God in a damn difficult sittiation…' Rain clouds were piling up. The crickets in the tall weeds at the side of the road accompanied us, and now and then a night-bat would fly past too close to our faces, and we would stand still, or duck our heads, until its thick flapping wings disappeared. Then we turned the corner and came out on the Front Road. The guest houses were quiet now. People were eating. And the road was quiet too. There were no prams, no nursemaids from the village, no evil dogs with evil white boys, nothing but the peace of the sea and the skin-screeching crawling of the crabs on the walks of the Hastings Rocks, moving and scurrying and scavenging like chalk on a blackboard. It was quiet and peaceful – even the waves, which romped like children spoken to, climbing the shore and the side of the Rocks, and then losing their foothold, and slipping back into the sea again. And all this time, my mother was quiet. Only her breathing was walking beside me. But there was something in the way she walked. I glanced at her breast, and I saw the rose. I lagged behind, and I could sense some odd feeling in the way she put her foot forward and brought up the other one alongside it, and then made another step in front of that foot… some plan, some plot was being measured out of those footsteps.

We passed the Hastings Rocks, and the Rocks went out of sight. Our corner was coming up next. Just before we turned the corner, my mother looked at the Marine Hotel, and made a loud mental note, 'Girlie must be still working.' And we moved on, in the darkness, with the clouds lining up. She reached down in the darkness, and she grasped my hand. The darkness always bothered her. But something about the firmness of the grip – the grip was usually a touch, a touch of recognition, a touch of familiarity, of closeness – this grip was firm and sudden, and cold. The white world was behind us now. We were on our road. She began to suck on her teeth, noisily, with great annoyance. 'What you think I is, at all, boy? You make me come all the way 'cross this place, in the white people' district this time o' night… you make me go up there to the headmaster-man and make myself look like a damn fool…' I did not even see the whiteness of her palm. But I felt it, wham! That one landed on my hand. In the darkness, I tried to move out of her range, but the blows landed anyhow. Wham-wham! 'Take that!' she said, 'and that!' Wham-wham! 'You make tonight the last time you try to make me look like a damn fool in front o' that gentleman, you hear?' But I was gone. Gone into the darkness, away from her.

'Milton? MIL-ton?' She was alone in the darkness; and she was terrified of the darkness. I had her beaten. 'Mil-TUN, boy, come back with me! Milton Milton Milton…'

And her voice, like the voice of a church bell in the distance, disappeared from me as I ran across the street, our street, away from her, to be free…

4

The moon was running hurdles between a barricade of clouds. Sometimes, it would appear from behind the clouds, and guide me; and at other times, it would stay behind the paling of clouds and sneer at me, and leave me stranded in the deserted, free road. Once or twice, the headlamps of a motor car hit me, and I scampered into the gutter.

It was late. And it was chilly. But I was on my own. And I was glad. I could tramp down to Gravesend Beach any time, at any hour now, with Lester and the boys. I could play cricket until the dusk came, until the cricket ball and the darkness were one colour. I could go out in Lester's father's fishing boat and look at the sea and look at the fish, and look at the island changing from an island to a dot in the sea. I could do anything. I could even hide in the darkness of the wall of the Marine Hotel and watch the tourists dance clumsily to the swinging beat of the calypso. I could do anything.

But where was I to go tonight? Where would I sleep? My father! No. My father would be under the tamarind tree with his face close to the raging flame from the bottle-lamp, and his eyes would be on the few shillings under the canvas cloth, where the money was placed out of the eyes of P.C. 202, Edwin Jones, alias the Gestapo. I know! The white lady who gave her clothes to my mother to be washed. She must be lonely. And I could keep her company. No. Yes! No! Yes!... And then, and then... perhaps she might give me an imported biscuit from her imported tin of biscuits which came from England and which had a lion and another white animal which had one horn sticking out of his head, and which had a red flag wrapped around the tin, and some braid and some plaid... Or perhaps I should simply visit Miss Brewster, and help her clean the cockroaches out of her larder, and help her sweep her yard, or… (Girlie's first child, Rachel, had run away from home, too. And she was only eleven years old. And I remember that the moment after she ran away, Girlie and my mother and the rest of the village called her a jezebel, because only jezebels ran away from home and spent their time on the wharf welcoming every man-of-war and tourist boat from England and America. But we never heard from Rachel for a long long time. And when she was out of everybody's mind, she became something like a martyr to the other children whose parents were cruel. And then one day, the village erupted with praise and surprise, and laughter and forgiveness, when Willoughby the postman brought a first-class, registered air mail red-white-and-blue envelope with United States written on it. And on the envelope, with a picture of Abraham Lincoln, the man who freed the slaves, was Rachel's handwriting like a spider which had got rambled in a pool of ink. Everybody, including Willoughby, read the letter. A large technicolour photograph of Rachel, fat and shining and jewelled, plump smack in the middle of two fat black children; and behind them was a fat prosperous man. Rachel was married. Rachel had succeeded. Rachel had two legitimate children. Two boys. Rachel's mother, Girlie, had six children in all, and not one of them was legitimate, and not two of them from the same man. Inside the letter, folded the same size as the stamp with Lincoln's picture on it, was a real ten-dollar bill, made in the United States of America, with 'In God We Trust' printed on it. I can still remember how Girlie turned her bloodshot eyes around and around in her head at the sight and at the possession of the money. 'Lord Jesus in heaven, have Thy mercy!' Girlie shouted. 'I have win the first prize! Oh Jesus God, I got the first prize I win a sweepstake!' And immediately, she hid the money in her soiled brassière strap, in the crux of her breasts. 'My girl-child marri'd, my child marri'd a big 'Merican-man! But Mistress Sobers, look how that little thing gone and get marri'd to a big 'Merican-man! She gone way way up in that big country and marri'd a big big doctor-man! Well, Jesus Christ, ain't that something, though.' And then she had beaten her leg, saying with the action, that she was sure something good had come of her child, Rachel. 'Mistress Sobers, I knowed it, I knowed it! I knew it all the time. When we was combing the dark streets, walking night after night by the sea, by the Rocks, down by Gravesend Beach, thinking that maybe the waves in the sea wash' Rachel out... and them long dark nights walking the lonely lonely roads, lis'ning for something or somebody to come outta the cane fields, thinking that perhaps a man had take' my child in them canes, and had do what the hell he like' with Rachel... Mistress Sobers, deep deep down in my heart, I knew, and I calling on 'pon He up there above to bear my witness, I did know all the time, that Rachel was out of harm's way, and in someplace like Amer'ca. And to show you that I was right all these years...' 'But how much years gone by now, that Rachel have run 'way from home now, Girlie?' my mother asked. And Girlie got vexed and chastised my mother. 'Do not slander my daughter, Mistress Sobers, please. Rachel not run 'way no place. You can't call it run 'way, now. That child was only escaping from the systum, darling. Is a' escape, Mistress Sobers. And escaping is a diff'rent thing altogether from running 'way.' 'I beg your pardon, darling. Pardon me,' my mother said, with a razor blade in her voice. 'Do not let we worry our heads over Rachel now. Rachel all right. She happy. Rachel prosper' like nobody's business. And she have two nice-looking childrens. But how you like my gran'childrens, though? You think they take after the gran'mother, or they take after the mother?' 'They take after the godmother, Girlie!' My mother was Rachel's god-mother. And that was the story of Rachel's flight from our village.)... or would she let me sleep in her thick bed of chicken feathers? The night was chilly. And it was late. I had no place to go, in the midst of my freedom. Tomorrow, I would spend the whole day on the beach, or picking sea-eggs, or watching the white people play tennis on the Garrison Savannah, or watch the stiff toy-soldiers of men change the guard at the Garrison Barracks. But tomorrow was too far off. And tonight, today, was such a long day.

The clouds had gathered around the moon now; and there was a threat of rain in the skies. In the glare of another set of motor-car headlamps, I saw Miss Brewster coming towards me. She came out of the light like a tugger coming out of a thick fog. Before I could run, she was on me.

'Hey, you! Is that you, Milton? Your mother do not have any more decencies than to send you out in a night like tonight?' Before I could say a word, she was reproaching my mother; and all young mothers in the village. 'Do not say a word. Do not say one word. Come, come with me, Milton.' And we set out for home, Miss Brewster's home. 'The manner your mother bringing you up, boy, is not no Christian-minded manner o' bringing up a child. You had your supper? Okay! I will give you your supper. You must be hungry. You is hungry, ain't you? Sure, you hungry!' And talking like this, answering her own questions, she led me across the dark road.

We turned the corner by the Bath, named the Bath Corner. A clump of men was shouting at the tops of their voices, arguing about the best heavyweight boxer in the world. The night before, Joe Louis had fought Rocky Marciano. And Miss Brewster, used to the foulness of these arguments around the Bath Corner, and anticipating some of it now, applied more pressure to my hand, and pulled me faster, away from hearing the profanities. But I lingered with my ears, and even rehearsed some of the choice words in my mind. A man was presenting his case:

'No, man! Not in this world nor in the next world to come, nor, be-Christ! in the nextest after that! So, I saying to you, that no fucking white man could lick no black man! It ain' true!'

'Boy, take a look at your hist'ries, boy!' another man was saying. We were twenty yards from them. 'Take a peep at the hist'ry books, and you have to agree with me that, gorblummuh! you do not know what the hell you have just say, and utter'.' All the men gathered around his words like flies on a bag of sugar in a shop. 'Lissen to me. Lissen to me! I is a man, the onliest man in this here present company barring none, and none exempted, I say I is the only man what travel this kiss-me-arse world from East, be-Christ, to West. North and South.' The men bawled. And I felt Miss Brewster flinch. Within my heart I was enjoying the man's voice. It was like the voice of a drunken man singing a descant of Psalm 23, standing in the graveyard of St Hastings Church, just behind the organist's alto pedals. 'Man, I have journey' so damn far on this earth that one time I went up in Russia, and I have see', with my own two eyes, Stalin drinking vodkas outta a chamberpot!' Miss Brewster tensed her body.

'And I still say and affirm in a positive kind o' way, that no kiss-me-arse white man could lick a black man inside the ring, or outside the ring.'

'Did not a man name' Marciano lick-in Joe Louis' arse last night? And did not a next fellar, Max Schmeling, lick it in too? These is commasense-facts and hist'ries I putting to you.'

'I put it to you, Willy-Willy, I put it to you. Is a black man more stronger than a white man?'

'I will not 'pon a point of order or principles, answer that arse-hole interrogative, man…'

'Words! words! words!' shouted the men. 'Words! Christ, Willy, man, you like you swallow' a Oxford dictionary, man!'

'…What kind o' arse-hole question you putting to me after I have relate' certain ins-and-outs of a particular sittiation… Goodnight, Miss Brewster, ma'am! God go with yuh! How-d'-do, and goodnight, ma'am. Get home safely!… 'cause, Robby, I looks at you, and be-Christ!…'

'Continue, man, Willy-Willy. Continue.'

'As I was saying, I was living up in Harlem New York City, Amer'ca, and I had a cleaning bill what was taller'n Moun' Teverest, and the little piece o' pussy I was then keep-on the side, she belly start climbing the hills o' pregnuncy, and every morning and evening, she moaning and groaning, Willy-Willy, the baby coming, the baby coming – although she is only two weeks in the fambly-way…'

We were too far from them to hear more. Miss Brewster never did stop grumbling about her upbringing and the upbringing of this generation. '…And when we was little girls, we never could be seen loit'ring 'round the Bath Corner. Oh no!' Her attitude to the men was like a block of ice; and it seemed she was frozen with an unknown fear that would come to her, one day perhaps, when all these bad men like Willy-Willy would take over the entire island. 'When we was girls growing up into young womens and ladies, there wasn't no such things as gathering 'round Bath Corners.'

'There was lights in them days, Miss Brewster, ma'am?'

'Lights? We had to be in our parents' parlour by six o'clock. In them days, it was charraids and decencies! Decencies and charraids. And not one of we girls ever took unto herself a man, saving it was approve' by our parents…'

'Was you married, then, Miss Brewster, ma'am?'

'The modernt generation of today! Lord Lord Lord in heaven!'

We were home now. Miss Brewster tiptoed through the darkness of the house, a long cavern of old Victorian furniture, through treacherous alleyways of china cabinets loaded with the hope-chest contents of her two sisters, now dead, now hopeless, and without ever having had the experience of a man's warm lips on their prim mouths; and through the short passageway crowded with pictures of Miss Brewster's family and family tribe of uncles, aunts, sisters, first, second, and third and fourth cousins. And the largest framed picture was that of her own godson, the educated man from the village. It was a life-sized portrait. I was so happy in this house! I never wanted to be inside a house as much as I wanted to be inside Miss Brewster's house.

'Miss Brewster, I will help you do your things, and clean the yard and scrub the house, and go at the shop for you, and…'

'Milton?'

Her hands, fumbling in the darkness, touched a lamp. And the lamp fell. And the glass chimney was shattered. I remembered my mother's chimney which I had cleaned this evening. I wondered whether she was watching the chimney now, as she always watched it, when she sat alone in the small house grown vast with boredom. She would sit for hours and watch the flames lick the sides of the chimney, and leave little black tongues of dried flames which ran all the way up the fat belly of the lamp chimney.

'That chimbley was a precious thing to me, Milton,' she said, sweeping up the broken pieces, and guiding them towards the open door which brought in some light, although not much. I could see the stains of tears crawling across her cheeks like two small dry rivers. She changed her mind about sweeping the broken glass outside, and instead, she put it into an envelope. She took the envelope with the broken pieces, and she put it safely into a drawer of a large ornate chest, which had dolphins, now a long time dead and wrinkled, embossed all over it. She hid the envelope at the back of the drawer. 'A' old woman don't have much things to hang on 'pon, Milton. And I is a' old woman now. My mother give me that lamp chimbley fifty-sixty years ago…' She was crying again. Crying like an old woman would cry; so quiet, so ashamed of herself for crying in front of a small boy, that you had to listen very carefully to hear the changes in the rhythm of her breathing. In such a big house, this woman crying. In such a big house, with so much food in it, this old woman crying. In such a comfortable house, filled with furniture that my eyes had never seen before; a house many times larger than our shack, and here, this woman, so proud and so dignified on the steps of her girls' school, crying before me, a little boy who had run away from home, because home was too cruel, too poor. 'I guess you want something to eat, eh, Milton?' She shuffled out into the kitchen which, unlike ours, was joined onto the rest of the house, on the same level. In her kitchen was an artillery of shining pots and pans whose outsides were brighter than their insides. And there were plates and saucers piled high and evenly, like the strata in the rock quarry in which my father sometimes worked, cutting stone.

She brought me some homemade coconut bread and some aerated drink; and I immediately attacked it. The bread was polka-dotted with raisins and currants and prunes; and I could smell the rum and the vanilla essence which she had bathed the bread with. As I ate, she sat looking at me. It was a far-off look, a piercing gaze, distant and puzzling; a kind of look which my mother always had when she was debating whether to flog me or kiss me. Sometimes, the headmaster looked at me that way too. I glanced up from the saucer which was patched with plaster of Paris, and she was still watching me, as if I were the cat, and she the rat… or she the cat and I the rat.

She got up from the rocking-chair in which she sat watching me, and in which she was rocking herself, and she took off her shoes and threw them under the bed. And then she began to undress. In front of me! I wondered why she would do this. Perhaps she was really blind. Perhaps she did not remember that I was still there with her. My mother had told me that one day Miss Brewster ate her lunch in front of all the assistant mistresses in the school's lunch room, and then sent home a little girl to fetch her lunch. That was how forgetful she was – twenty years ago. Perhaps she had forgotten that she had brought me home with her. But she ripped her dress in half with the zipper which travelled the length of her body, and as she unzipped the zipper her heavy bowels and breasts fell out into her underslip, like the entrails of a pig spurting out when the knife of the butcher had ripped it in twain. She wheeled around, and faced me with her rolling body. I closed my eyes. But I could not keep them closed too long. And when I opened them, she was looking at me. And when she saw me looking at her, she turned around again, in a funny way, as if she was telling me with that action, that I should stop eating and come around in front and see her, and watch her. Now, all I could see was the heaving heaviness of her behind, and the large worms of blue-black veins in her legs. She untied the canopy of the bedstead. The canopy dropped like a thick fish-net, and she went under it, leaving only her legs exposed to me. Her dress went up out of my view, like the bottom of a curtain in a theatre. And then, all was flesh and veins.

'Milton?'

'Yes, Miss Brewster, ma'am.'

'You like girls?'

'Girls, ma'am?'

'Yes, girls. Have you ever see' a girl yet?'

'No, ma'am… yes, ma'am! Lester have a sister who is a girl. I see her only this morning, ma'am.'

'What is the best thing about a girl that you like, Milton?'

'The best thing, ma'am?'

'You remember on them nice bright Sundee mornings going down at Gravesend Beach, and seeing them nice little girls running 'bout on the beach; and playing hop-scotch in the sand and shouting and screeling and hollering and *naked*?'

Her body appeared like a bulk, like an oversized bag of sugar all the time she talked to me. The curtain rope of the drape dropped further to the floor and I could no longer see her legs. But I could see her feet. They looked like two slabs of very thick rubber, the tops of which were black and the bottoms of which were pink. And each time she moved, they expanded and contracted like the bellows of a concertina.

'Come here, Milton, a second.'

Behind the canopy, she was as still as death. The room was still. My breathing was still. And when I watched the canopy for a long time, deciding what to do, the bulk became larger and larger and larger still, until all I could see before me was the bulk of her body which filled the entire house.

'Milton?' she called out, in a sing-song voice.

Perhaps Miss Brewster was calling me to suck my blood. Or to kill me. Willy-Willy had told me tales of women who lived alone, who sucked little boys' blood until all that was left was skin and bones. Old women were vampires, he told me. They would trap little boys in their houses and pretend they were their godmothers or fairy godmothers and then tie them down to the bed and suck out all of their blood and drink it. The more I watched the canopy the more I thought it was changing from red satin to black crepe. Out of the roomful of black crepe came Miss Brewster, undressed, and no longer fat and wobbly, but thin as a razor blade, thin as a vampire or a witch. Her fingers were long and they had nails on them; and her hair was long and flying about around her shoulders. And when I looked again, she was no longer naked, but dressed in a long flowing white dress. Miss Brewster was not walking like a human being now. She was rising and falling in the air. Rising and falling, and still each time she rose and fell, she was nearer to me. She held out her hand, and said, 'Come, time to go to bed!'

'No no no!'

'Milton, what is the matter with you?'

'No no no! I don't wanna, I don't wanna!'

She reached out to me and I darted aside; and I hit her as I darted aside, and something fell to the ground with a small, dull noise, like a small pin-cushion. Miss Brewster gasped. I looked at her head, and she was bald. Miss Brewster was bald.

'No no no! You is a man! You is a man. I wanna go home!'

'Milton, please! Milton? Please!'

'You's a man! You's a man!'

'It is a wig, Milton! A wig!' She was sitting dejectedly in her rocking-chair, holding the clump of hair in her hands. 'I had a bad sickness when I was a little girl. It is a wig, Milton. A wig… please, don't tell nobody, Milton. It is a wig…'

And when I dashed out of that house, in the drizzling rain, with the lightning flashing like pieces of steel all about me, I could still hear her voice in my ears, and see her tears coming down her cheeks like that time when a group of us choir boys poured water on the face of the wooden statue of Mary Magdalene, painted in ebony. I ran and I ran and the splashes in the road filled my eyes with mud and water. And still I ran in the direction of my father's house, across the Pasture, Rudder Pasture.

Before me stands the clammy-cherry tree. It is big and thick around its waist like my mother. Its branches hang low low to the ground; so low that I can hold up my hand and grab a branch and swing and swing until my head gets giddy from the excitement and the glee.

It is late now. The night is like a monster out of a story book; and it is terrible like Miss Brewster. There still is the tree. Standing and blocking my way. But I have to pass it in order to get to my father's house. There is no other way there.

I can see the shadow of his house just in front of me, keeping quiet, as if it is waiting to frighten me. But I walk on, looking out of the corner of my eyes, seeing everything but seeing nothing. Imagining everything, but seeing nothing. Hearing everything, but seeing nothing. The dogs are growling. The rain is falling now. Vampires are flapping their wings and sharpening their teeth, and Miss Brewster is among them, and she is undressing and coming after me… the lightning is flashing like a torchlight… and the old toothless headmaster is caressing behind his back a rose tree branch that has no rose on it, only prickles – *I have just passed the tree!* – and nothing happens.

I reach my father's door. The rain is pouring now. And I knock on it, and call out with all my voice for him. But not a sound, not a word comes out of my mouth. The lightning is flashing again. And I am like a block of ice, with fear. But a window opens. A shadow peeps out, sees nothing in the shadows, and slams the window with a bang that was louder than the thunder that roared over the hills. 'Some rotten-able bastard! Nathan, has you put the salt around the house tonight before you lay down? You cannot trust these bastards what lives near you as neighbours, hear?

Nathan, has you sprinkle' 'round this house with salt, like I ask you?' A man's voice grumbles something; and that is all I hear for a long while. I knock again, louder, and my knocking frightens me. 'Nathan? NATHAN Nathan Nathan? You hear something? What I have just tell you 'bout sprinkling the salt 'round the house at night to keep away them spirits, 'specially Beulah, from preventing me from catching a proper night's sleep?' The man grumbles again; and I can hear him walking about inside the house. 'Nathan, I have a mind to make you throw-on a jacket 'round your shoulder' and go out there right now this minute and sprinkle the salt 'round the house. 'Cause, be-Christ Beulah dead and gone now three years running inna four, and she would not stop haunting me and riding me, riding me, when the nights come.'

'Gorblummuh!' the man said.

'Something out there! Somebody out there!'

'Medlin, lemme catch some shut-eye, good-Christ, nuh?'

'I want you to go out there and sprinkle 'bout some salt, and tell Beulah that she dead now, and she don't got no damn business 'round my house, haunting me.'

'She right like hell to haunt your arse! If you didn't put something in Beulah' food, Beulah might still be living today!'

'Blow you! Looka, blow you in hell! You stating that I p'ison Beulah! Say it again and lemme hear what you just said. You stating that I put something in Beulah' food?'

But instead he poked his head through the top half of the window and shouted, 'Who the hell you is out there?'

'Daddy? Daddy, is me.'

'Milton? Gorblummuh, boy! That is you out there? You mean to tell me your mother do not have no more blasted sense than to send you out in a...'

'Daddy?'

'Come back tomorrow morning, Milton, man.'

'Daddy, Miss Brewster is a man...'

'What? Boy, you does see duppies?'

'...I tell you, Daddy, she is a man. I see her with her real head... real hair...'

The woman's head appeared at the window. 'What what what? Who' he? I hear him say he want' to sleep here?'

'For Chrissakes, Medlin, lemme tackle this alone.'

'Look, Nathan, he not setting foot inside of this house! This might be your house, but he not coming in! Be-Christ when he step in, I step out!'

'Medlin, lemme tackle this for Godssake!'

'Look, Nathan, shut that window, do! I catching a draught in my shoulder-blades. Shut the so-and-so window, do!' And she made an attempt to shut it herself, and I saw a shadow move, and then I heard a slap, and Madelaine shrieked. 'God blind you in hell, Nathan! You make just now the last time you ever raise a hand 'gainst me!'

'Shut-shut-shut-shut up! You hear? Or I turn yuh damn face behind your back with a next slap. I is the man here!'

'You can't slap me up nor shut me up, you bastard! You think I frighten' for you or for that dead bitch Beulah or for that other bitch what mothered your idiot-child out there!'

'Have little respect for the boy, woman. Talk proper' in the presence o' the boy, please.' But she went on talking and swearing. 'Milton,' he said, when he must have realized that it was useless to plead any more with Madelaine. 'Milton?' he said again, as if he was not quite sure of himself. By this time, Madelaine had moved away from the window. But we could still hear her moaning and cursing in the background.

'Daddy, Mister Blackman cut-up my back with a...'

'Blackman cut-up your back?'

'Yeah.'

'For what?'

'Mister Blackman cut-up my back all 'cross my shoulder and across my back, for...'

'What for, I ask you? What he do that for?'

'...and my mother take me up to Blackman' house for satisfaction but he give her a rose and she turn' back and when we was getting near home she just turn' 'round and start' beating me up, and...'

'Milton, that is your mother. She have the right to do that, boy.'

'...but I didn' do nothing, though. And after she start' beating me I run away and I went over by Miss Brewster but Miss Brewster turn' inna a man and I run out and the rain start' falling and I get wet and that is why I come to sleep here, 'cause I do not know where else to go and sleep.'

'Man, Milton, look, man, I sleepy as hell, boy! So, look, come back in the morning, eh, and we could talk-over this thing, 'cause sleep got me cripple-up. What you say to that, eh?'

'Tell him that! tell him that! What the hell he mean waking-up people all hours o' the night, for?'

'Shut your arse, woman! I talking to my son, so you keep outta this! Milton, my eyeballs sore sore with lack o' sleep and night rest, boy. So, come back in the morning, eh?'

'But Daddy, the lightning flashing and the rain…'

'In the morning, eh? In the morning, bright and early, I going come 'cross the road and see your mother.'

'That first-child idiot out there not heard you say in the morning? *In the morning, boy!* In the morning. Night-time is make for sleeping in. And the morning-time make for talking in. So come back tomorrow morning, please God.'

'Medlin, this is two times I have ask' you to shut your fucking mout'. The third time I not going to tell you *nothing*. I just going to knock every blasted teeth outta your bloody head. You understan'?'

And suddenly, Madelaine started to sing aloud,

> 'Rock of Ages, cleft for me-eeee,
> Let me hide myself in thee-eee.'

My father left the window to do something inside; and she took the opportunity to come back to the window, to spit outside. 'Hawwwwwk!' her throat said. 'Hawwwwwk! Take that!' And the slimy dribble dropped on my forehead.

'Look, Milton, catch! Hold up yuh hand in the air, and catch this little something.' '…Let me hide myself in thee…' 'Buy a coconut bread with it in the morning to drink with your tea, man.'

I saw the flash flash like a small firefly and then the flash disappeared into the blackness at my feet.

'Take that cent, man, and see what you could do with it, Milton. Come back in the morning. Come back in the morning, I going try to be here, man…'

'– cleft for me-eee,
Let me hide…

'That billy-goat still out there?' She closed the window; and all I could see then was the pasture of trees, creeping towards me. Inside the house, they were quarrelling. She was saying, 'Twelve o'clock midnight! And he come knocking on my house! At twelve o'clock in the middle o' the night!' And all he said was, 'But oh Christ, Medlin! he is only a little boy, and twelve o'clock ain't so damn late, though.'

Beulah was not like Madelaine. Madelaine was not like Beulah. I loved Beulah. Beulah used to live in the house with my father. Beulah used to laugh a lot. Beulah would stand in the frame of the door, her hands rammed into the fatness of her hips, akimbo, her legs spawning the doorway as the Pillars of Rome spawned Rome, and hold her head back, showing the ringlets in her neck, and she would say aloud as if the entire village had come to listen to her, 'Oh jumping Jesus, Nathan! your dear boy-child out here! Boy, come here, do, and let your dear aunt kiss you. Come come come!' And I would run and place my head against her stomach; and her stomach would heave like a palm full of jello. And she would squeeze me close to her, until I almost disappeared into the sweet billowiness of her bosom. And she would kiss me, on my face, and on my head; and all the time press her hand tight tight tight into my hand; and then, when she held me arms' length from her to look and see how big I was growing, and I was so very very happy… and when I had the courage to open my eyes and look into my palm, I would see there, the shiniest, newest shilling ever made. Beulah was the only person in the world who did this to me.

But Beulah is dead now. Dead and gone. Dead dead dead, and gone – gone, my father told me, as he wiped his eyes with tears in them, with the large tablecloth of a handkerchief which only the day before, Beulah had ironed for him with her own hands. Gone for ever, up above with the clouds and the birds and the air, and God, my father told me. Gone gone gone, is Beulah to Beulahland. When Beulah died I was seven years old. And they told me that she died because she had something growing inside her belly, which grew and grew and grew, and which was not supposed to grow, but it grew nevertheless. And the thing which grew the wrong way caused her death, my father said. One bright morning, just as she had cooked and washed and starched and ironed that handkerchief for my father, she sat down to drink some ice-water, and bram! cramps, bad-feels, giddy-head! And before my father could say, 'Beulah what' wrong?' Beulah was gone...

5

I was running through the thunder and the lightning and the rain now. Through the silken shades of the driving rain I could see a few dog-tired bus drivers and conductors sleeping on the seats of their buses parked in front of Pastor Best's Christian Mission Church in God. They were waiting for the endless revival meeting to crawl to an end in this stormy perspiring night. A crowd of men and women were standing outside, sheltering under the large open windows, listening in awe to the brimstone voice of the pastor. Everybody in the village came to hear Pastor Best during revival meetings in his church. My mother would sometimes attend. She might be there, inside, right now, listening and asking God to return her son to her. I could never understand why she went to this church. She was already christened, and baptized in the big, ivy-covered stone mansion of the other church, the Church of England. But one church was not enough for her. She had to have another church. And she chose the Christian Mission Church in God.

Pastor Best was talking about hell-fire roasting up all the sinners in the village. I was frightened; and I looked around for somebody I knew, somebody I knew was wicked like me, who would be roasted like me. And I saw Willy-Willy, sitting on a large stone, just a little distance from the press of the crowd, ignoring the rain as he vomited and cursed as he vomited. He was talking to the vomit as it spurted out of his mouth in a rush, and then trickled off into a long dribble like chewing gum in a child's outstretched hands. And then he wiped his mouth with the back of his hand, his head hanging as if on a piece of cloth, and then he hawked loudly and spat like a sprinkler.

'Pastor Best, shut yuh fucking mout'! You talking arse!' The men and women standing beside the church whispered to Willy-

Willy to keep quiet; and Willy-Willy said, 'All right all right! Willy-Willy… shhhh!… Willy-Willy going keep quiet!' And without warning, like the thunder, he exploded, in a loud voice, 'Pastor Best? Pas-TUR BEST, shut your… so-and-so mout' up, and go home and live with yuh Sisters!' And the crowd grumbled and felt ashamed and embarrassed for their souls and for Willy-Willy. I remained hiding in the shadows.

The vomit spurted out again; and he watched the dribbling chewing gum of spittle twirling on the ground in front of him. He raised one foot, and mashed his bare heel in the vomit. 'Goddamn! God-damn!… this rum drinking and night-dew don't make me into a Charles Atlas! You hear me, Pastur Best?'

'Shut up, Willy-Willy!' a man said. 'You don't hear the man o' God saying something?'

'Man-o'-God? Man-o'-God?… and living with every marri'd woman in the village?… But I going burn-down this blasted church!… Pastor Best, I going burn-down this blasted church if you don't take your hands offa my woman, Annie… I going burn…' and he vomited again; and his voice died down as if he was now talking a secret to the vomit, and holding it as a conspirator… 'down this blasted church…' He was quiet for a while. Suddenly, an eruption took place inside his chest, deep down. He beat his fist against his chest. And that rackled the cough. It was becoming lighter now. And I could see the contortions and the pain printed on his face as he struggled with the muscles in his guts and in his chest to squeeze the cough and the cold out and up into his mouth so that he might have more control over it. But the more he coughed, the more the cough played with him and taunted him. Eventually, he surrendered his whole body to the uncontrollable rackling. 'Gorblummuh, Pastur Best, I coming in there for Annie's arse!' The volcano inside him was erupting again. He placed his fist against his chest. And he beat on it. And the men and women standing by the windows begged him to make less noise. Then the eruption came. Something was coming up into his mouth, and he sprang up off the stone, and walked off a few feet from the side of the church. He held his head down, low low low to the ground. And he spluttered the greenish stuff on the ground and on his bare feet.

'Gorblummuh! And Annie have lock' the door, and I can't get in outta this night-dew! Whilst she in there, in Pastur Best' church, getting in the blasted spirit. But be-Christ! if I count to twenty and that church not over, Annie' backside going 'o be stiff with licks tonight... Pas-TUR Best?'

And when he shouted, the men rushed to him to silence him with their hands and fists, but he wobbled off in my direction, and I had to escape under the cellar of the church. I felt doomed under the cellar. (The Gestapo had arrested small boys for 'breaking and entering' church cellars, to do 'rudeness' together.) In the cellar it was dark like the Hell the pastor was preaching about above my head. All those people, all those grown-up people above me, were safe and saved. And I was lost in the everlasting darkness of the cellar. And then, cobwebs took my mind off cellars and hells. And they tickled my face. And they tickled my ears. And I wanted to laugh out as I always laughed out when cobwebs tickled my ears. But the pastor's voice poured through the floorboards and drowned me with a new fear: a fear of becoming nothing when I died. And I could see, through the cracks in the floor, the upper softness of the women's legs; and the white bloomers, frilled, and heavy like washed-out white flourbags. And I could see the shining black old suits of the men, the Brothers; and the grey ash of the boys' legs, exposed by their short trousers, showing just where the lakes of coconut oil and hair grease ended on their skin. Some of the boys and some of the girls were bowing their heads like scales weighing potatoes, because they could not follow the words of the pastor's message which was too heavy and too dull and too boring for their young minds that flittered like butterflies. Every now and then, a woman's foot would explode and rip the floorboards above me. And I became frightened again; and I saw the church tumbling down in the middle of this fever of emotion and religion. And I saw the End of the World coming. And the trees tumbled down. And the winds roared like in the Bible. And the sea, the same sea that washed the Esplanade and the Hastings Rocks, the same sea rushed over the Front Road and through the back roads and came through the island, the town, the village and it washed everybody into the sea, into Hell, and only the people in the church were saved. And the school house tumbled down, and Lester and I laughed; and my father was ripped out, ripped up with his guts tied around that tree in the Pasture where he lived; and Miss Brewster was killed praying on her knees, and then I heard Pastor Best's voice roaring down the hill under my cellar, and a woman's voice in the church screeled out: *'No no no! Oh Gawd, Jesus Christ! No!'*

And Pastor Best's voice said aloud: 'Yeah! Yeah, Lord! YEAH! Brothers and Sisters, I bringing you a message tonight that going rip-loose and tear-loose and capsize inside your guts… tear OUT all the nastiness there! and cleanse you… yeah! CLEANSE YOU! cleanse you cleanse you, like nobody's business…'

And the woman's voice said: 'Nobody's business save God' business!'

'Yeah, that's right, Sister Sobers! You tell them! Nobody's business save God Jesus Christ' business!'

'Ahhh-ahhh! hallelooo! praise Jeees-sus!'

'Yeah, Sister Sobers! You tell 'em. You is a woman with a broken heart tonight! Lord help us to pray for this Sister! This Sister, Lord, have loss her son! But praise Christ, Brothers and Sisters, Jesus send back the prodigull son, and God-dammit, He could send back Milton!' The pastor was facing the congregation now. I could see him through a large crack in the floor. He was facing his people with only half of his body. And he would bob and weave his body about like a boxer throwing punches. And each time he punched the congregation with a moan or a grunt of rejoicing, the congregation yelled out, and screamed, 'AAAMEN!' His lips were red, like arrows in a forge. And he would shake his whole body this way, and then that way, moving like a sparring partner in a ring with a destructive champion. Rivers of sweat were washing his face, and when he shook the words out of his mouth, the sweat sprinkled the Brothers and Sisters, like Holy Water.

'Lawwd, help us! Lawwd, help us!' He held the Book in his hand and banged it many times on the railing that railed off the congregation from him. And when he was tired of banging it on the railing, and when the echo had died like a shout in the sea, he brandished it in their faces. And then he gave off a laugh. 'Heh-heh-heh! I say Gawwd bring back the prodigull son, and He could bring back Milton. Suffer the little childrens… suffer the little little childrens to COME unto me… saith the Lawwd!' He was talking rat-tat-tat-tat fast now; not taking any time for breath nor for thoughts. 'Tonight is a night for exposing all the rotten-ness in this damn village. Tonight is exposing night, and I talking-out everything tonight. 'Cause tonight, praise Jee-sus, they is two sinners, yeah two confess' sinners in the midst o' this holy congregation. Yes yes yes! YES, Lord! They is a sinner down there sitting down what has loss her son. And they is a next sinner sitting over here, who have come in here tonight, thank Jee-sus, to find solace and a harbour in a time o' trouble and tribulation from a man who gone wild out there in the wilderness o' the world!' His voice died down. Low low low. Now it was a con-spiratorial whisper; he was telling them things which not even the person next door ought to hear. It was a confidential whisper, a plotting whisper. 'You going wonder how I get this freedom o' speech tonight! You going wonder how one man get all this freedom o' speech to expose all the worthlissness, all the degra-dation in this place, in this village. I have get this freedom, 'cause I own this house o' God. I owns this house, 'cause this house is the House o' God, and I, praise Christ! is the messenger o' God!'

'Freedom o' speech, Lord! Freedom o' speech!' shrieked Annie, who pounded up and down the aisle in front of the altar. Then she dropped flat on the floor, writhing and worming around like a large green worm dropped from a bad pod of peas. 'Freedom! FREE-dom… freedom o' speech and freedom o' pow'r!'

'That's right, Sister Annie! Freedom o' speech! I have free-dom o' speech! That is British! The British owns my freedom o' speech! Yeah! The British! But I is British! Yeah! And I owns my own freedom o' speech! Yeah! That is logick! And it is British, too! Yeah! YEAH! But! Praise Christ! I want freedom o' entry! Yeah! FREEDOM! Yeah! O' entry! Yeah! FREEDOM O' ENTRY! Freedom o' entry to enter in your souls! Yeah! Lord, gimme that freedom, 'cause that sort o' freedom is Yourn!'

'You got that freedom, Pastor Best! That freedom is yourn already! You got it. You have it! 'Cause it is yourn!'

The church was shaking. The men and women standing outside in the dying rain were shaking too. And it was hushed. Inside the church, all I could hear was Annie writhing in the pain and ecstasy of the spirit. Above her, standing with the sweat of his words sprinkling like a hose, was Pastor Best, waving and beckoning and imploring his congregation of sinners to come up and say a few words to God, in silence.

'A loss son-*nuh*! Yeah! Dress in gold-*uh*! With riches-*uh*! And raiments make outta the best-*tuh*! Lord help us-*uh*! That son-*uh*! Lord-*uh*! Now loss-*uh*! That son is now loss-*uh*! Let us pray for that boy-*uh*! Loss in the outside world o' these savage savage nasty brutal bad streets-*uh*! We ask Thee, Lord-*uh*! Put courage-*uh*! COURAGE-*uh*! In this Sister's heart-*uh*! Lord-*uh*! For though the journey is long-*uh*! And ardrous-*uh*! We know-*uh*! Yes yes yes yes yes YES-*uh*! Though the journey! Is long! And hard-*uh*! Jesus Christ is watching! He is watching-*uh*! Yes-*uh*! Watching-*uh*! You and me-*uh*! The great and the small-*uh*! He is watching! The white and the black-*uh*! The rich and the poor-*uh*! Them who live out the Front Road-*uh*! And them in the back roads-*uh*! In the Marine Hotel-*uh*! In the Pasture-*uh*! And praise Christ! them poor peoples in the Poor House! He can save you-*uh*! And me-*uh*!' His voice was rising and falling, rising and falling; controlled and uncontrolled; musical and savage; soothing and rasping; comforting and frightening. And every time he said '*uh*!' he gave whatever was in front of him – the railing of the altar, or a pew, or a Sister's back – a smack, and when there was nothing in front of him, he slammed the Bible against his thighs. And each time he slammed the Good Book there, and uttered forth his cry of painful association to God, the Brothers and Sisters moaned and gasped, and called on Christ to save them. And then, all was like a graveyard in the church. Only the breathing. Only the breathing of men and women who had run a long hard race to victory. Only the creaking of the pastor's shoes as he walked up and down the small church. And then he began again. His voice still in its conspiring tone. 'I going ask you… mens, womens and childrens… suffer the little ones-*uh*!… to come. I going ask you Brothers and Sisters, and them out there standing up by the winders, to come, and kneel down, and talk with Jesus. Not with me. I could only listen. But God could answer! Yeah! God could listen and answer. I see we have the headmaster o' the school 'mongst us! Don't hide, Mister Blackman! Don't jump down offa that rock-stone and hide! You could hide from me! But not from God! Come, one and all! If you is a headmaster and you could enter a school house, then you could enter God's house. So, come in, Mister Headmaster! Take off yuh hat and come in!' And like a miracle, all the men and women at the windows started to file inside the church; and the Brothers and Sisters got up and walked slowly, humbly up to the altar rail and kneeled down and were quiet – everybody except Sister Annie, who jumped up in the air, and started to peel off her clothes. And nobody looked at her. Not even Pastor Best.

'I see we have a white gentleman still standing up outside! Don't be frighten', Mister White Man. You can come in here! 'Cause I know where you went tonight! Yeah, Lord! They can't hide nothing from You! Mister White Man, if you could go in the Cat House, you could come in the Spirit House!' And the face of the white man faded in the blackness outside the church. I was frightened. All the moaning and the groaning, and searching for help; and the people inside finding it; and I, outside, and beneath, trembling and not knowing what to do. 'Let we pray for that white gentleman, Lord! He come-*uh*! In our streets-*uh*! Looking for flesh-*uh*! The flesh of our womens-*uh*! But, Lord-*uh*! He is 'fraid for Your presence-*uh*! God save him-*uh*! And Milton-*uh*! A loss boy tonight-*uh*! In the byways and lie-ways of death-*uh*!' – a woman's voice screamed, and Pastor Best waited until the scream tore the pants off the night, and exploded in a long hysterical laugh, before he went on – 'let we bow our heads in pray-*uh*! For our headmaster-*uh*! Mister Blackman-*uh*!…'

…Something long and crawly was crawling on my leg. It was dark black under the cellar. No light from the Good Book, or from the cleansed, chastised people above me. Nothing had seeped through the floorboards but terror. But I could not mistake the crawl. I had felt something similar before. And my mother had always warned me, never *never* to move, when I felt one of them crawling on me. I pretended now to be dead. I lay still. Dead-still, as if Pastor Best's words had killed me. And as I experienced this play-play death, I tried to follow the progress of the thing crawling up my leg, counting all the time each one of its hundred legs as they moved like a very slow magic lantern, or like a picture taken at too slow a speed. The centipede crawled right up to the top of my leg; stopped; waited, as if it were waiting for the traffic lights to change from red to green; or as if it was undecided which way to go: up my left leg or my right leg; my left hip or my right hip; and then it made up its mind to continue up under my trousers. It was a giggly ticklish journey under my trousers. But it was terrifying too. But I remembered I was dead. And I had to remain dead. Into the softness, into the shrubbery around my young manhood, oh, heh-heh-heh-hee-hee-hee!… ticklish ticklish! How I feared that this beast would try to eat off my manhood! (It had happened before. My mother told me this bedtime story once.) Up up up it went until my belt around my waist created a road block for it. And the centipede had to make a detour and travel right back down the way it had come. And just as it got near the end of the subway created by my leg and my trousers, something, someone was coming under the cellar with me. Paper was being rubbed together… a larger body was crawling… Pastor Best was tearing up the people above my head, 'God, look down tonight! At this wickit wickit wickit world o' Yours! And behold the corruption! And crime! And whoring of all mankinds-*uh*!' – the centipede began to sting. I grabbed my trousers, my leg, and the centipede in one trembling handful of panic, hearing the storm above me, just as a match was struck and a fzzzz-ing noise was beginning and the cellar was filled with smoke; and another match was struck, and Willy-Willy's face was shown to me in a halo of the match, and sweat and madness; his eyes fiery with blood and rum. He saw me and he stiffened. And then he came at me, and grabbed me by the leg and pulled me out of the cellar after him.

'Get your arse outta here! I going blow-down this kiss-me-arse place, 'cause I tired waiting for Annie to come out! Get your arse outta here!'

We got out, and Willy-Willy, smelling like an open cask of bad rum, started to laugh, as we watched the smoke rising from the cellar and engulfing the whole church. And I thought of that Good Friday afternoon, in the crowded cinema in Bridgetown, when I saw the clouds of smoke, or something, rising rising, and out of them came a Cross.

'You ain't seen me tonight, hear?'

'No, Willy-Willy!'

'You ain't know my name, neither, hear?'

'No, Willy-Willy.'

'And be-Christ! I not seen you neither, hear? 'Cause, gorblummuh! if you utter one word!… one iota-word outta you!' His hands were around my neck, choking me. 'One kiss-me-arse word outta you, I know where you does live! And buh-doooommmmm! your house blow-up in the blasted sea!'

'Yea, Willy-Willy!'

'I tired as arse waiting! So I blow up the blasted church! Now, get yuh arse home!' He coughed and spat. 'I waiting to see this house jump be-Christ, sky-high up to Glory! Heh-heh-heh-heeee!'

As I left him, Pastor Best was still raging, ignorant of the smoke encircling the house of prayer: *'Build me a' ARK! BUILD ME A' ARK! Yessssss! Build me a' ark! Christ knows we need a haven, a' ark, tonight in all this storm! But hallelulia, we inside, we inside, we inside in God' tabernacle! And them who unfortunate enough to be outside tonight, yess, Lord-uh! it is hell! for the end of all flesh is at hand! Yeah, Lord-uh!'* A woman's voice screamed in a cry of joy and of pain; and then she started to sing, a soft song, 'Nearer My God to Thee'. The people were so transfixed by the soft beauty of her complaining voice, that they allowed her to sing almost the first verse by herself, before they joined in.

'God is here tonight, brethren!… God is here!

> *'Near-rerrr my God to Thee,*
> *Near-reer my God to Thee-eee*
> *Near-er my God-duh…'*

6

The street was crowded with people. All the people were black people. And the street was paved; and was wide, wide as the sea. And there were large motor cars such as I had never seen in Barbados. And in the middle of the street was something like a large long flowerbed with red rose flowers in it. And the flowerbed stretched and stretched the whole length of the street, outdistancing my eyes. And there were policemen. The policemen were the only people who were not black like the people. They were white policemen. And these policemen were walking about with guns; and the guns were real guns; not like the guns of pieces of sugar canes with which Lester and I used to declare war on each other; not like the guns we played cowboys-and-crooks with; not like the guns I saw the high school boys from Harrison College and Combermere and the Lodge School carrying on their shoulders and shooting off their mouths with, one day at the Queen's Birthday Parade on the Garrison Savannah. Not like those unreal muskets in the hands of the black people in the island. These guns were hanging out of the policemen's holsters, as if they were too large for the holsters. But the policemen did not behave as if they knew their guns were dropping out of their holsters. They were walking and sauntering up and down the street looking at the black people congregated at the corner of the street which I thought was our Bath Corner. But it was not our Bath Corner. It had a funny name. Not like Bath Street, or Bath Corner, or Bath Place. It had a funny, foolish name, like 125th-Street-and-Seventh-Avenue, and still it looked like our Bath Corner. And there was even the old slave house which we used as a Benefit Society for saving pennies once a week, and as the Village Penny Bank from which you could borrow, or loan, or trust, or deposit a cent, or a penny... and years ago, so my mother had told me, Willy-

Willy had even dared, and did, deposit a farthing. And there was I, in the midst of the flowers and in the midst of the thistles and thorns of men, barefooted. And there was something like white sand on the ground. It was all over the street, all over the sidewalk, all over the people's hair, as if some careless grocery man had lifted a large bag of salt, or flour, and all had capsized all over the place. It was something like sand. But it was not sand. It was like flour too. But it was not flour. And when I touched it, and picked some of it up in my hand (all the time listening to a man that talked like Pastor Best but who resembled Willy-Willy) the thing was very cold. Br-r-r-r! Was it cold! Br-r-r-r! And I had to drop it out of my hand, forthwith. And a small willy-willy of a man beside me said, 'Man, ain't this preaching a bitch!' And I looked at him and asked him with my eyes what he meant. And he looked at me, straight in my face, and spat out something like soapy tobacco juice which landed an inch from my bare feet; and he said, 'Ain't you just like a nigger! Ain't this nigger a bastard? Candy, ain't this a brash brazen bold uppity nigger for ya?' And the woman called Candy looked like Miss Brewster; but she was not Miss Brewster; and she said, 'Son, where your mother? Where you from? You ain't no Harlem nigger, is you really?' And she held back her head far far back so far that I could see the silver ore of fillings in her teeth; and she shook her head from right to left and she looked at me with pity in her large brown eyes; and held back her head laughing, and then her hair fell off in the white road. And she was then a man! And when she mentioned Harlem, I knew I was in the dreams of Willy-Willy's country, that I was dreaming. But I could not stop the dream because I was dreaming. I was to wait for Willy-Willy in front of a house which looked like a church. But it was a house. Miss Brewster's house. And he was to take me up the long climb of marble mountains to Miss Brewster's bed, covered with garbage and debris and spittle and water from human beings and from animals. But I searched and searched and could not find Willy-Willy. And I was tired. And I lay on the street. But the street did not feel cold. It was more soggy than cold. As if I was lying on grass wet from the rain. It was like lying on a dirt floor, or under a cellar, rather than in a cellar. The dirt in the cellar was warm, warm as my blood, or my forehead after a race from school to home for lunch. And then I heard a pastor's voice, yelling at the people. But it was not Pastor Best. The man was standing on the stilts of a stepladder. And the black people were answering him and saying and shouting, 'Right! Right-right-right!' each time he asked them, 'Right-or-wrong?' He was a man with brain. A brain nourished, as my mother had told me, by eating many many fish heads boiled in soup. The man was saying, '...*and Will Rogers, yeah! use' to go to the stoo-dio in a station wagon...*' (What was a station wagon?) '*...use' to go to the stoo-dio in a station wagon! Right-or-wrong?*'

And the people yelled, '*Right!*'

'*Will Rogers use' to go to the stoo-dio in a station wagon! Will Rogers is DEAD, but he left back MILLIONS! MILLIONS! It even take a Brinks truck to move half o' Will Rogers' bread from a bank account in the First Nation'l Bank to the Chase Manhattan Bank! Right-or-wrong?*'

'*Right!*'

'*Step'n-Fletchett still LIVING! Yeah! Right-or-wrong? Yeahhh! Step-'n-Fletchett had a Doozenburg... a DOOZEN-BURG!... a chauff'r!... a footman!... a FOOTMUN!... a white woman, yeah!... a WHITE woman, and a dawg!...*'

'*Oh Jesus Christ!*'

'*Will Rogers left back MILLIONS!... Step still living somewhere up in Harlem here!... Dooz-EN-burg GONE!... FOOT-mun gone!... WHITE WOMAN GONE!... white woman GONE!... DAWG GONE! DAWG GONE GONE GONE!...*' And the people yelled and yelled and yelled until tears came out of their eyes; and they clapped their sides and hands and cried. And the woman called Candy, who was like Miss Brewster, yelled, 'Step-'n-Fletchett? Ain't he that nigger what had so much o' money that he uses to wear gold slippers?... Even before he get to Heav'n?' And just then, two policemen, a black policeman and a white policeman, came with their holsters empty (their guns were in their hands) and they pulled their triggers on the people, and water came out of their guns... water, like the water from a fire hose. And suddenly the man's words changed from hot air to fire. And fire was on everybody's head. And the water shot all the people to the ground, soaking, wringing-dead; and they yelled and they turned

105

around and wiggled and shook the water out of their corpses and out of their freshly combed-and-processed hair, like wet birds clapping their wings. And they all fell down again, wet and DEAD. And you could see transparent right through the plastic of a woman's dress, and touch with your eyes the beautiful rolling trembling vigorous vigour of her black body. And a voice from a woman, Candy or Miss Brewster, who was DEAD, wet soaking dead, asked, '*Where that blasted little boy I seen just now? Where that blasted little boy who ain't never seen snow and winter and fire and water before? I wonder if he get burned up in the fire last night?*'... and then Harlem changed into the Bath Corner. I could see the old slave house again, in flames now; and the Benefit Society in which every Saturday at seven o'clock at sundown, my father and my mother, like all the fathers and mothers, uncles and aunts, women and men in the village, deposited a penny saved from a penny and a half, to be put aside in case... and the tall ackee tree with its fleshy leaves and its fleshy fruits sweet as limes, on fire with the flames like leaves falling around it... and the Bath itself. This was the Bath, where, every morning, depending on my mother's whims, I would go to have a bath. And now here I was, Milton, entering through the entrance marked MEN. And I stared at the entrance marked WOMEN, and wondered what went on in that section. And the old man, Mister Alonzius Waterman, kippered-up with age like a red herring, and black, was sitting down on a wooden chair out front, with his thick double-lined book ruled in red ink (the same colour as the flames in the ackee tree) with the names of all the men, women, children, boys and girls in our village – only thing, our village looked like the street in Harlem – who were too poor to have a bath inside or outside their own houses, and who therefore had to come, as I had come in this dream, to this public bath... where we came, if not to bathe, at least to write our names in the double-lined book, smashing the boundaries of the parallel lines with our rebellious handwriting. And Mister Alonzius Waterman was looking at me with a long withered scowl, wondering whether to let me in, or leave me out in the dusty, dirt-ridden village morning. And he shouted at me and told me not to 'waste the white-man water and to get my blasted nasty self outta the white-man water in exact' five minutes', that if I bathed for six minutes, he was going to throw me out in the road. And I laughed in his face, and nothing happened. And I couldn't quite understand, because the day before I had sucked my teeth at him and he drove the double-lined book in my behind. But this morning, I climbed up onto the top of the partition of the MEN'S section and looked down into the section marked WOMEN and satisfied my curiosity about the women who were bathing. And when I saw the old woman, naked, naked and rippled, with her tough skin and loose flesh hanging like the neck of a cow, all skin, I closed my eyes and Miss Brewster came into my vision and I came crashing down on the cement under the torrents of the large shower. And the older boys laughed. And they laughed on and on, and their laughter brought Inspector Waterman, still holding his double-lined book between his thumbs and fingers. And he did not laugh. He banished me from the Bath for twenty weeks. 'You is a savage, Milton! A savage do not need a bath. You is a African! And Africans do not know what water mean. You big, idiot-headed black cannibull!' And suddenly, everything went blank, and the flames enveloped everything, including Mister Alonzius Waterman. And I went home crying to my mother, and my mother laughed and gave me a red rose flower. And then it was daylight again, a new morning, although there was no sunset or night dividing the two. And it was early in front of the Bath again. So early, that the first man had not yet come for his early cold health-giving shower. And then the first man appeared. Mister Blackman. He was on his way back from Gravesend Beach and his underpants were hanging like real bathing trunks from the handlebar of his old green Raleigh bicycle. He came early to bathe in peace in private before any of his students or any of the women teachers or the civil servants came to get theirs. The Bath was shut though. And in a rage, he rushed across the road to the rum shop and grocery owned by Mister Fuguero, and that too was closed. And he held the door like he had held Mister Fuguero's little son, and he shook it and beat it with his foot, and Mister Fuguero came out in his pyjamas and poured blows into the headmaster like a woman pouring green peas into a gallon pot. And Mister Blackman ran across the road, and Mister Fuguero disappeared in flames. And as Mister

Blackman ran (he left his bicycle on the steps of the Bath), he looked at the houses and knocked on them; and the houses, painted in the colours of the rainbow, and standing precariously on loose foundations of coral stone, resembling a child's alphabet castle, burst out into flames... and he disappeared like on a Resurrection morning. And I was left standing in the white cold street in front of my godmother's house, on the top of the little incline near the Bath Corner. She was sleeping inside the large empty house with the moonlight coming through the spaces where shutters used to be, long long ago. Throw a stone on the roof and rattle her out of her sleep, and make her run out into the dewdrop morning in her nightgown, Willy-Willy said. Heh-heh-heh! Take a clothes peg off her clothes line and clip the peg on to the breast of the old cow which gives her milk which supplies the village with milk mixed half-and-half with water, Willy-Willy said. Perhaps you can sleep with – at – your godmother, Willy-Willy said. She is your godmother, and because she is your godmother, she is the mother which the vicar through God, said God gave to you to help you grow up to be a man of God with; and since, moreover, she is your godmother, it means she is better than a mother who is only a blood-mother, since God is better than blood, Willy-Willy said... '*and Step-'n-Fletchett dead and gone! Step DEAD DEAD DEAD DEAD... Right-or-wrong?*'

'*He ain' dead no dead. I seen him out there on the Pasture last night. And he wasn't dead, 'cause I is one man who don't see spirits. He come by my house asking for a night-lodging.*'

'*You seen that boy?*'

'*Yeah. I seen him last night. But Good Christ, Ruby, I is only his father. I is not working now, for months on top o' months. And the woman I living with, Medlin, seen him asking for a... well, hell, Ruby, you know Medlin is not no nice sort o' person.*'

'*That's your worthliss business, Nathan,*' the woman's voice said, with a shriek in it.

'*But where the damn boy is, now?*' the man's voice asked. '*Where my son?*'

'*Your son?*'

'*I say MY son.*'

'*You have now realize' he is your son? He have been your son,*'

*Nathan, since that night when you first lay-down on top o' my belly
and breed me with Milton. And then you had the decencies to turn
'round and left me swell'-up big big big like a breadcart full o' bread
with Milton inside my belly. And, niggerman, you now referring to
him as your son?'*

'I breed you with him, so he is my son.'

*'Looka, niggerman! get to-hell outta my eyesight this bright
Fridee morning, do. Don't come in here and take 'way the spirit
outta my soul, please! I is a person touch' with the Holy Ghost.'*

'You believe in that sh—?'

*'Believe? I was there! I was there last night, in Pastor Best'
church! I seen it with my own two eyes. I seen with my two eyes the
clouds rolling up in the air like waves in the sea. And the noise, buh-
dammmmmm! like when you blowing stones in the rock quarry...
and I open' my two eyes!... and Pastor Best fall down on the altar...
the people in church run outside. And I stand my ground. 'Cause I
could have feel God touching me. That's what I mean when I refer
to myself as a child o' God... and furthermore, I have a tub-full o'
washing and ir'ning to do for that whore out the Front Road.'*

*'Gorblummuh! Ruby, you is as stupid as two mules and jack-
asses, though.'*

*'I have see' God, Nathan, with my own two eyes, on this earth!
And that is all I have to say to you. So, Nathan, you not talking to
a commonclass person no longer. You looking at a saint. Saint
Ruby, darling, if yuh please! And that is the manner o' way in
which you shall address me in the futures.'*

'Saint Ruby my arse!... You hear' who blow-up the church?'

*'God blow-up the church, Nathan! That was a' act o' God. Not
man! 'Twas a miracle and a lesson and a warning.'*

*'Miracle my arse!... 'Twas a warning, all right! But 'twas a
warning to Pastor Best to get up offa his arse and work and stop
living offa the womens in the church! God was warning, in
thruth!... but He was warning Pastor Best to get off offa Annie'
belly, heh-heh-heh!...'*

'Nathan, you is a sinner.'

'Sinner my arse!' And I heard something fall; and I turned over
in my sleep. And the bed I was lying in was very gritty, as if
somebody had thrown a donkey cart full of pebbles in my bed.

And when I turned over on my other side, I felt for the bed covers and my hands came up full of dirt. And I sat up in my bed, and bump! my head crashed against the ceiling of the cellar. And spin by spin my head began to tell me where I was.

The talking inside, on the second floor of my castle of dirt, went on, raving like the waves in a storm. Now and then, a chair tumbled to the ground, like a tree crashing in the wind. And the voices would rise like the wind, and then die. And then there would be a laugh, and a sigh, as if the sea were washing everything back far far far out into the far distance of the horizon.

'But look now! If you was the proper kind o' woman, Ruby, though, you think you would have take' that boy up to the headmaster' house, and not tell the headmaster the purpose and intent o' your mission?'

'Don't cross-up my blasted morning, eh, Nathan?'

'Lissen to me, woman!'

'Man, Nathan, I have tell you already that you don't have no damn rights coming inna this house and humbugging me, yuh. I does not live with you! I never have. I don't sleep in the same bed with you, and be-Christ! Nathan, you hads better leave me to myself. Me and you done-with long long time ago!'

'I come for satisfaction 'bout my child!'

'*Your* child?'

'Yes! My child.'

'Now tell me, no! come, tell me!… How much money?… How much child-money you has ever put in my hands since I borned Milton, October the twenty-six', nine year' pass? How much child-money have you bringed and put inside my hand? Man, have you forget that Magistrate Chandler had was to call a police' for you and lock you up for one entire seven-days before you would even fork-over the two shilling' what the Court put on you to supscribe to Milton' upkeep? You have forget all that nasty, bad hist'ries in regards o' me and my child, Milton?'

'Ease-me-up, Ruby, girl, oh Jesus Christ, ease-me-up! Good God! Man, Ruby, man, ease-me-up! Gimme a' ease-ment! I is not a working man now. I is' not a working man as I uses to be. But I going promise real' hard though to bring in a couple shilling' next Sa'rday and put them in your hand. Medlin now gone saying she have not see her menses, and be-Christ! she like she is pregnunt now. So, I asking you real' bad, Ruby, ease-me-up. You see a man before you what have a woman in the fambly way.'

'But lissen to he! He… you come in here telling me what? That is your and Medlin' stinking business. I have God to worry about. Not man!'

'But oh Christ! Ruby, I coming to you on bended knee! I penetunt as hell now, man!'

'Penetunt? Is penetunt you penetunt? You sure and certain-sure you have not come in here with your tongue longing-out for *one* thing? You sure sure sure? That Medlin have not throwed your backside outta your own-own house because she have find herself pregnunt with a fatherless child… that you now coming smelling-up under my shifts?'

'But oh Christ, Ruby, I sencere!'

'How sencere?'

'Sencere as arse!'

'Sencere, eh?'

'Real' sencere! Sencere sencere sencere.'

'For thruth?'

'In thruth. I sencere as arse, man.'

'And what your motives and motivations is?'

'The onliest motive and motivation in my heart, Ruby, is love and…'

'God blow you in hell, Nathan! Get out! Get out get out get out! You mixing-me-up! You trying to turn my head topsy-turvy. Man, I have fling you outta my heart long long long ago!… and only Jesus Christ above habitating this heart o' mine now. From last night.'

'But take me back, nuh? Oh God, Ruby, I off'ring you love and sencereness… and, maybe if God work' out things betwixt me and you, maybe, and I saying maybe real' serious' now, maybe… maybe I will take you down that blasted aisle.'

'Come come come now! Nathan, take off your hand offa me. Come! No, Nathan, man! It ain' true. No, oh Christ, come! it ain' true at all! Take your rotten hand' offa me. And stop feeling-up my behind before I don't throw some o' this hot tea in your damn face! You put something there? You don't know nothing 'bout me, man.'

'But I love you real' bad, though. I dying for you real' bad, Ruby.'

'Well, you will have to *dead* then!'

'Be-Christ! you don't know, Ruby. You don't know, Ruby girl, but the nights comes and goes and finds me tossing and turning all blasted small hours o' the night on my piller, at night. Can't sleep no kind o' how, no kind o' sleep. Sleep won't come no-kind-o'-how! I rests my head 'pon that piller at nights, man, and I ain' shame' to tell you, but the sleep does be far far away over the hills and mountains counting sheeps up to three million... ten million, and be-Christ! all I does be seeing all the time in my nightmares and dreams, is sheeps sheeps and gorblummuh! more sheeps. Never sleep!'

'You should 'ave been a preacher-man. You does talk so damn smart and sweet, Nathan, that I think you should have went in for the preaching ministries. You has great honey on your lips, Nathan. But be-Christ! and I telling you now, this bright blessid Fridee morning, you hasn't got no damn honey enough 'pon your lips for me to come crawling back to you and lay-down beneath you, whilst you treat me worser than a Lazoretto dog! Not me. Once bitten, twice shy. It never happen'!'

'But who is talking 'bout laying-down? *Has* I open' my mouth and say anything 'bout laying-down?'

'You smelling 'bout in here for something, Nathan. But get out, 'cause nothing in here do not belongst to you.'

But oh Christ, Ruby! Don't move 'way from me, man. Come closer, more closer, man. Oh hell! Ruby, let me just put my hands 'pon you and touch you up, girl.'

'Take off your hand' offa me! Take off your worthliss hand' offa me!' And there was a dull ring, *brunnnngggg!* and then he said, 'Jesus Christ!' and he started to laugh. And then, there was a noise in that part of the house, above my head, that part where my mother slept. They were fighting and throwing pillows around. And whenever he stepped on the bed, in the middle of the sagging straw bed, the ceiling of the cellar shook. And she would give off a laugh. It was not quite a laugh, like a happy laugh, like how people laugh. But a half-laugh that seemed to say she was taunting him while she knew all the while that she was not going to give in to him. And the storm subsided. And all I could hear was the breeze whispering through the tired, wind-beaten trees, *shwishhhhhhhh!* And the bed started to vibrate in rhythm, in a constant movement as if somebody was up there jumping on it, one-two-one-two-one-two-*three*! Then the beat increased in tempo, and it grew louder: *one-two-one-two-one-two! faster faster*. As if there were many policemen in Harlem running after the men and women who had stood in the street listening to the man who resembled Pastor Best, on the stepladder talking about Will Rogers and Step-'n-Fletchett. And then, all of a sudden, there was a scream. Not a real scream. But a scream for joy, as if she was reaching for a fruit at the top of a tree; as if she had been stretching and stretching for a long time until almost out of breath now, she had just touched it and then missed it by a wish's breath and her hand had begun to snap out of its socket… she had just reached the fruit with the tips of her fingers and something within her, some desire which made her grow that fraction of an inch more… and then she grabbed it and then she exploded and then she collapsed with a great satisfaction.

'Gorblummuh, Ruby! You do not taste no less sweeter than you was tasting that night, nine year' ago, Febry gone…'

'Come come come, Nathan! Get up offa me now!'

'Oh God, Ruby! Ruby, oh God!'

'I is a damn busy woman today, with a hundred and one things on my mind to do. God moving 'bout inside my spirit, so come, get up! I have to get up!'

'Let we lay-down here a sec more, and think and plan things, Ruby. Let we stand right here in this bed till next year come, I so damn happy and full-up with a sweet fullness. Let we lay-down here, right here in this bed and dream and see things what all these blasted years I been keeping outta your reaches because Satan get-in my backside and make me run after the wrong breed o' womankind and cause me to leave you outside in the cold, by yourself. Let we plan 'bout Milton. Milton getting to be a big boy now. And he should have a man in the house to guide him and teach him how to hold a cricket bat, and make a fish hook outta a common pin. Milton getting to be a big boy now. He should have a real father. Not only a man what living with his mother on the side, like Willy-Willy. He need' a father. And I is his father, so…'

'You is his father? You not kidding! For thruth?'

'…he should not be out walking 'bout in the night-dew like he was walking 'bout last night when he come by my place. And be-Christ! it burn' my heart real' sore that I could not even open my own door and let in my own son, knowing that the bitch I happen to live with…'

'And you is really his father?'

'…but let me and you put we two heads together and work out something positive for that boy o' ours. That boy is going to be as bright as a new shilling with eddication. I understand he could count up to fifty already!… But it is a funny-arse thing, though! I myself do not have no eddication. When I should 'ave been sitting down in Blackman' school house, I was sitting down under the clammy-cherry tree out there in the Pasture, throwing dice, catching fish 'pon the beach, be-Jees, or else diving sea-eggs… and on top o' that, swelling-up womens belly, as I have done yours, Ruby. But all that is past tense now, and we have to look at it that way. Though now that I 'pon the subject o' eddication, you is not a woman in possession o' too much eddication yourself. So, Ruby, do not let we be guilty o' making the selfsame mistakes and errors three times, and bring up the boy, the only boy-child we possesses to be a gardener-boy in no damn white people' place out the Front Road. That gardener-thing too is past tense, Ruby, darling love.'

'Nathan?'

'Yeah, Ruby, darling.'

'Nathan? Nathan?'

'I laying-down here, with my two ear' open, lissening to what you saying, Rube.'

'Nathan, you know what I have in mind for that boy?'

'What you have in mind for that boy, Ruby?'

'I want to see that boy-child o' mine, o' ours, riding 'pon a brand new-brand three-speed tick-tick bicycle, wearing his nice starch'-and-ir'n' khaki trousers and white shirt stiff stiff like a dealboard and white like Blanca, whiter than the snows... brown shoes shining like a dog's stones in the moonlight, and that school tie... the same tie as what the vicar' son, Billy, does wear down to Harrison College. I want Milton to go to Harrison College too...'

'But how he doing in school? Harrison College, I hear, is a damn hard place to get in to... they does set some blasted stiff sums and arithmetics down there, though, Rube.'

'It do not matter, Nathan. Milton going to Harrison. I going send him to Harrison College next year before he turn' ten years. I do not mind living in the past tense as you say, Nathan, with tribulations and poorness going to bed with me ever' night. But Milton, that boy-child o' mine, of ours, he must have the best o' every-damn-thing possible.'

'And you know what, Rube?'

'What, Nate?'

'I have the selfsame calculations and figuring-outs in mind for Milton.'

'For thruth?'

'Yeah, in thruth. He is all we possesses. So, we have to sp'il him with goodness and kindness. And this is something I intends to put to that blasted racoon when he march' his arse back inside this house. I intends to explain to him the ins and outs o' life in this blasted island. And is this. I have come to a damn serious understanding during my travels in and around this blasted past-tense village. A man could live in this backwards place, Barbados, and still could walk 'bout the place as he like' and pleases. A man could maybe go to a high school. A man could maybe never go to a high school. He would have to spend the rest of his breathing days 'pon this earth walking 'bout the village barefoot! A man, on the other hand, could commit a murder, or commit a larceny as the Gestapo does call it. But concentrating 'pon the man what went through high school. After all them years, and he come out with them papers inside his hand testifying to the fact that really and truly he did come through in a certain fashion, learning-wise. Well, you could hold-down a big-arse job. But it is a funny big-arse job. Is a job reserve' for people like me or you, or Milton, or Blackman... or even Miss Brewster, or...'

'What that stand' for, Nate?'

'What? People? I mean and intends to mean, the people o' the earth. The real people.'

'But people is people!'

'Not in this contest and not in this sense. But continuing. A fellar like that... maybe in a couple years, that fellar might be Milton... he could have a civil servant job. A schoolteacher job, like Blackman or Miss Brewster. He could even come out as a saniterry inspector and walk all through this blasted village in a khaki suit and white cork hat with a white enamel ladle in his hand' to dip down inside the poor people' shitty closets with. But be-Christ! after all them school fees I pay out, and all them dollars spend on books, I hopes, I hopes to-hell that Milton do not come out as no damn inspector, looking for a million and one larvees in no blasted person' outdoor closet, or to see if they have young musquitoes in their drinking-water buckets. That, Ruby, according to a fellar I know, with who' I have had a long conversation regarding the ins and outs o' things in this past-tense village, that, Rube, is the lengths and the advantages Milton could go to in this kiss-me-arse island after he find' himself in the possession of a high-school eddication. Be-Jesus Christ! it ain't so diff'rent from being a professional gambler. But anyhow, I did not have no eddication, and he have to.'

'You talking the Gospull-thruth, Nathan, boy. You have talk' what God wanted you was to have talk' nine year' October gone!'

'And if Milton is a boy what have a singing voice in his head, I want him to sing in the cathedral' choirs 'pon a Sundee. Oh Christ, I could see that bastard now, Rube, darling love! I could see Milton right this very now before my eye' wearing them red robes and that thing 'round his neck like a... like a... like a piece o' white paper roll' up neat' like a piece o' white toilet paper that I have see' once in a guest room in the Marine Hotel... roll' up just like a bellows...'

'You means a ruff, Nathan.'

'Yeah, a ruff!... and walking up and down that cathedral' aisle with the choirs and the Bishop o' the islan', and singing them psalms and carols and songs ancient and modernt so damn sweet, more sweeter than if he was a blasted humming bird!'

'That is our son, Nathan.'

'Be-Christ, Ruby, you have just say a mouthful! Milton is our own. Our own-own flesh-and-blood possession!'

'Yes. Every boy should go and let the Bishop say, "*In this... In this...*" What he does say now, Rube? I didn' get confirm' myself, when I was a boy, so...'

'I don't know neither, Nate. I didn't get confirmed neither and the Lord Bishop didn' lay on his hand' 'pon my head neither. Heh-heh-heh!... But look the two o' we here...'

'Heh-heh-heh-heh!'

'Heh-heh-haaa! But I like it, though. 'Cause it is something that is Anglicun, and it sound' damn nice. It look' too damn nice to see them little boys and little girls walking up slow slow slooow like if they sliding up and not really walking at all, up up up the aisle to the Bishop dress'-down in his rich pretty robes with that big shiny thing on his head and that big ring 'pon his index finger and, and... it is one o' them same fingers as what he lays on their heads when he bless' them and say that thing what neither you nor me do not remember just this minute as being what is he really does say.'

'And if Milton learn' good, perhaps we could think 'bout sending him to Blackman for a little private tuitions and lessons after school in the evenings.'

'That cost' money though, Nathan!'

'I knows that, Ruby.'

'And where the hell that money going to come from? I is only a washerwoman, Nathan, remember that!'

'That's true too! All these damn dreams we dreaming cost money.'

'Money money money.'

'But the money going have to come, though. I gotta get my hand' 'pon some money, and it gotta come. Even if I have to thief it.'

'Oh God no, Nathan! Saying things like that makes my belly burn me, man. Let we just live as God say' we poor people is to live and exist in this village. Don't let we fight 'gainst the pricks o' God nor man. And if we prove weselves to be patient people, well, maybe something may happen. He *must* provide. He bound and 'bliged to provide. Christ, man! Don't you see how He does provide for the birds o' the air? Have you ever see' a bird lining-up in a food-line or a soup kitchen down at Madame Ifill place begging for food? Have you ever see' or hear' a bird living on welfare, saving it is God' welfare?'

'Of a thruth, Ruby, girl, is commasense you talking. But I going to go 'round by the Marine and beg for that night-watch-man job today, as soon as you give me little warm tea to belch up some a' this damn gas inside my guts. I intends to go 'round there. And when I come back, I going to march 'cross to that school house and tell Blackman a word or two 'bout resting his blasted hand on my child, and if he do not…'

'Don't say nothing 'bout that! Nathan, do not go 'cross the white people' road and bring shame and sorrow on my head, please.'

'I do not intends to bring neither shame nor sorrow on your head, Ruby, and I is in a position to take some o' that said shame and sorrow, if mayhaps I was such a' arse as to bring it on your head. But I was thinking 'bout the private tuitions for Milton.'

'Oh! I thought you was going to mention the beating Blackman give Milton, 'cause Milton must have deserve' it, and according to…'

'And, Ruby, a little Hist'ry and Geog'fy and maybe, Latin? 'Cause I have hear' from somebody who ought to know 'bout these things that to be a' eddicated man in this day and age a person cannot carry on no kind a' eddicated conversation nor speech if that said person is not in possession of Latin. You maybe could become a' inspector o' closets with the Department o' Health, or even become a civil servant. But nothing important. And I say already, I do not want that for Milton. Milton too damn bright already, according to Blackman.'

'Of a thruth, Milton have something better in him. Blackman told me so when we went up by his place last night. He say' to me, "Mistress Sobers," he say'…'

'He call' you Mistress Sobers? Oh Jesus Christ! Heh-heh-heh!'

'That's my blasted business what he call' me, and what I answer' to! But he says, "You have name' Milton after a real borned genius." Some man' name he call' in similarities with Milton'

118

name, but I can't rightly remember if the man was a German-man, or a Yankee-man… and really and truly I don't think I want Milton to be name' after no damn Yankee-man, 'cause them Yankee-mens too slick. Look at the one that marri'd Girlie' daughter, Rachel!… Maybe the headmaster did mention a' Eng-lishman, like one o' them big-shot mens what comes over here from the Mother Country. And if it is a fact that I have name' my poor common simple child after one o' them big important English-mens, well, all I have to say is that I have try my best to give Milton the most proper name a mother could buy. Blackman told me all them things to my face, and in the hearing o' Milton, that Milton more brighter than a what.'

'*That* is my son, Ruby!'

'Something special in store for that boy, Nathan.'

'That is *my* son!'

'But I wonder where Milton is now?'

'Leave him, Ruby. Leave him. Maybe even now, Milton hearing every word, every damn iota we been saying 'bout him in his favour. He going come home, Ruby. He going come home, 'cause this is home, and he bound to come home…'

'You mean like what they say in that school book we uses to read out of in First Standard, 'bout the little girl with yellow hair who loss the sheeps and she left all them sheeps and they come home bringing their tails behind them?'

'Be-Christ, Ruby, you has something in you too, yuh! I give you credits for that. Heh-heh-heh! now how the hell you could think of a thing like that all of a sudden out of the blue? Jesus Christ! something good, something basic like genius borned inna this fambly. And gorblummuh! this have make me damn sorrowful to think that I have neglect' to pay attention to my fambly and to my business all these nine years. I sorry sorry sorry, Ruby, and I hope to-Christ that you have a full realization as to the degree and amount o' my begrievement.'

'You's forgiv'n, Nathan. You forgiv'n. You have repenteth. You come with your tail betwixt your legs in penetunce for your past-tense misdeeds and I have forgive' and forget. And I know God forgive too. 'Cause a strange feeling o' happiness resting light in my heart this peaceable morning. Christ knows I could

119

jump up in the air and screel out for bloody-hell and murder! It is so damn funny in a good way that I feel this morning. Nathan, I could get up right now and wash-out a' oceanful o' clothes for that white lady. I could get up right now outta this bed, from laying down under you, Nathan, and march my backside 'cross that Front Road and stand up with my two hand' in my kimbo, so! and look that white whore right in her two eye' till my eye' and her eye' makes *four*! And be-Christ, Nathan, I could skin-up my dress in her face and tell her plain and simple, "Kiss my arse, please!"'

'Heh-hee-hee! oh Lord, Rube, child!'

'This is the brand o' happiness you have place' on my heart this morning, Nathan. Something brave and courageous resting light like a fowl-cock feather and nice inside me, today. And after last night, and the descending o' the Spirit in that church, God-love-a-duck, I could move mountains!... and I regard that white woman out there as one such mountain, 'cause she cheap as hell!'

'But don't do what you have just suggest', though. Don't throw-out the bath-water with the baby still remaining in the bath-water. Ruby, that is sp'iling your nose to change your features, and as poor people we have to travel a damn lonely precarious road, sometimes.'

'Hee-hee-heh-heh! I was only joking.'

'Be-Christ, I hopes so! 'Cause that is money, dollars and cents you was just joking with! You have to continue bringing in money till I get my hand 'pon a job. But anyhow!... and you know, Rube, in a funny-arse way, that is the same way I feel too. Gorblummuh! a piece o' woman, a regular piece o' woman does do, and could do some funny-arse things to a man' head. 'Cause, harken I could get up right this very now, drag on my trousers and shirt and roll up my shirt sleeves and walk 'cross there and grab Blackman by his arse, drag him outta that school house, fling him on the ground, and gorblummuh kick his arse till I see blood!'

'Heh-heh-heh-hee!'

'Heh-heh-heh-heh!'

'Nathan? Nathan, come close. I have something to intrust to your ears. Nathan, I glad glad till I don't know how to say it, that you have come and unlock' my chastity belt and ripp'-off them old rusty locks I had 'pon it, and you have bring me back inna the realm o' being a woman. I glad for that. 'Cause love is like the fresh air we does breathe in and breathe out. The more a woman have, the more she wants. And I thought I was strong when I lock'-out man from my heart. But now that I have open' the door o' my heart again, I is a more stronger woman, Nathan. At least, it is a good thing that Milton loss, 'cause Milton being loss have bring you back.'

'Look, let we stop this dreaming. I think we dream' long-enough.'

'Yeah.'

'I going and look for a job.'

'Nathan, you think Milton get wet in the rain and thunder and lightning last night?'

'Milton all right.'

'I should tar his arse, though!'

'Easy on the boy, Ruby.'

'All last night, grief in my heart, till I went in that church and heard the word o' God.'

'Ease-up the boy, Ruby.'

'I asking everybody, "Has you seen Milton? Has you seen Milton?"'

'We have turn' over a brand new-brand leaf, Rube. A new chapter about to begin.'

'Yeah, that is the thruth.'

'Well, let we behave so, then.'

'Okay. You run 'long now, and I going left back some salt fish and b'iled potatoes till you come back, and I going leave it by the fireside in case I not here till you return. And Nathan? If you see Milton in your turning, give him one damn blow and tell him march his backside in here, forthwith.'

'Ease him up, Ruby. Even now, Milton right here in ear-distance hearing you talking 'bout him. And he going come. He going come just like that little girl with the yellow hair you have tell me 'bout, bringing her tail between her legs.'

'But if you see him tell him don't tarry.'

'I going.'

'Go! In the name o' the Lord, go.'

'I going.'

'You have say so two times now, Nathan. If you not seen me when you come back I will be up the Corner by Milton' godmother helping her sweep out the house. She getting to be old now, and she is good to me. Last week she even put a handful o' rice, long-grain rice and a slice o' butter, real butter from somewhere call' Australia… and a bottle o' milk, in my hand.'

'She does still mix-up the milk?'

'Don't be too rough 'pon poor Aunt Maud, Nathan. She old. And life to her must look real dismal.'

'I not vex'. I only wish I had half the brain Maud have.'

'Come now, drink this little warm green-tea. It was left back for Milton' breakfast, but Milton outta sight now, so you drink it up.'

I could hear him drinking the tea noisily. And then he belched like a foghorn.

'Say excuse, Nathan.'

'Excuse, Ruby… Ruby, darling love?'

'Yes, Nathan?'

'Ruby? You think that maybe you could see your way with a six-cent piece? I need a rum, and cigs. I have not taste' a cig'rette, be-Christ! in a dog's age.'

'Look under the lef'-hand corner o' the tablecloth on the table in the front house, and you going see two shillings and a six-cent piece. Take the six-cent piece. I borrow' that change last night from Girlie when we was combing this village looking for that little bitch. She has owe' me a dollar, and she don't remember she have borrow' that change from me since last Old Year's Night, and this is June now. So, I borrows it back from her and she ain't no wiser, 'cause I makes her think she lending me something.'

'Thanks.'

He said it quickly and curtly. And as quickly his feet moved through the second floor above me. And they jumped down on to the dirt floor of the kitchen section. Through the portholes of the castle of my cellar I saw him. His left trouser leg was rolled up just below his knee. His cap was on his head with the peak turned over one ear. His shirt tail was flying like the tail of a kite in the breeze on Easter morning. And he was tossing the six-cent piece high into the air, catching it expertly with his hand behind his back, as he walked. And before he went out of my sight, he burst into a song, 'Brown-Skin Gal'.

> 'Brown-skin gal, stay home and mind ba-bee!
> Brown-skin gal, stay home and mind ba-bee!
> Ah'm going away in a sailing boat,
> And if Ah don' come back, STAY home –
> And MIND ba-bee!'

And something about the way he said 'stay home' made me think that my mother was never going to see him again, alive, with the six cents. Or with the job. Or with any of the promises he had weaved with her about me. And inside the house, my mother raged loudly in the lullaby of a different song:

> 'Near-errr my God to Thee,
> Near-errr my Gawd to Thee-ee,
> Near-er my God to Thee,
> Near-er-errr to Theeeeee!'

7

Some ants were carrying a bulky piece of salt fishbone from the side of the house foundation where I had been lying all the time my father and mother were talking. They were marching across the hilly terrain of the ground, across a bridge made of a piece of dried rotten shingle, and towards the storehouse of their nest. I watched the foreman in front doing nothing but directing; and giving instructions to the other labourers. He ran on a little ahead of them like a scout, like something my headmaster called a 'reckon-noiter', when he was teaching us a poem called 'Go To The Ant, Thou Sluggard'. The 'reckon-noiter' was running forward and backward and guiding the team of toy mules over the rough ground, running along the tired line, cheering up some, whipping others with his voice (I could hear him shout) and then returning to his place in front. *Go to the ant, thou sluggard!* ... they had travelled miles and miles of their journey and when I thought they would rest for a break, they kept right on. Now they are about three miles... three inches from my right foot. I wonder if they will walk over my foot; or whether the foreman is smart enough to have them march around my foot. Perhaps even sting me out of their way. But they are marching around me. And in a short time, they are already in front of their storage warehouse... *Consider her ways, and be wise...*

I had forgotten about my mother above me. Now I can hear her tramping and trampling the lonely regions of the house, lonely now, because she has a man again, and he is not here; because the man who was in her bed is not here; because the man who is in her life again is not here. The house is lonely. The way she walks about the house is different already. Her footsteps are lighter now. Love which taught her how to camouflage her two hundred pounds of avoirdupois so that she could walk like an elephant has now schooled her into walking like a cat with fur slippers on its feet. It is love. Love has now placed a dancing-ness, a feeling of expectation in her footsteps. My mother is a woman once more. She is moving about the house like a woman expecting her man, my father. But I cannot enjoy with her her happiness. To me, a father is like the coming of a rival in a love affair. My mother has been my lover all these years. She had remained mine, alone with me, mine only, all those nine miserable terrible years of romance, of ups and downs, but mostly downs. All through my bouts of chicken-pox, of measles, of typhoid fever when she could have baked a chicken on the oven of my neck... all through those days when I had cut my toe, my second toe after the big toe; and the cut had turned into a 'life-sore' because it never improved or healed slightly in two years, no matter what she did with it. She had put lizard droppings on it; she had rubbed it in chicken droppings and afterwards wrapped it in oil leaves; she had bathed it in cold water, hot water, lukewarm water; she had washed it in warm castor oil, lukewarm castor oil, hot castor oil; she had put healing plaster on it; she had taken me to the obeah woman, a Madame Miranda from the island of St Lucia. And nothing happened. All I remember from the visit to Madame Miranda was a small image of an African princess... Nothing my mother could do with it, or to it, would heal the cut on my toe. The ants have disappeared into their nest... *consider her ways, and be wise!* And then one morning, Willy-Willy, passing the road, heard my mother screaming and heard me screaming as she tried to dip my foot in a basin of hot water; and he came and he looked at me and at my mother and at the foot and he saw a piece of broken glass bottle; and with his thumb nail and his index-finger nail, he pulled the speck of glass out, and within two weeks my cut was healed... *go to the ant, thou sluggard!* My mother has now exhausted 'Nearer my God' five times. She has sung the first verse (the only one she has sung) over and over five times. And satisfied at last with her conquest and wreck of this beautiful song, she turns her attention to destroying the harmony of 'Ride On, Ride On, In Majesty'. She would sing a phrase, leave it until she had lifted a cup maybe, or a chair, or had dusted a speck of dust off the hands of her rocking-chair, and then she would return to the phrase in the exact wrong key as when she had first abandoned it; and then she would continue until maybe she reached the second phrase, when, midway in the phrase, a fly might land on the phrase written in her mind and take her attention off the song for a moment while she smacked the fly, 'You bastard!' and then she would return again to her majestic journey which contradicts itself for being lowly and majestic in the same breath. Now I can hear her riding on, riding on, riding horses of her imaginary love affair with my father, perhaps, riding on... not the clip-clop-cloppity clop horses in the roof of her mouth, but the horses of the Spirit, spiritual galleons which God always sends for her to journey on... riding on, riding on these mares to meet her death. What a terrible thing to do! How brave for my mother, though! That she, a woman big enough to stand in front of an elephant and you could not see the elephant; who was still scared pissing-stiff of a mouse; and for this brave child to suggest that she might mount a horse and ride away from her misery in the village to majesty! My mother who was scared to suggest to the white lady out the Front Road in the mansion house that she should receive five *plus* five *plus* five shillings (at least!) for washing her dirty linen in the secrecy of our backyard, instead of *five* shillings... this woman, this mother, this coward of a woman is now riding on, riding on, riding on, to die! Die for what, I wonder. Perhaps it was the new love in her heart, born from the rejoining with a man whom she had burned to ashes at the bottom of her heart for nine weltering years. Love is a funny thing, Willy-Willy said. And women, too, he said.

'Girlie? Girlie Girlie Girlie? I in love! Girlie, I have something secret to 'trust to your ears.'

I heard my mother laugh as she waited for her friend to unlatch our back door and enter, after crossing the road and coming around through the cluttered vines that painted our house.

And when she entered, she exclaimed, 'Lord Lord Lord, Ruby, what has get in your tail so early this morning? You singing down the whole n'ighbourhood with them songs o' death? And, Christ! look how you have your house clean'-out so damn early. In ten-eleven years I was living next door to you as your n'ighbour I have never see' this destruction in your place! Lord Lord Jesus!'

'I is a woman in love, Girlie.'

'In *what*? With who, though? With what? God?'

'With He too! But I in love with a person on the earth.'

'Christ, child! if being in love does do a thing like this to a woman, God have His mercy, no love for me, darling! Love! Love?'

'I in love.'

'Love? You say love, Ruby?'

'Love love love love alone!'

'Well, look, darling, you talking 'bout madness, eh. 'Cause only a man who is a damn mad insane woman would shine and polish every glass in her house at ten o'clock in the morning. You losing control over yourself, Ruby?'

'Is love, Girlie!'

'You talking 'bout *man*. Not love! You had a man in here last night, I bet. You has had somebody in this bed last night, Ruby.'

'I was here this morning singing my praises to God, and worrying my head over Milton, when...'

'That boy not marched his tail back here yet?'

'He still running 'way, but I have forget him. My mind on things *above*. But as I saying to you though, Girlie... I was in here on my bended knees prostrated before God, singing and asking Him when He intend' to send back my child, plus a shilling. I in here complaining 'fore God concerning my sorrows and tribulations when, *bram!* darling, God answer' my prayers and answer' them in a damn funny fashion, as only God in Heaven could answer prayers. I was begging for the return of the prodigull son, and God turn' 'round and grant' me a *husband*.'

'Jesus Christ, Ruby!'

'A husband, darling love!'

'What the hell is this I discerning?'

'Sweetheart, a husband.'

'Who? Who who?'

'Milton' father. Nathan!'

'No, Ruby! yuh lie!' And from her voice, I could see Girlie clearly in my mind, shaking her head from side to side, refusing to believe what her ears had just heard. 'You mean to inform me that worthliss Nathan offer' you the wedding ring? Worthliss worthliss Nathan what have so much o' womens stinking-up Rudder Pasture, *walk'* out here this early in the morning *on his own oars* and propose' to do the thing with you!… Looka, Ruby, Nathan smelling for something, yuh!'

'Is Nathan, darling love. My husband about-to-be!'

'Oh Christ! no, Ruby, man! I refuse to believe that. I have to hear that in front o' my eyes to believe that. I have to see that before I would believe that!'

'It is the Gospull.'

'And when the wedding set for?'

'It ain' set. Girlie, don't be a damn fool! It is not set, and I not setting it! I not setting it, not the wedding date, till Nathan has work'-off his behind for me and have sweat'-off some perspiration o' finance and help for a fraction o' them hours o' sufferation and grieviancies which he make me go through whilst he was out cattawoulling behind every whore he rested his eyes on!'

'Heh-heh-haa! I could see love has not make you stupid 'cause you has not loss your head through love. You now talking like if you was a real white lady.'

'You think I borned yesterday?'

'True!'

'I not borned yesterday, Girlie darling. I did not call Nathan. Nathan walk' in here bright and early this morning. Nathan creep in here confessing and confessing things I did not e'en know he was guilty of. And he come saying he sorry, so I figure' that if he sorry he must really want to feel sorry for himself. I have nothing to loss. If he is sorry, well, he want' to feel sorry. But I am going to make Nathan *pay* for being sorry. Girlie, I am going to take a turn in Nathan' arse – pardon my vernaculer so early in the morning, please – I intends to fix Nathan in such a manner and fashion that he is going to bring all his money and lay it inside my palm, look! right in his left-han' palm! and then he going have to turn 'round and *beg* me to give him back cig'rette money and rum money. Girlie, I done fooling. My child getting to be a big man and I have to see him launch' and harboured in Harrison College.'

'You have every damn right to think and figure the way you

thinking and figuring, Ruby. I have give' up trying to force the man what fathered two o' my beasts to put a ring 'pon my finger. I resign' to living a bachelor's life – a' old maid's existence. So I have to congraddilate you although I also envies you a little bit. But it is only congraddilations I have for you inside my heart, Ruby. You have wait' a long time for this to happen to you. Oh Christ, is *nine* years! But you bear it like a lady. You is the champ!'

'Is God, Girlie! You must have hear' 'bout last night out in the church, Pastor Best' church? Well, it is God. That was God, and now this is God a second time, and I telling...'

'But, no, Ruby! The papers say that somebody try to blow-up the damn church last night, yuh. It ain' God, darling. It is man. It is a' enemy o' God. I just come from out the Bath Corner, and never before in my borned days have I see' so much detectives and police!'

'You mean I was under the wrong illusion concerning the events o' last night?'

'You was wrong, Ruby. But be-Christ it do not make no damn diff'rence if you say it was a miracle. It really and truly was a miracle that you and the rest o' people what remained in the church after I left is still alive and in the flesh this morning. That is the miracle!'

'Oh Lord in heaven!... but anyhow, we talking 'bout life now!... as I was saying to you... I intends to keeps Nathan dangling 'pon my finger. I intends to hold out that wedding-ring finger in front o' Nathan' face all the time that he bringing in the money. And I intends to let him eat outta this hand I holding out to show you now. You stupid, woman?'

'How you does do it, though? Give me a lesson, nuh. I cannot understand mens. Christ I cannot understand mens! Every time I manages to get one o' them beasts through that door o' mine and in my bedroom, I ends up on the wrong side o' the cash book. I ends up giving 'way my flesh *free*. On credits Jesus, Ruby, if you think you bad-luckid... looka, if I ask one o' them for three shillings for spending the night with me, and he say' he only have a six-cent piece in his pocket, you don't know it is me who start' crying and feeling sorry for him, and I even says to him, "Do not mind, love. Don't mind. This thing betwixt my leg' is mine and

129

if I giving it 'way free, you must not mind. Bring back the change next time.'"

'And I bet you never rest eyes on the bastard!'

'Who tol' you so good, eh? They *never* come back. I is a woman with a heart, Ruby, and say what you like, although I sells it, I love it bad bad myself. So, what the hell! Get pay for something that you like doing? That ain't a Christian-minded thing to do, man.'

'But, Girlie. You have to start using the head God put on your shoulders, man. You getting on in age, and you do not have…'

'I shall dead as a' old woman, and when they take me from the almshouse up in Christ Church, I going have the biggest loveliest funeral you ever set eyes on!'

And all of a sudden, Willy-Willy's voice was shouting out for my mother. He was running. He was in a hurry. He was in an evil mood, like when I had seen him last night.

'Ruby? Ruby? Ruby?' he called out from the road.

Inside the backyard, my mother told Girlie something; and Girlie left. Before she left, she warned my mother about Willy-Willy.

'Take a piece o' advice from me, Ruby. Don't let that brute cross-up your life now, Ruby. He is a damn black cat. And all he could do to you now is throw bad-luck in your paths. If yuh needs any help just call. I going be liss'ning for your S.O.S.'

'I could handle Willy-Willy. Thanks though. And come back when the bitch leave'.' And Girlie left as quickly as she had arrived. And my mother changed her manner and welcomed Willy-Willy with laughter in her voice.

The gate was slammed behind him. For a while all I could hear was his footsteps walking up and down the yard.

'Gorblummuh!… gorblummuh!' he said, as if he were a gramophone record stuck in a bad track. 'You say you haven't see' Milton? You haven't see' Milton since last night, yesterday evening after school?'

'I have not seen the…'

'Gorblummuh!'

'But, Willy-Willy?'

'Be-Christ, don't Willy-Willy me! Don't Willy-Willy me,

Ruby, 'cause you living a damn double-life behind my back. I hear' you had a man in here last night.'

'But, Willy-Willy, man, how you could think... how you could *even* think a thing like that 'bout me? How? How how how?'

'The walls have ears, Ruby! The walls have ears. And the way I feel now, with ever' blasted body behind me, I could lash your arse to threads. Ruby, I could take down this window stick offa this window and break it in fine fine pieces in your backside! I could do that right now, Ruby! You two-timing me, yuh.'

'Oh Christ, Willy-Willy, don't...'

'You two-timing me?'

'Oh loss, man!'

'You haven't sleep with a man in here last night? Lemme look at them sheets, then. Lemme inspect that bed o' yourn, 'cause I know...'

'Look, Willy-Willy, all right! All right! But I had to do it. And I going tell you just why I had to have them motivations and motives concerning the doing of it. But I do not want you to get in a vexatious mood and temper and shed no more blood when I have tell you what I have to tell you...'

'Gorblummuh!... Gorblum...'

'It have grieve' my heart bad bad that I had was to work out things in this fashion. But let we look at the facts o' life a minute...'

'Gorblummuh, yes! Facts! Them is what I interested in!'

'Let we look at the facts this way, Willy-Willy...' There was a long pause, and I felt they were plotting some trick against me. But I was going to remain under the cellar until I died from starvation like that man in Indian History, about whom our headmaster told us. 'Willy-Willy, answer me if I is wrong. Tell me if I was wrong. Looka! For nine years almost going in ten years this month or the next, for *nine years* we have keep a secret betwixt ourselves. We have gone to sleep and wake' up with that secret tight tight tight in our fist' like a real secret should be kept. Now, I asking you, Willy-Willy, as a man in the particular condition in which you is, I asking you, will you be such a stinking bitch as to do something 'gainst me what would prevent me from getting happiness.'

'But oh Jesus Christ, Ruby! you knows full well that all I have in my heart for you is love, and…'

'*Good!* Now that secret we have keeped so long, you think that under the circumstances it ought to be shouted out on the house-top?'

'Oh Jesus Christ, no!'

'*Well!* And if I can arrange a something what going to take off your shoulders the burdens and the yokes o' obligations and duties, would you refer to me as a' enemy?'

'No! Oh Christ! no no no! But I still don't see what the arse you driving at, though! You up to some-damn-thing what I can't discern at the moment, but what I could smell, 'cause it damn stink.'

'*Wait!* Is you in a position to married me and make a home for your child?'

'But Jesus Christ, Ruby, looka, I come over here to ask 'bout Milton… oh hell now, Ruby, looka, heh-heh-heh!… I have a couple shillings in my pockets, I going even give you a couple for the child, and next week…'

'*God blind you, Willy-Willy, lissen to me!* Lissen to me, man, and shut up your blasted mout'! I talking sense!'

'All right all right… all right!'

'*Lissen to me!* You can not married me, right?'

'But, oh hell, Ruby, I is a man unemploy' and…'

'Canst you?'

'Well, hell no!'

'Good!'

'But oh hell, Ruby! You know my sittiation, and…'

'It grieve' my heart to tell you what I have to tell you. Willy-Willy, but Nathan have come back.'

'Nathan?… come back?'

'He come back asking me to let him come back.'

'And you take him back?'

'I have take' him back 'cause he offered me the ring!'

'But gorblummuh! after you hold-on and spend all my bonus-money from the Benefit Society? After you spend-out all my savings from the Penny Bank, and… and… gorblummuh, Ruby! I going have to ask you to please give me back that white sharkskin dress I buy for you from the Indian-man… I could sell that dress to Annie and buy a rum with it. Come come!'

'Look at it this way, Willy-Willy. Look at the facts this way. Nathan offering the ring. You is Milton' father. But I have wait' ten years whilst you put me off and put me on, and now I relieving you of your burdens. Willy-Willy… every woman want' to know she have her own-own man sleeping 'side o' her at nights… and I not any diff'rent from any other woman… thousands o' womens thinks in that fashion. A wedding ring does do wonders to a woman' heart, Willy-Willy, and I need a husband.'

'But you forgetting that a piece o' Milton belongst to me?'

'I know that.'

'And how the hell… gorblummuh, Ruby!'

'Look, Willy-Willy, Nathan has gone 'cross by the Marine asking 'bout a night-watchman job. He soon come back. I don't want no fighting and bloodshed in my house… and what Milton going think when he hear' that his father ain't really and truly his father? Think o' Milton, man.'

'You see' Milton?'

'Not since yesterday.'

'And you say you is a mother?'

'But Willy-Willy, Milton has run away from home, and…'

'Where you look' for Milton? You went 'bout looking for my child?'

'I look' and I look' till I was tired as a horse, and then I went in Pastor Best' church to ask God to bring back Milton, and…'

'I could kill you be-Christ! dead dead *dead*! Ruby, I could put my two hand' to your blasted neck and kill you dead dead dead like I almost blow-up…'

'What you say? Willy-Willy, what that I just hear' you say?'

'Ruby, I in trouble! Ruby?… Ruby, I talking to you!… Ruby?…'

'Willy-Willy… did you?…'

'I is a man in hiding, Ruby.'

'You is a murd'rer!'

'Now, look, Ruby! Ruby?… You lis'ning? Look, Ruby, no-body ain' dead… nobody ain't hurt…'

'Somebody coming!'

'Look! Milton is the onliest witness! I have to see Milton!…
before anybody talk' to him!… Milton is the onliest…'

'*Quick*, somebody…'

'I out by the Bath Corner!… tonight… 'round ten!'

'…body coming! I going be there!'

'The Bath Corner… behind the Bath Wall… *Find* Milton!…
Ruby, find Milton before he go to the police.'

'Ten o'clock, Willy-Willy, and…'

'By the Bath Wall. And be-Christ! don't be late!'

My mother lied to Girlie. Girlie came back asking what Willy-
Willy wanted, and my mother told her he had come begging for
money. Girlie cursed Willy-Willy all the way through hell and
back again, calling him a no-good, 'short-nee-crutch', 'young old
man'. And my mother went on to say how she was glad to get rid
of him at last; that her life was taking on a new turn: she was going
to be married. And she stood up in the middle of the backyard,
with a piece of wringing wet washing in her hand, talking all the
time she wrung the clothes. She asked Girlie whether she had
figured about her future, and Girlie said no. She advised Girlie to
visit the obeah woman, Madame Miranda, and Girlie almost lost
her breath. And my mother had to implore her to lower her voice
in case somebody heard them talking. And Girlie continued
shaking her head from side to side (I could see them through my
portholes), marvelling at the marvel that she had lived so close to
us and did not know that my mother was a believer in obeah. Ants
of hunger were eating away my insides; but I had to let them gnaw
in peace. The women went on talking as if I were not missing; and
I promised them to remain missing until they thought more
about me.

'Has you went down by Gravesend Beach to see if Milton
wash'-up in a wave, drowned?'

'Milton not drowned, not drowned, my dear, eh! Milton
somewhere hiding. He ain' that kind o' child to go and drown
heself on purpose. Christ, child, Milton can't even swim!'

'Has you thought of going by the school?'

'No. Nathan gone 'cross there.'

'In the church? In the belfry?'

'Milton can't climb!'

'Jesus Christ! that is your son!'

'Look, Girlie, I still have to finish this tubful o' clothes, yuh! Confuse myself with Milton? If he dead, I will hear.' And she changed the conversation to talking about her own life. Girlie, previously in a hurry to run along to her work in the Marine Hotel, remained glued to her feet, mouth drooped in astonishment as a new chapter of life was exposed to her by her neighbour with whom she had romped and played on the fringes of starvation and crime for so many years. Did she know that Miranda, Madame Miranda, could do wonders? Did she know that Nathan was in the hands of an obeah woman for *nine years*?

'Jesus God? Nine years? God God God!' Girlie screamed.

Nine years were a long time, my mother said. A damn long time. But the results were there. 'Obeah does work, just like God, Girlie,' she said. 'Slow, but *sure sure*! Nine years last Good Friday night, me and Miranda sit down in her living-room in front o' them cards and that crystul ball thing and talk'-over things to God. We had Nathan inside our hands even from that first night. But things was hard with me. You have remember' that bout o' sickness what flinged me flat on my back for three months with influenza? And I had was to ask you to see that the white lady get her clothes starch'-and-ir'n' every week? It is then that I had to stop-off paying Madame Miranda, 'cause Willy-Willy and me had a bad quarrel that had bloodshed in it, and he stop' giving me money for Milton through that...'

'Jesus God, Ruby! Willy-Willy?... And I living next-door to you all these years!'

'This is confession-morning, Girlie, and I intends to wipe off my slate clean clean.' But she had to put Nathan right. And as soon as she was on her two feet again, financially, she dragged him back to the Madame; and the two of them spied at the cards for days and days until...

'Superstition-things scares the shit outta me, Ruby.'

'You is a coward, Girlie?'

'I am not no blasted coward, Ruby!'

'You is a coward, Girlie.'

'I ain't no blasted coward I tell you, Ruby, 'cause I not frighten' to walk home from that Marine Hotel by myself at the latest o' hours, and...'

'You is a coward 'gainst the mysteries o' God. Wake up! Wake up, child, and clean-out yourself,' my mother told her. And she went on to tell Girlie that it was only the stupid black people who did not take advantage of the mysteries of God: they should indulge more in the greater, higher mysteries of the things of life. 'It is only we stupid arses who do not get the full benefits from the things what God put in this world for we to get the full benefits from. You hear what I saying? Wake up and clean-up yourself! I saying to you, Girlie, that it is only people like me and you, black people and the rest what are scared stiff to take up God' Bible in their hands and read it like how God make it to be readed. That Bible... look, I have one o' them right here!... I keeps it on top o' this china cabinet... in the highest place in this house. Look 'round this room, and see if you see anything *anything* at all... even that picture o' me as a little girl in pigtails... tell me, Girlie, have you see' anything inside this house o' mine hanging from a more higher and exalted place? No! 'Course you not seen anything more higher and exalted than the Bible. And you know why? Because it is God' words.' And I could hear her giving the Bible three heavy tremendous bangs with her hand. 'God write this Book for me, for you, for that white lady out there in the Front Road... for each and everyest one o' we mortals to read outta. And, Girlie, if you can't understand how to read it, let me take you to Madame Miranda and let the three o' we sit down and figure-out a way how to read it then.'

And with this, Girlie jumped down from the back door, and scrambled out of the backyard, saying, 'Jesus! I late for work already. I going have to see you again in the turning, hear...' And my mother, disappointed by Girlie's ignorance and terror about the mysteries of life, sighed heavily and cursed Girlie. 'You borned a whore and you going *dead* a whore!' And then she too left the house. In the wind, the gate was slamming every two seconds...

8

All I can hear now is the *clip-clop-clop-cloppity-clop* of the old brown hobby horse from Ned's Dairy. It is limping across the road and mashing little pools of water that gleam in the sun. Last night's rain is still on the ground. It comes towards our house from delivering milk to the white houses in the Front Road. *Twelve o'clock and school's out!* Always around twelve o'clock the hobby horse passes in front of our school which is halfway between our house and the corner of the Front Road. And always, we boys would stop listening to our masters and mimic the *clip-clop-clop-cloppity-clop* of the old hobby horse by pulling our tongues against the bridges of our mouths. And even if the headmaster was glaring at us, we would still fool him because we did our *clippity-clopping* within the free joyfulness of our hearts, where he and his tamarind rod could not enter. And sometimes, we would run races, clipping-and-clopping, until our mouth-bridges were tired and sore like the hoofs of the hobby horse walking all that hot, dusty, waterless distance between the homes of the white rich and poor black; but the white rich were the only ones in our village who did not jump on a bicycle and ride the quarter mile to the dairy yard and get their milk-and-water three cents cheaper. And once, Lester, my arch-friend in everything, decided to challenge me to a race. It was the Queen's Stakes of clip-clopping. And all the boys were there, anxious, betting used matchsticks – four on me and six on Lester – and the headmaster was miles away on the platform correcting books; so far from our minds that he seemed overseas. And our class, for once happy, for once quiet, no more Commandments, no more Arithmetical Tables, no more Scriptures, no more '*Jesus was born in Bethlehem of Judea*' – '*Too loud, boys! Too LOUD! Too soft, now! Louder, LOUDER! Not so loud!*' – just twenty harmless, happy boys sitting at the railing of the race course, while Lester and I trotted out the horses in our mouths, took them up to the starting tape, got ready for the starter, gave our horses a few taps with our riding canes, and faced the starter... nervous as horses on the Garrison Savannah Course where real racehorses ran... and then, THEY'RE OFF! *clip-clop-clop-clip-clippity-clop! clip-clip-clip-clop!* Lester was turning the first bend first, out through the classroom of the Big Boys, the boys in Seventh Standard, down the playing field and out along the tar road, free and in the sun and away from Mister Blackman... and I, close behind, enjoying this brief reprieve of the race from the whip... and I tore my whip into the laziness of my horse: *clip-clop-clop!* And suddenly, the cheering in the grandstand of the classroom stopped. The onlookers in the middle of the racecourse went dumb. The breeze blowing against my face was still. And a new breeze within the room was heavy and stiff and dramatic.

'Go on go on!' It was the headmaster, standing like a steward in the paths of our horses. 'Go on! Go on, you two idiots, and lemme see who going win this race. Mister Lester the Jockey? Mister Milton the Jockey? Or me, the Headmaster? Okay? On yuh marks! Get set! Go!' – and the whip, without waiting, was falling plax-plax-plax-plax! on our behinds and the headmaster was running behind us all the way through the cluttered alley-ways of our class right up to the platform. Our horses had disappeared. Only we boys felt the sting of his whip. And from that day we always ran private, silent races with the horses in our mouths prancing around the racecourse of our minds.

It is twelve o'clock now, Friday, and children are streaming out for lunch. The girls from the girls' school near our house are walking and talking about their teachers. And I can hear one of them saying her teacher does not know how to dress. And the boys are screaming out, plotting and planning their games of cricket and marbles which they will play after school. I can only see the legs and hips of the children, masculine and feminine. From the hips down to the dust-covered bare feet of the boys and the ashes around the ankles of the girls, some of whom are wearing canvas shoes. I can see the whole bodies of the small children from my rampart in the cellar. There is Lester. Lester,

Lester, oh Lester! walking like a little billy, like a little bully. And with him are some of the boys in my class. They look so different now, seeing them through these portholes of the stone foundations of my house. Lester comes full into my view. I imagine him in the middle of my submarine spying-glass. Closer, Lester! Closer CLOSER! 'Fire one!'... BOOM! Lester keeps walking on. 'Fire two!' BOOM! Lester keeps walking on like a little England taking everything; and talking everything he knows about Mister Blackman and the rose in the school gardens and about Shortie... right into the muzzle of my biggest torpedo exit, and comes to stare me in the face. But he does not know his fate; he does not know this. And then he shouts, 'Milton is a billy-goat! Milton is a billy-goat!' He is point-blank now, near death, and I aim, aim well... aim... aimmmmm!... three, four, five, six, seven, EIGHT torpedoes... boom! booom! boooom! booooom! boooooom! booooooom! boooooooom! BOOOOOOOOM!... and when the noise clears away and the smoke clears, and the hate and the bitterness, I still hear his voice, 'Milton is a billy-goat! Milton is a billy-goat!' And I begin to cry, and close my ears with my index fingers so that I would not hear his ugly voice. But his voice, and the voices of his friends, my one-time friends, come to my ears still.

'...and did you see how Blackman run outta the school when Milton' father appear' through the door?... Blackman' face turned white white white like a pillow-case, and...'

'...he ask' Milton' father to spare him... parden parden parden Mister Milton' Father! Parden!'

'And all the time the teachers was laughing at the headmaster, hee-hee-hee! and all the time the stick was playing fireworks in Blackman' arse!'

'...and you see how Milton' father hold the stick over Blackman' head, and make Blackman say "parden"?... and then, and then...'

'Milton have a real father, though, boy!'

'I wish my father was a Bad Man like Milton' father. But my father is only a fisherman, and he could only catch fish. He can't beat up a headmaster pretty like Milton' father...'

'Lord! and didn't the blood pour down offa Blackman' face and head and forehead!...'

'Lordey! Lordey!… and didn' that blood look real' pretty! So much blood pouring down offa Blackman, and all the time Milton' father pelting that big stick, wham! Parden, Mister Milton' Father!… wham! I going to kill you, Blackman! I going to kill you!… wham!… Parden, parden, Mister Milton'…'

'And Jees! after all o' that, Blackman won't even give us half-day from school! Blackman is a real stingy man, though!'

'…and when he come back in the school and the blood was still running down all over his white suit and the red blood was making the white suit look pink… And Blackman' face was black-and-blue, and… But you wait till Milton come back to school… just wait! He going to be a real hero.'

'He going to be a hero.'

'Milton going to be a hero all right! But after Blackman throw' the tam'rind whip in his…'

And their voices disappeared and faded, and hunger took the place of their voices. And there was nothing for me to do; and nothing to listen to but the ants of hunger grumbling inside me. And suddenly I began to feel very closed in, cramped in my little shallow castle; suddenly all the fears that had haunted me last night while I was running away, all those terrors – Miss Brewster, my father, and the headmaster – came back to me. And I yearned to be out of my prison under the house, to be above ground like Lester. Now school was like a heaven. I missed the headmaster, and the whizzing sound of his whip; I missed the buzzing noise of the recitation of the Ten Commandments; and the hum of voices saying the Lord's Prayer over and over again until the words meant nothing to me; and I missed the young, uncracked, mellow singing voices singing spirituals from the southern states, spirituals that stretched the length and breath and breadth of a land which not one of us could ever see… spirituals that told us about women and men and whisky and pain and cruelty and freedom and the lack of freedom…

Inside our little house seemed very strange to me now, al-though it was only little more than one day that I was away from it. The touch of the tables was different. And I ran my fingers along them to get to know them once more. Along the back of the rocking-chair in which my mother sat, not rocking, at sundown. And in the bedroom. Why did I rush in there expecting to find something distasteful? What did I expect to find there? Was it the evidence of the imprint of her body and Nathan's body on the bed sheets? Or the evidence of the action I had heard early this morning? But I found nothing there. Nothing but the white windblown expanse of sheets which looked like snow and the two pillowcases like two ugly sand dunes. And then I went into the kitchen. The food was there. Food for Nathan. And green tea for me. And the money!... Where was the money?... Under the tablecloth... at the right-hand corner? or the left-hand corner?... Where was the money?... Suppose Nathan had taken, had *stolen* all of the money?... the money... cigarettes... two shillings...

Trembling, my hands fumbled under the cloth, and the money was there. I was disappointed that Nathan was so honest. He was honest but I did not hate him less. With the money in my hands, all I could think of was Nathan coming back tonight, and taking off his dirty smelly clothes that were like the perfume of the soil, throwing his clothes over my mother's rocking-chair, drinking hot green tea from a half-gallon tin tot, farting loudly and belching loudly, and then dropping into bed with my mother, on top of my mother, as if he were my father... and I hated to think of it. The money felt good in my hands. I rattled it and rackled it, and held it and ran my fingers through it and over it, running them through it in my pockets as if I were the headmaster on the afternoon of payday. The food! I must eat all of the food. And I went into the kitchen and ate all of the food, with my fingers because the spoons were all dirty from last night. I would go away. I would go away to sea. I would go away to sea and land in Harlem. I would go away. I could break every plate, glass, saucer... set the house on fire, set the bed on fire to purge it... I could do anything now, because I was going away. And I could not find anything to do. Nothing to tear up, nothing to destroy, nothing to throw my bitterness on. And so I wiped my fingers on the clean shining linen tablecloth, as I had seen Nathan do. And I stood staring at the grease, at the four lines pointing in one direction but pointing to no destination. And then, for no reason, I made the four lines into four arrows which gave meaning to the lines, and then...

footsteps were coming around the paling. I rushed under the cellar. Before I was out of sight, the footsteps changed their mind… the gate was touched, and the footsteps went back out towards the road. And I could hear abuse and disgust… and the wind reminding the gate that it was still unlocked. Sleep came soon to me. Heavy and sluggish after the food, in a short while, with my thoughts spinning around in my head before they were born. And then I thought I was setting out on a journey in a far land where all the policemen were black and where the people standing on a crowded corner were all white. And I walked up to the speaker to beg him not to set the people on fire; but before I reached the speaker (this speaker had no face) I slipped on a slab of ice and fell through a manhole. And then all was darkness.

Someone is jumping on the lid of the manhole. Up and down up and down, all over the cover. And the more I grip the lid and try to reach the top the more the lid shakes and the further down I am falling into the slippery underworld of darkness. There are voices, confused voices that echo and re-echo. There is a noise, a noise as if many persons are trying to talk at the same time. As if each person has a very important point to make. But as if neither person regards the other's point as being sufficiently important. And a verbal argument boils up and changes into a physical argument. And someone shouts, loudly as if to smash his lungs, 'God blind you in hell, Nathan! You is thiefing black bastard!' And when I hear the voice, I reach the top of the manhole and the lid comes off in my hand. I am awake now. I am awake because I can feel dirt in my mouth; and I can see the ants crawling over my hands and dragging pieces of rice with them. The voices belong to Nathan and my mother. She is shouting and screaming and her voice disappears for moments under the passion of her cruelty.

'But Ruby!… oh Christ, Ruby, you have me wrong! You have me wrong wrong wrong.'

'Nathan, get to-hell outta my eyesight before I screel-out and bring every police' to get you for committing a rape on me, yuh! How *dare* you say Milton thief my money? I know Milton.'

'But good Lord, Ruby! Rube, I telling you the thruth… I take up the six-cent piece as I ask' you… Look! No, come, look… I have three cig'rettes and a half-smoke' butt still left back…'

'Look how Satan smashing up my…'

'But, Rube, I not so heartless that I going bite-off the hand that put food inside my mouth! I not so damn stupid, Ruby.'

'Get out, Nathan! Get out!'

'Okay okay, Ruby! So I rested my hands on the extra change. But you know I is a man unemploy', Ruby. Good Jesus Christ, Rube, ease me up, oh God, ease me up a pivvy, man! Looka, Ruby!… Rube? Lissen to me, man!… Look, Rube, as soon as I get that night-watchman job I going pay…'

'You have just tell me you didn' get the job!'

'No no! I didn' tell you…'

'You lying dog! You didn' just tell me… you change your mouth again?'

'Yes yes!'

'Yes? You thief my money?'

'Yes! No! Oh Christ, I damn mix'-up…'

''Course you mixed up! You mixed up bad.'

'But Ruby, I promise I going make up the deficits… look, Ruby, I is a man on bended knees before you…'

'…I needs clothes. I needs things a woman need'. Look, I can't even go to the doctor shop and purchase some period-pads for when my time o' month comes… I so blasted poor!… and now for you to come now and take this kind o' advantages of me!' She was crying now, crying tears of blood, so hurt was she by his behaviour. And I was crying too. I was crying because she was crying. I could feel that she was being swallowed up by her tears and grief.

'Ruby? Ruby, darling? I going make it up to you, I promise you. I promise you, Rube.'

'You promise? You promise? You thief it and then promise? Look, love a duck, Nathan! I could kill you! I could kill you if you don't move outta my eyesight! I going kill you!… kill you dead dead dead DEAD… as a nit!' And then, just then as she said 'dead', something fell. Perhaps it was her rocking-chair. Perhaps it was the table. Perhaps a chair. Perhaps a body. His body.

Fear made me creep to the edge of the cellar near the entrance

143

to the kitchen part of the house and the steps leading into the house. My mother was sobbing, weeping… crying as if it was the only thing left to do, as if she had just that moment come to the end of her ability to express her emotion further. And then she screamed. She screamed a scream of childbirth.

'Girlie? Girlie Girlie?'

'Mistress Sobers, have you call'?' Even Girlie's voice was tired. Worn out no doubt from work and lack of sleep. 'What can I do for you?'

'Girlie, come here quick! Come come quick!'

'Ruby Sobers, guess who spending tonight with me in my bed? Guess who just agree' to pay me…'

'Girlie, I think I kill Nathan. I think Nathan' dead!'

'Jesus Christ, Mistress Sobers! You is a mad woman, or what?'

'Come quick, I think Nathan' dead…'

9

The road before me was dark. And I was becoming tired. The day before, I had travelled this same dark road, in the same condition of fear and of hatred for a parent. Now I was running away again. Always running, always running...

There was going to be a funeral. There would be a funeral. A large funeral... no, a small, very tiny, small funeral for Nathan. For Nathan was not a likeable man. And the large village hearse, black as the devil in hell, would drive up to my mother's front door, like a large worm easy as grease on a slippery road. And the black undertaker would get out, wipe his fat jowls, sweating and fussing and saying that my mother should have bought a larger prettier brown walnut coffin (although there were no walnut trees in our village or in our island), with lots more silver things on it; and that she should have hired three more cars for the family instead of the one car that went with the hearse. And they would take Nathan away, and bring him back later that same night when everybody but the mourners and the rum-drinkers who drank rum and sang bass at every funeral in the village would be there, singing and drinking; and Nathan would be smelling funny with that funny essence of death hanging around him and around the house. And then, the rest of the neighbours, both enemies and friends, would all become friends now that Nathan was dead. And they would come and take a sip of rum and peep in at the coffin through the oval hole at the top, and say as they had said when Girlie's sister died from double pneumonia, 'My my my! He look' nice! He look' the selfsame way and manner as when he was in the flesh. Nathan make' a nice dead, though!' And they would start up their singing, 'The Day Thou Gavest, Lord, Is Ending'... and the bass voices of his gambling friends loud and wandering away from the chords of the tune because of the rum, straying and mourning and mournful... and the women wailing and singing in soprano at one and the same time, so that you could not tell where the tears ended and the singing and the beauty of their voices began. And the children herded into the midst of all this suffering, all this weeping to peep in through the little oval hole in the top of the coffin and see what Mister Nathan 'look' like now that he dead... and the women white as snow in white dresses made in a hurry and fitting evil; and the men, some in borrowed suits, some in old suits, all black and fitting them like coats of mail, with white shirt collars too small and too stiff with starch, hard as cardboard; and the old ties with lines of silver slashing them from the large ugly knots down to the top of the navel... and all of the men and women smelling like whiffs of English lavender, and bay rum from British Guiana, and carbolic soap. The mourning and the weeping. The weeping and the mourning. The sighing and the coughing. The screaming and the falsetto singing. The words of memory spoken by the minister chosen by my mother, Pastor Best... Nathan would have died in such a way undeserving of a burial by the vicar... and the pastor himself black and dressed in black, his seven-days-go-to-meeting-suit, telling the world that Nathan was a good Christian-minded man while everybody in the village knew that Nathan was a crook; telling the neighbours that God was now taking Nathan up into His bosom, in Heaven, and that that was a good thing, while everybody knew for certain that Nathan was bound for Hell on a fast donkey cart. And the women, like so many dead people, would sigh and think of the day when they too would be carried on the wings of a angel-plane up up up above the white clouds, up beyond the blue sky, to knock on God's door, to get St Peter up, still sleepy and tired as a watchman with watching, and ask him to unlock the Gate and let Nathan in. And now that Nathan was dead and gone, it was no time to weep, because weeping meant that Nathan was bound for Hell, which everybody including the pastor knew for certain, but which everybody including the pastor could not say in front of the mourners who were still alive. Pastor Best could not say this because he was in the habit of saying that every black man when dead had to go to

Heaven because he had spent all his life on earth in Hell. And my poor mother, unhappy not because Nathan was dead, but because Nathan had dared to die in her house, and had left her holding the heavy costs and the burden of the expense of burying him… she would tell Girlie when the last car had come back from Westbury Cemetery in the evening dusk, 'Jesus Christ, child, Nathan costed me more as a dead man than when he was in the flesh and living!'… unhappy also because Madelaine cursed and abused and swore at everybody who said Nathan was her man; and that she ought to have buried him. But Madelaine would have said, 'No no no NO! Nathan ain't my man. Never was. And never will be! Nathan didn' dead in my house, so he can't be my man!' And in the midst of all these thistles of grief, my mother would be sorrowful because she did not know what was inside the envelope that contained the mysteries of Nathan's will – or whether Nathan had remembered to write a will. Did Nathan leave back a will? People have a habit of dying without a will. Did everything remain for Madelaine? Or did he change back the will, and leave everything for my mother when he changed his heart about her? It would be such a battle between my mother and Madelaine if, after my mother had shouldered the costs of the coffin, she then found out that Nathan's house and his land and his chairs and his tables and his painter's brushes and his dice and his small savings in the Penny Bank and his subscription card at the Benefit Society, all belonged to Madelaine. My mother would kill Madelaine. And if Madelaine had any children from an outside man, she would have to kill them too, just like the man in the Shakespeare book, a man our headmaster told us about, who had to keep on killing people like snakes, scotching them in the rosebud of time, because he had made one mistake of killing one, and now his hands were red with the paint of the incarnadine seas. But if my mother did really and truly kill Nathan… if she had killed him… committed a murder, would she get anything from the will, if there was a will? But if there was a will, there would have to be a way…

There were not many people in the street this night. Those who were lingering in front of houses watching the night come; and those who were talking to the silhouettes of heads printed against the dim light cast from the kerosene lamps, paid no attention to me running across the road to reach the Bath Wall. And a sudden fear came over me, like the fear that swamped me when I was under the church. Suppose nobody cared about me? Suppose nobody knew I was not dead, as Nathan might now be dead? To whom could I run now? Miss Brewster?… and let her drink her loneliness out of me?

A knot of men were assembling near the top of the hill where my godmother lived with her cows. They were talking about cricket. One man was saying, 'Worrell is a more better batsman than John Goddard, and be-Christ! when Lin'wall from Australia and Bedsuh from Englunt was firing-down them fast balls who the hell you think stan'-up like a man and face' them? Goddard?' And another man was saying something about somebody standing up and 'making three hunder-red runs in India' backside, though!' And then I heard a man saying, '…be-Christ! you gotta come to Barbados to find out 'bout cricket! Littl' Englund, man! You don't know, be-Christ! that more world records break right here 'pon that piece o' turf call' Kens'ton Oval than anywhere else in this Chinee world…' and then I saw light coming from my godmother's bedroom window, through the jalousies. And I could make her out, fuzzy and shadowy, moving about her lonely room, preparing herself for the long cold night ahead of her; getting her deserved rest in order to face the cows and the customers who complained about too much milk in the water she sold. And then I reached the Bath Wall.

There was a shadow sitting on the kerb. A woman. She sat with her dress tucked vigorously betwixt her fat legs which looked like two hunks of wallaba wood. Right up to the crux of her thighs I could see. And in her hand was a short stump of sugar cane. She was peeling the cane with the knives of her teeth. *Sssssssplit!* I went in the darkness to wait for Willy-Willy. A piece of cane blade went flying through the air like an aeroplane without wings. *Sssssssplit!* another piece. And so on until the cane, sticky and juicy, knotted every two inches, remained in her hand. She fumbled somewhere in the bundle of cloth that was her lap and brought out a knife; and with the knife she screwed around the cane, broke off a piece, put it into her mouth, closed her eyes and chomped with glee until the juice and the sugar from the cane trickled down her chin like dribble. And then she wiped her chin with the back of her hand, the hand that held the knife, and continued screwing off pieces of the cane, and placing them into her mouth and chomping on them. '...Blasted cane real' sweet though!' she mumbles to the cane. '...Hads better buy a next piece from that thiefing whore.' She chomps again. 'We produces... cane... Cane is our... agricult'rul... stable-crop. And you mean to tell me... that I have... to *buy* a piece... o' cane, or my mouth... won't... taste none o'... this sweetness what the... Gov'munt always sending outta the islan'?... Four inches o' cane... for a damn big penny? A *whole* penny?'

And then I heard a shuffle of steps in the darkness behind the Bath Wall. Shhh! there is someone there!... shhh!... perhaps it is...

'Ruby? Is that you, Ruby?' The shuffling becomes more anxious, as if walking on hills of gravel. 'Ruby?... Ruby?...' And then the silence of anxious quiet, a quiet that prepares itself for something dramatic. I can hear the woman at the kerb peeling cane, and hear the slits of cane dropping on the ground; and the chomping on the cane. The street light came on, and Willy-Willy rushed out of the darkness at me.

'What the ar—!' He stood watching me without talking. Just watching me, as if he was deciding what to do with me. 'Who send you here?' he said, gripping me by my neck. 'Who send you here? Nathan? Nathan send you here?'

'Nobody.'

'And how you know I here?'

'Nobody.'

'You tell anybody?'

'No.'

'You tell anybody 'bout last night?'

'No, Willy-Willy.'

'Gorblummuh!'

'I ain't tell nobody, Willy-Willy.'

'Gorblummuh! If...' and he tightened his hands around my neck, 'if you tell anybody...' and he said no more. We stood facing each other: he looking at me not knowing what to do with me; and

I, wishing he would call me his son. And after a lifetime of silence, he said, 'Milton, you have to help me out. I in trouble.'

'Yes, Willy-Willy.'

'And you have to bear witness for me.'

'Yes, Willy-Willy.'

'Gorblummuh, or I kill you!'

'I not going talk.'

'Talk and I cut out your damn tongue like them sinner-men!'

'No, Willy-Willy.'

'I have to tell you something, Milton, boy. I is a man in hiding from the laws o' the land. I is a hunted man, Milton. And you is the onliest person on this living earth what know' what happen'. So, if you talk, Willy-Willy *gone*! You know what that mean'?'

'Yes, Willy-Willy. That mean' prison, and…'

'Maybe fifteen years if the judge in a good mood.' He guided me back into the shadows of the Bath Wall. Then he said, 'And you won't want to see old Willy-Willy in that predicamunt, would yuh?… 'Cause that mean' death! And, Milton, I is a young man, and I not ready to dead yet. So, I asking you to keep your tail betwixt your legs, 'cause you have not see' me last night, or never. Hear? Good! Seal' and sign', Milton?'

'Yeah, Willy-Willy.'

'Good boy!' and he held me by the hand and led me out of the darkness and we came abreast of the woman still sitting on the kerb. He looked around him nervously as though expecting someone to arrest him. I could feel his blood pumping through his fingers into my fingers. We saw the woman sitting with a pile of chewed cane pith in front of her. Large brown ants glistened in the light from the street lamp. They were moving logs of the sugar-cane pith, and she watched them silently and did nothing. Then she took up a piece of cane blade, and with it she guillotined a large brown ant, cutting its torso in half. And for a time, the ant was still very industrious (*go to the ant, thou sluggard!*) thinking it was still alive, moved and then found that its rear half was not coming along with its front half, and it tried to turn back but could not. Then it collapsed, dropped, paused, wriggled and died. The woman laughed. Willy-Willy tightened his grip on my hand, and we walked on. He took me to the back door of Mister Fuguero's

Rum and Grocery Shop. He knocked twice on the door, and a little knot-hole of orange light appeared and in the middle of it was Mister Fuguero's eye. The door was opened; Mister Fuguero looked around inside the front of the shop, and then came back. There was dirty sand on the floor; and dead beetles and bees from the sugar bags were crunched into the sand. Willy-Willy lifted the part of the shop counter which could be lifted like a trap-door; ducked under it, held it high until I passed under it, closed it and then shuffled nervously in the dirty sand. Mister Fuguero came and stood beside Willy-Willy.

'The coast clear, Willy-Willy, you old backside!' He patted Willy-Willy on the back. 'I hear' the detectives coming back in the morning though. So, look out.' He swallowed something in his mouth, and I saw the lump ooze down his swallow pipe. 'A half bottle?' He looked me squarely in the eyes. 'The son growing real' nice, Willy!'

Willy-Willy said nothing.

'That is your boy, Willy-Willy. I can see Willy-Willy written all over this boy' fissiogomy!' But Willy-Willy said nothing. 'Half bottle o' Three Stars, then? This boy have your features. Both o' you ugly as arse, though! You couldn' hide be-Christ, Willy-Williams, even if you did want to hide. Flesh and blood. Spitting image o' you. Chip offa the blasted worthliss block, eh, Williams?' And then he shuffled through the sand to fetch the rum. He came back, and banged the bottle on the counter. 'And Willy-Willy?… when this thing blow' over, come 'round sometime. The paling in the back 'gainst that whore' house coming down. She swear' blind that my fowl-cock breeding her hens, and that my pigs shitting up her yard. So, come 'round when you in the clear some time in the daytime… I going keep my mouth shut! Could yuh make it?' Throughout all this, Willy-Willy was silent; and I could see hate in his eyes for Mister Fuguero. I did not know a pair of eyes could contain such venom. 'Five shilling'?' Still, Willy-Willy was quiet. 'Oh Christ! you old black Jew! Alright, ten shilling' then!'

Willy-Willy raised the trap-door of the counter, held it high until I stooped under it, then he stooped under it, and then he let it drop, *bram!*

'Looka, Willy-Willy, stand clear o' the law, boy! You shouldn' be walking 'bout so early in the night, man. You is a damn good carpenter when you ain' have in your rums. I needs you, boy. So stand clear o' the police.'

'Make it fifteen shilling', Fuguey!'

Mister Fuguero stared at him, as if he had forgotten Willy-Willy could talk.

'Fifteen shilling'.'

'All right, you thiefing bitch! I can't hold a hammer straight, so I have to let you rob me, you bastard! You old, old…'

'Thanks, Fuguey,' Willy-Willy said, and we were moving through the darkness again, back to the Bath Wall.

We were on the Bath Wall. We were sitting as we must have sat countless times before. I was looking at the stars, counting them. In all this time, Willy-Willy had not spoken; either to me or to the bottle of rum he was drinking. Below us, still on the sidewalk, and nodding now, was the woman who had sucked the sugar cane and crucified the large brown ant. Willy-Willy pushed the bottle into his hip pocket each time he took a nip; and he smoked and inhaled deeply and noisily as if the smoke contained small pebbles which he had to get through his nostrils; and he held the cigarette in the cup of his hand as they did in a blackout during the war.

'Take cover! Take cover, Willy!' the woman said. For a while I did not understand; but later on, footsteps were coming towards us. It was a man. He came out of the darkness and stood up in front of us, away from us hiding in the darkness. I could see him looking down at the woman on the kerb. He seemed unable to make up his mind whether to talk to the woman or to ask her to come aside with him. Willy-Willy had by now pinched the burning ash from his cigarette as they did in an air-raid during the war. The man was waiting. And then his patience gave out.

'You coming home now?' the man asked.

'No!' the woman said, as if she did not know the man.

'You coming home now, or you going lemme lick-in your backside with this stick?'

'Lick it in! Lick it in! I have witnesses.'

152

'You coming home? Or you going let me shut you outta the house?'

'Shut me out! Shut me out!'

'You intends to come home and feed the child? Or you intends to let him screel-out his damn lungs and dead?'

'Let the baby screel till he pee himself. Let him *dead*.'

'Jesus Christ!' he said, defeated by the woman. He walked up and down in front of us for some time. And tormented by her, and not knowing what to do, he made a feigned blow at her neck with the stick he held in his hand. The woman did not move. And the blow landed nowhere, not on her neck, since it was not meant to land there. 'You don't know, gorblimey!… I could beat you inna a pulp be-Christ, till you come like putty? With this stick I have in my hand I could par'lyse you… I could beat you stiff right here now, woman… you don't know I could kill you even?'

'Kill me!'

'I could really kill you for truth, you don't know?'

'I invites you to do it. Kill me.'

'I could do it.'

'Well, yes! You haves my permission.'

'Looka, woman, you coming home and minding that blasted child o' yours?'

'I not coming.'

'You intends to sit down here 'pon this kerb like if you is some, some… whore or something?'

'Your worthliss mother is a more bigger whore than me!'

'You calling my mother a whore?' His voice was getting louder and cruel.

'Have you hear' me call your mother a whore? That lady? That princiss?'

'Please! Come home, eh… for the last time. You coming home?'

'You have not see' me sitting down here 'pon the white man' kerb?'

'Oh Jesus Christ!' And he rammed the stick against the concrete of the wall, and the jar drove pins and needles of shivers through me. And then he walked away into the blackness of the night, reappeared again once as he came under the yellow street lamp near Pastor Best's church, faded again like a movie coming to its end, and the ticking stick which he dragged along the railings of the houses along the street became inaudible as his footsteps died in the night. The woman got up, held her hands to her belly and laughed.

'The coast clear!' she said. And Willy-Willy came out of the darkness, and we sat in the shadows of the wall again. He held the bottle to his mouth and kept it there while the rum fell into his mouth down down down like sand in an hour glass. And just as the last second of time was about to fall, he took the bottle from his lips, held it up in the air like Mister Smith at the doctor shop measuring a prescription of medicine, and held it over to the woman on the kerb.

'Come, Millicunt! Drink this little blasted rum, do!'

'Thanks boy, Willy-Willy?'

'Thank *you*!' He held his hand around my neck, dragged me off the wall, and said, 'Come!'

We were coming near, Willy-Willy and I, to the crowd of men who were still arguing about cricket. And we passed them and continued along the side of the road, ducking into the gutter each time a motor car approached. Perhaps Willy-Willy was taking me to put me in the care of my godmother. I would like that. I would sleep on one of her three old-fashioned Victorian chesterfield sofas in the living-room which smelled like a funeral parlour, with all those artificial flowers flourishing like real flowers growing wild in old embossed vases. And I would have all the milk in the world, in the cows, to drink. And there would be buttermilk and cakes; and I would tinkle her tinkling old piano which had lost all but one of its keys; and I would play with the birds motionless in flight on the wall over the dining-table in the living-room which had smear-proof oilcloth on it... and look at the painting of a very gloomy day, a day not in our island, but a day in some foreign country where houses had straw or something that looked like straw on their roofs, and where children wore shoes made of wood and where the cows were red and white instead of black and brown as the cows in our village... and there was that young girl with whom I was in love, so beautiful and so white with long reddish hair as if she had sat too close to the logs in the fireplace, hair that stretched down to the tips of her long black stockings and across her shoulders like the golden paint of a sunset. And on her shoulders, with the sunset hair, was a bar made of wood, and attached to the bar were two small pails, full of milk. And the old man, probably her grandfather, standing at the door for ever, with a large pipe in his mouth and volcanoes of smoke billowing forth from a briar that burned like an eternal flame…

But we have passed my godmother's house now; and I am still watching the old man standing at the cottage door, as I had watched him for nine years. Perhaps Willy-Willy is going to the police station to give himself up, and give me up. Perhaps he is tired of hiding and living in the shadows of the village. The police station in our village is like the inside of the storage room at Goddard's Grocery, cold and vast and full of people and police-men and things which seem dead. There is always a large black constable spawning the desk, on the point of falling asleep for good; and always there is an old-fashioned nib pen in his hand and with the end of this he beats time, for time is everywhere in this station. Sarge (we call him Sarge because he has been in the police force so long that he could have been a sergeant if he had the brains) is a man who has looked on crime so long and so often during his long sleep at this desk that only if a man is brought in who killed God, only this impossible extreme misdemeanour could make Sarge get up off his backside and avoirdupois and show enough emotion to make you certain he is still in the flesh and not of the quick and the dead. One time, I was taken to this very police station by the Gestapo who told me 'to testify and swear a' oath, touching the Bible with all two of my hands, that all I henceforth say is the truth the whole truth and nothing but the truth so help me God'; and I touched the Bible with my hands still wet and sticky and aromatic with the essence of Miss Price's mangoes on them, and the Gestapo told me to say that I was a 'burglar'. And I had wondered and worried about the meaning of the word, 'burglar', and the Gestapo did not tell me because he did not know the meaning of the word; but he used it neverthe-less. What was a 'burglar'? Was he a man? Or was he a woman? Or a man who thought he was a woman? One time, a man called another man by a name which sounded like 'burgler', although it might not have been 'burgler', and the man so called beat that man until he could not breathe. And once, somebody said a man named Sugarcake was a something… did he mean 'burgler'? But when the Gestapo took me into the station he changed the word 'burgler' to larceny. Larceny, the Gestapo called it. Petty larceny. And Sarge looked up at me without moving his eyeballs, without moving his eyelids, did something with the old-fashioned pen, looked at me again, got up, went outside behind the tall huge unpainted desk, came back with a piece of slender bamboo in his hand, and drove it into my backside, *whap-whap-whap-whapp!* And Christ! when I stopped running, my trousers were soaking wet! I never told my mother I had a criminal record of petty larceny.

And coming into the shadows of the police station, I thought of the time when the man named Sugarcake was taken to the station in a sugar bag still crawling with ants and bees attracted by the grains of sugar still left in the bag and not by Sugarcake's sweetness. And Sugarcake was naked. And the policemen told Sarge that they had 'catch' him with a little boy', and that the boy's 'thing was bruised bad bad, real' bad because this worthliss Sugarcake had done something *bad* to the little boy'. The confession of guilt ripped from Sugarcake said with so-help-me-God-truth that the said Sugarcake had trapped the little boy. The Gestapo said Sugarcake confessed that he had trapped the little boy; and he had given evidence without placing his hand on the Bible. He had lured the little boy on the day in question, aforementioned, into the same parlour of his spider web of wickedness with an aerated drink and a penny cake that had sugar on it. And when the little boy, the defendant, out of faith for Sugarcake, the aforementioned accused, so the Gestapo said; when the said little defendant boy who was defenceless, out of his faith for Sugarcake, had eaten and had drunk and was merry, then wicked wicked Sugarcake like Satan in man's clothing, turned around and 'did this evil thing' to the little defenceless boy who was the defendant. And Sarge growled with his eyes, and kicked Sugarcake in a very delicate spot in his sugar-bag suit; and Sugarcake screeled for blue murder in the police station, and the

Gestapo shut the windows to keep in the screams and then he nailed Sugarcake with another charge, disorderly conduct. And just when Sugarcake screeled out, Sarge yelled, 'I have a damn good mind to *cut* out what you got! Man, you is a *man*, too? You is a liability. You is a savage! You is a blasted African savage! You is a damn sagaboy! You is a... you is a... burgler! (or something that sounded like that). *You love boys!* Man, I got a kiss-me-arse mind to throw acid in your damn face... if, if-if-if you don't get outta my sight I kill you dead dead, 'cause I have a little boy at home, and and-and-and...' And Sarge put his shoulder to the wheel and kicked Sugarcake again and again and again. And then a van which we called the Mae West came and three tall policemen who looked like monsters came out, and the tall policemen snapped something silvery on Sugarcake's hands, and dipped his hands into a blue-black bottle of ink and made him write his name on a piece of paper, using only the tips of his ten fingers to write with; and then a camera went plix-flop! and a thing like a small bulb with frozen milk on it fell on the floor, and one of the telephone-pole policemen kicked it right into Sugarcake's face and they pushed him, Sugarcake, the accused Sugarcake, into the Mae West and slammed the door in his face and did not say, 'Pardon'. And Sarge, like a man after a hard day's work on the plantation, rubbed his hands whistlingly together as if washing them with invisible incarnadine water and said, 'Oh Christ! a little nine-year-old boy! Nine years! And mashed-up for life! That, that... that-that-that... *cannibull*!' And Sarge started to cry because, as he said, his boy at home was nine years old too...

As the large raindrop of a light bulb in front of the police station faded behind me, I knew for the first time, with extreme terror, that we were going home to my mother. Something within me said it was time to stop fighting, to give up, surrender. And I felt tired, very tired; and I felt glad that my punishment, the end of my fatigue was at hand. I could feel the warmth of my bed and the sting of the whip on my body at the same time, and I was happier. Surrender. Surrender and look into the soft loving eyes of your mother, son. Surrender, because you are weary now with guilt, and burdened down with a conscience of sorrow. And I thought again of Sugarcake, himself so tired and weary from the assize of trials and cross-examinations for his crime of misleading a little defendant boy… answering all those questions all those hours; and answering them truthfully, admittingly, and finding none of the policemen believing that he was telling everything… so long, so wearily long that it must have been a joy to be punished. And I thought of the headmaster who warned me about 'birds of vengeance picking out my eyes if I broke the Fifth Commandment' – or was it the Fourth? – the one which frightened me to *'honour thy father and thy mother that thy days may be long in the land which…'*

We turned off the main road and into the alleyway of vines that led to our house; and then I saw my mother's body filling the doorway and the heavy window stick and the shouts and the screams and the perspiration and the spittle and the red tongue and the teeth and the sweat and the hands moving up and down like a piston in the engine room at the plantation and the house stifled in darkness with all the windows open letting in a lighter darkness… I could see the shape of the large mansion-needle tree outside. And I could feel the quiet; the quietness of the house; somewhere in that quietness, somewhere in that darkness, my mother was lurking for me. Somewhere, blended in with the darkness of the spirit of the house, were the anger and the wrath. And the wrath and anger would change into a horrible Thing; and the Thing would come at me. And the Thing would change into my mother as it got near to me; and like a crab – but larger than any crab I ever caught on the beach – the claws of darkness would reach out like prongs, like the prongs of a large ice-prong made of steel. And my mother would grip me…

But it was only Willy-Willy standing beside me, not holding me now; only standing there looking down at me as he had watched me when I appeared out of the darkness behind the Bath Wall. Terror was in his eyes. He was just standing there looking at me, as if he had done the wrong thing to bring me all this way home. He too looked as if he had surrendered.

'Son,' he said, as if he meant it, 'Son. Yuh mother waiting. Don't keep yuh mother waiting, son.' And he disappeared in the darkness. And even if there was no darkness, my eyes could not have seen him for the tears.

10

She was sitting in the darkness, in the rocking-chair. The house was quiet. The rocking-chair was quiet. I had been standing by the door through which I had entered for a long time, and she had said nothing. The kerosene lamp on the table behind was low, so low that every five seconds or so, little flames of stars sputtered from it. Through the opened window at which she sat, I could see the large mansion-needle tree in the yard of the girls' school. And there she sat not talking, not rocking, not breathing; and there I stood like a fool, condemned. A hot bath in a tub of salts would have been more welcome than this punishment of silence. The hours under the church cellar, and under our cellar, the hours in the rain, my whole lifetime of running away from the thistles and thorns of poverty came before me, but I could not make sense out of it. It just came like a very bad dream: in which I saw Nathan.

And when she did speak to me, she said, in that disinterested manner, 'Boy, where the hell you went all the time, eh?'

'Nowhere, Ma.'

'Nowhere, eh?' The rocking-chair gave a creak. She was coming at me. But the creak turned into a rock. 'Look, get your arse out at the pipe and bring me a fresh bucket o' water. I ain't had fresh water since, since... Thursdee. That lady' clothes still have to be washed.'

'Yes, Ma.'

'And... has you seen Willy-Willy?'

'No, Ma.'

'Milton?'

'Yes, Ma.'

'I have something to tell you.'

'Yes, Ma.'

'Something important, Milton. Something what every mother shouldn' be in a position to tell her own child, but what every mother should expect every child to know for granted, and to take for granted. I have to tell you, Milton, that after tonight you going to have a father. A father living in his house with you. You know what that mean'?'

'Yes, Ma.'

'What, then?'

'I having a father, Ma.'

'Yeah. You having a father. After nine years! Nine years it take' you to have a father, Milton. And your father' name is Nathan.'

'Yes, Ma.'

'After tonight, you address Nathan as Daddy. You hear me?'

'Yes, Ma.'

'Now march your arse 'cross the road for that bucket o' water. And come back in here and take off them dirty musty clothes and get in bed.'

In the kitchen part I could hear her complaining about me. 'I clothes that boy. I feeds that boy. I sends that boy to school. I does everything God allow' a poor woman to do… he not lacking for Sundee School clothes… every Sundee he marching himself outta this humble abode, dress'-down like a little doctor. He is a choir boy in the Anglican church. Not the church out the road, not Pastor Best' church. But the Anglican church! I joined him in the Scouts… oh Jesus Christ, Milton what more is you demanding outta me? What more?' Going around the paling this dark late night, I was looking down into the shining bottom of the galvanized bucket to see what hope, what fortune was lurking there to save me.

From our house to the stand-pipe across the road was a distance of one hundred playful yards in the daytime. At night, one hundred terrifying yards. I had run, I had skipped, I had rambled this distance all my life. The way I went from our house to this pipe varied according to the impetus of mind, the incentive and the motive for going there. It varied also according to the closeness of mother and whip behind me. Tonight, it was late and dark. I was running the whole distance. But I would have to walk the return journey; because the bucket would be on my head, because it was too large and heavy to be carried in my hand.

This stand-pipe was an outstanding monument in my life. In fact, it was also outstanding in the lives of everybody in our village. Here my mother had abused Girlie so rottenly that Girlie turned into tears of shame. Here Girlie had abused my mother until the water dropped from my mother's eyes like pearls of sorrow. Women washed their clothes under the pipe. Here they gossiped. Here you could stand for five minutes and know everything about the white people who lived across the Front Road. You could find out how many tourists had come to the island from Britain, from Canada, from America; how many had come from Venezuela to learn English; and you knew on sight those who were cheap and tight with tips. You could learn, by standing here in the company of women, how many of Vicar Adamson's shirts were patched at the elbow; how many were only shirt-fronts and shirt-cuffs, and how many were without backs. Vicar Adamson's wife was seen going out late one night with a man, the gardener (that was before the gardener was fired by the vicar and before Lester was hired in his place). And here the story was told of how they walked in the shadows of the side of the Front Road, white hand in black hand (which the men called 'mixing'), all the way down Hastings Road after dark, to the Garrison Savannah pasture, and how they stopped under a tree, a berry tree and stomped the essence and the juice out of the fallen berries as they held 'mixing' hands; and how they lay on the damp grass and laughed and laughed at the vicar, and talked things and plotted things about leaving the poor vicar of our church with our church and with the poor of our church. Here for the first time, I learned everything about the origin of children. They did not come in baskets which black witches placed on doorsteps, as my mother told me. And they did not come down chimneys either, as the young white Sunday School teacher from England told us in kindergarten. (And Lester had reminded her over and over again that our houses in the village did not have chimneys, and yet there were more babies than mothers could afford, babies, ''gitimate and illigitimate'. Our Sunday School teacher still maintained that 'babies come down chimneys', in that voice of English legal tender which we always respected and paid our respects to; and believed, because it was English.) Here also, my mother regaled the neighbours about a certain doctor's wife: this lady had only three or four underpants; and they were always dirty, my washerwoman mother declared; and the women cackled like hens, and the men laughed without letting any sound come out of their mouths. Here it was said by the people of the village with one voice that 'white people is damn funny funny people'. I remember it was near this stand-pipe that I was used as a rope in a tug-of-war for parental custody by my father and my mother, as they tried to settle out of court the custody of my bastardy. All the women had said my mother had the right to keep me. All the men said a father should keep his son, and teach him how to drink, and how to fish, and how to bowl a spin ball in cricket, and how to get on with women; that a son brought up by a woman, a mother, turns out always to be a she-she boy. At that time, there were more women than men in our village. And the women won. And my mother kept me from that day. But she had threatened anyhow to kill my father (at that time I did not know who my father was) before she would permit him to lay his nasty good-for-nothing hand on her clean boy-child.

Here now there is no one. Not one living soul; not one soul living or dead. No women are quarrelling now. No women are washing their underclothes under the pipe. No men are washing their faces and hands and feet before falling into bed. Not one. Only me. And it is still. Still as the graveyard on Gravesend Beach where long ago the sailors of an English man-of-war mistook a lantern in Sam Lord's tree for a lighthouse, and came in, and were stuck, and were shipwrecked, and were drowned, and were pulled out of the sea the next morning (some of them: the others were too heavy with the rum and the women of the island) and were buried under the grape trees on the beach. Gravesend Beach.

I can see the moon. It is far away, shining over Harlem, perhaps. And the stars. The stars I have counted all my life; stars I have seen while sitting on the Bath Wall with Willy-Willy; the stars I have seen and counted…

Twinkle twinkle, little star,
How I wonder how old you are...

My bucket is under the pipe and the water is dropping into it. But I watch the stars and wonder where and what they are. Jesus was found by a star, the headmaster said once. The Wise Men, two white men and a black man... two white men from England, and a black man from a place called Africa, the headmaster said... had travelled night and day all through hill and dale, all through and across Africa... One night, looking at stars alone from my window, I followed a star all across the road, through the Front Road, up by the Marine Hotel until I reached our headmaster's house. And then I stopped and stood up in the road, and passed water and then came back the same road with the star. *A star is a wonderful thing if you wonder!* And another time, I decided to take a longer journey with a star. I looked up all the time I was talking to the star. It was a Saturday night, and there were men and women and rum and beatings in my village. But I rode on in majesty on the hump of the camel of my imagination away from this noise, through the deserts of our streets like in the Arabian Nights, through pyramids of back alleys like those I had seen in a First Book of Africa, through muddy rivers of India like those big long ganges of rivers, full of snakes and things that had one name when they were on land, and another name when they were in the rivers, through the whole of England the Mother Country, where the Battle of Ten-Sixty-Six was fought and lost in history books, on paper; all through English History, our history, I walked with that star until a bicycle appeared out of the night without even a star for a headlamp, and *bram!* bicycle, rider and me were wrapped like ganges snakes in a cluster. That was the last time I ever travelled on a star...

'Tomorrow, bright and early, is clothes-day! And the rain coming. Your father took up ever' blasted cent I own and possess to my name, and the white lady out there waiting for these sheets and clothes!... He make Satan get up in my behind so bad that I had to fell him with a blow!... The rain coming, Lord!... I hope Nathan don't get wet in this night-rain!'

I knew I was home again. There are no stars, no camels of imagination, no wanderings through history in her voice. Her voice is the voice of thistles, of thorns. My mother's voice.

'Rain?' she asks the stars.

She raises her hand, with the back of it pointing skywards, and something wet falls into her hand. 'Rain!' she says, defiantly. 'Rain rain rain!' We ripped the clothes from the lines, and bounded into the house. My mother threw them into our best chair. And when she took my handful, she saw a large L-shape rent in a linen dress. But she did nothing; and she said nothing. She merely took them from me; took the rest from the chair, and with her foot she kicked them across the floor. I felt all of a sudden that something serious, something tragic would happen to her. But nothing happened. Perhaps what was going to happen, what could happen, had already happened to her, inside her mind. The rain was pouring now. My mother searched in an old clothes bundle for pieces of cloth to stuff the windows and the jalousies with. But she found nothing suitable to keep the driving rain outside. She stood looking at the floor, at the white clouds of linen dresses and white bed sheets; and I saw her eyes light up, and her hands move and her fingers stiffen... and in the midst of the rain and thunder which had begun to roll, all I could hear was the tearing of cloth. She stuffed the holes in her house with the white lady's clothes. The large hole above our bed was stopped up by a pair of panties. And when she had finished repairing the house with wads of cloth, she lit the kerosene lamp and then turned it down very low, until the wick almost disappeared among a niagara of sparkling stars. But then she raised it again, and searched for the Bible.

The thunder was raging. I was frightened because my mother was frightened. At times like this, we would sit together in a huddle of fear, knit together in love and in terror; and she would pretend that it was love alone which had bound us so. The thunder exploded right above us, and it made me look up; but I did not really know why I looked up instead of down, instead of burying my head in the pillows and sheets as my mother had done. And when it disappeared like a rock-crushing engine in the distance, I saw my mother trembling, kneeling beside me, and in her hands was the Bible, the fat, large, black, leather-bound Bible with the red edges and the gold-painted edges and the large cross cut in gold. Her lips were moving. But nothing was coming out. She looked so fragile now. So much like a large clump of mud, unshaped and dried in the heat of the sun, and ready to be crumbled and blown away by the first whiff of a sound in the heavens.

'I have done evil, son,' she said. She was fighting a long time for the words to come out. And I had seen them being fashioned and constructed at the tips of her lips. But it took her some time to express them outside the confusion of her mind. 'God is punishing me... I have done a bad bad thing.' I did not know which thing she was talking about: destroying the white lady's clothes, or beating my father, or all the bad things she had done during her life. But she kept on saying, 'I have done a bad thing, my son, and God is punishing me now.' She was still on her knees beside the bed. It seemed so natural for her to kneel beside the bed. She always kneeled beside the bed; and although she could have kneeled anywhere inside her house, and I would not have noticed it, yet to kneel beside her bed was so religious, so natural and so expressive of weakness and resignation.

'Kneel beside thy mother, son,' she whispered. 'This is a damn nasty night to be living in, tonight.' She put her arms around me and brought me within the safekeeping of her prayers. 'Where Nathan is now? Where Nathan is? I wonder where Nathan is?' I was so close to her that I could smell her body odour, and feel the life and the fear and the blood pumping through her body. 'Which part o' the Book that story 'bout the Flood is, son?'

'The Flood, Ma?'

'The Flood, son.'

'Ma, you mean the Flood that happen' in the Bible in the beginning of the world?'

'That is the onliest Flood I know 'bout.'

'Well, I don't know where to find it, Ma.' She was becoming angry again. I could see it in her eyes mixed with the terror. 'We haven't reach' the Flood part yet in school, Ma.'

'Search for it! Search for it!'

I searched and I searched. But I could not find the Flood. All

I could see were long words unpronounceable, swimming before the tears of my eyes like rivers. And in my nervousness, I dropped the Bible by mistake, and my mother shrieked and said I had no respect for the word of God. She snatched the Bible from my hand, and brushed it off, and placed it in my hands again. 'Is times like this, Lord, times o' storms and tribulations when every woman does wish she had a man, any man in the house…' and she sighed heavily, and said, 'Come, Milton, the Flood.' I knelt with that heavy book on my lap looking into its pages and thinking of how much I hated her, how great was my abuse for her. This woman, flat on her back with fear, and demanding a miracle of courage from these thin lifeless pages. Within me something was boiling, something bitter for her and for the thing that made her so stupid as to expect so much from such a book. I was bitter against the headmaster for telling us all those tales about miracles in the Bible, about men walking on the waves; about men turning loaves into a harvest to feed people; I was bitter because none of this happiness had ever touched me or my mother, and I hated her the more for expecting it would ever happen to her. But I had to search for the Flood, although I did not know where I would find it; but I did know that if I did not find it, my destruction would be greater than that of Sodom and Gomorrah. And a miracle happened. Turning the pages in wild frustration, and without eyes, for my eyes were swelling like rivers, the Book opened itself at the Flood. I started to hand it to her, forgetting that she could not read. She pushed it back to me, saying I had no manners; I should not push the Bible in her face.

'In the six hundreth year of Noah's life, in the second month… ('Ah-men!' she gasped. 'Say ah-men, Milton!' And I said ah-men, although I was thinking of running away from her, from this detestable resignation before a God who never visited me.) *'…in the selfsame day entered Noah and Shem and…'* ('I don't intends lis'ning to all that damn nonsense 'bout who enter' the Ark and who didn't enter the Ark! Read on, read on and lemme hear *if* and *when* they enter' the damn Ark. Lemme hear how the animals went in two-b'-two. Lemme hear something 'bout the actual Flood.') *'…and the Flood was forty days upon the earth and the waters increased…'* ('Yes! Yes, yes, Lord! Forty days and forty

nights! Read on, read on, Milton, 'cause you going good!') The rain was coming down now, like many large buckets of water out of the skies. The roof was leaking. Rain began to play drums on the floor, and kettles on the bed, and two large drops dropped on the page of the Bible. Suddenly there was a knocking on the back door. My mother made a start; and stopped breathing. Her eyes searched mine for strength. Fear returned to take the place of comfort. Love was in her eyes too. Love for me, love for my presence at that moment in the room with her.

'You think it is Girlie knocking?'

'I don't know, Ma.'

'It ain't Girlie, though. It can't be Girlie, 'cause Girlie left to go down in the country this afternoon to see her children' fathers…' The door was being tugged to and fro; and the rain and the thunder were so hard that the voice outside in the night sounded like a ghostly, frightening whisper.

'*Ruby! Ruby!*' the voice was calling. But my mother remained very quiet. She grabbed me closer to her, and her frightened fingernails dug into my arms.

'*Ruby! Ruby!*'

She whispered in a voice that came out as a shout, 'Milton, bring the Bible quick! God testing we tonight to see if we possesses any strength… God testing we as He has test' Daniel in the lion's den.'

Could I tell her that I was more terrified than she? That her fear was oozing through my body like large ringworms; that my fingers were fumbling through the Bible's leaves without seeing the names of the Books in it; and the knocking at the door was growing louder and louder and more frantic, more frightened and more frightening, like nothing I had ever heard before… and all the time, I was wondering whether the knocker was Nathan my 'father', or Willy-Willy my father; and hoping that it was Nathan and wishing that he would die in the storm, be washed away like the chickens in the backyard; and closing my eyes in fear and terror as the evil thought entered my head, closing my eyes to kill the wish in the manner of an ostrich, the feeling of guilt and the feeling of fear, the feeling of hostility towards my mother because she was a coward and superstitious; feeling hate for

Nathan and love for Willy-Willy; and wishing to throw the Bible through the window out into the storm...

'Son, read the part 'bout Daniel in the lion's den... please.'

...and the Bible in my hand was like a jungle without a track on which I could walk, so I was unable to travel through it, just to pacify my mother's silly desires; looking at the names of the Books in it for the first time: Genesis, rambling on to Exodus, Leviticus; and hearing the knocking and the storm tearing down the trees and the flimsy houses around us, and wandering through the Chronicles of Kings, then Second Kings, and being taken in my uncharted journey to Samuel. And finding, alas! that Samuel is useless, helpless, because there are no lions in Samuel.

'Ruby! Ruby!'

The storm is raging. You can hear the winds complaining with the trees and the trees crashing in the oceans of the road. Chickens are cackling before being drowned; dogs, eternal in our village, are barking; but their barking now has a death ring in it; and all the time the thunder laughing at us, and rolling in the distance, rushing upon us, capsizing like a quarry of dynamite and then fading away into the sea; and the lightning showing us the cracks and holes in our house and now and then my mother's face, stained with fright and tears; and the voice. The voice outside. The voice of the storm, and the voice in the storm.

'Oh Jesus Christ, Ruby! This is Willy-Willy!'

And she says nothing; she does nothing; only looks at me and with her eyes says she is not opening her door. Willy-Willy, my father. Willy-Willy, my friend, outside, drowning in the storm, and my mother and I, inside, sheltered, safe, secure, but cut into pieces by the lightning of fear. I searching the Bible for Daniel in the lion's den, and she searching within her heart for a miracle of courage.

...The Book of Psalms; and looking long and hard at the name now that I have seen it printed correctly for the first time in my life; Proverbs, which my mother always used to begin a scolding, and which the headmaster used as the basis of his boasts of intelligence; Ecclesiastes, and the Book of Solomon... Daniel nowhere in sight. ('Who you think is the most wisest man in the whole world?' Lester asked me once, in the playing field of our schoolroom. 'The most wisest man in the world is... ahm... ahmmm... Haile Selassie!' I told him that, because I had heard Willy-Willy say it the night before. 'No!' chirped Lester. 'Church-ill!' And I said, 'No no no! Selassie!' And Lester said, 'How could Selassie be the most wisest man in the world, when Selassie is *only* a black man? You expect a black man could be the most wisest man in the *whole* world?' But he insisted that it was Churchill, because, as he said, Churchill lived in England; Churchill was the only man, he said, who could polish off a half gallon of steam, smoke twenty-four cigars from Jamaica the same night and then turn around and face 'the House o' Commas the next morning and talk every man there and present, under the table. And to-besides, Churchill win the last war for the whole world!' And I remembered Willy-Willy saying that Selassie was the wisest man, because he was descended from Solomon the Great; and that the people who wrote the Bible for us to read did not want us to know that Selassie was really Solomon. 'Which Solomon?' Lester asked. 'Solomon, the man in the Bible? Or Solomon, the weightlifter?' And I said. 'No no no! Solomon that is now call' Selassie.' And to this Lester said. 'You is a' arse! Vicar Adamson told me that Churchill is the most wisest man in the world! You think that a common man like Willy-Willy could be as learnid as a vicar? You think a man like Willy-Willy could talk in Latin? Could Willy-Willy conduct a communion? Could Willy-Willy stand up in front o' the Gov'nor and shake hands like how Vicar Adamson does do? And Willy-Willy ain't even a' Englishman? And Willy-Willy didn't get eddicated at Oxford and Cambridge, neither! Willy-Willy is nothing alongside Vicar Adamson. Can Willy-Willy afford a servant-woman, a nursemaid, a cook to cook for him and a butler to pour drinks at a cocktail party, and a gardener-boy?' And it made me very sad to think that Willy-Willy had so many stripes against him; and the vicar had none. And all I could say to Lester was, 'Willy-Willy is the onliest man in this village what went all the way up in Harlem New York City, America, and sit down and drink rum with the great Joe Louis, and...') Search-ing still for Daniel, the knocking at the door, so close to my mother's chapel of prayers; and then the last cry from outside, 'Ruby! Ruby! Good dear, Ruby, man! Open the door, please!' and then footsteps like those of an ancient sea animal sploshing through the flood around our house; and my mother saying, with relief, 'Praise God, the bastard gone!' And then the lightning.

She grabbed the Bible from me. 'Where the arse Daniel is?' She wet her thumb, her right thumb with saliva. She turned-up her eyes, straining them in the bad light. She wet her thumb again, the same thumb, and then closed the Book. She opened it again, at the first page, the page which said something about a King of England asking some learned men like Vicar Adamson to write a version of the Bible in a kind of language called King James. My mother applied more saliva to her thumb, the Bible resting on the unmade, soaking bed, and she turned the pages one by one, one rustling page after another, searching searching for that portion of scripture which she knew within her heart would save us from this peril of God's wrath. A tree crashed outside, beside our house.

'What' this I got here?'

'Genissis.'

'You think we will find it in here?'

'Not in Genissis, Ma. That is where the world beginned.'

'Christ, if you know so much 'bout the world why you can't find... Look, don't let me lose my peace this blessid evening, eh boy? I looking for Daniel and you telling me damn foolishness 'bout when the world begin.' Her thumb stuck to a page and when she pulled it off, roughly, she tore the Good Book. 'Lord, have mercy! Forgive me for dispoiling Thy Book.' But she went on searching. 'Which one this is?'

'Judges, Ma.'

'And where the hell Daniel is?'

'Daniel in the lion's den, Ma.' (One afternoon in the steaming schoolroom, the headmaster was laughing. It was not often that our headmaster laughed. And Lester and I were looking at the pictures in *The First Reader For First Graders* which was our reading book in the fourth grade. Lester had wet his thumb like my mother had wet hers, and when he turned the page, the page was torn in half. We looked up at the headmaster. But he was still laughing. And then we looked down at the page and saw an old woman who was pushing a red-and-white cow up a ladder to eat the blue grass on the roof of a house. The ladder was leaning against the house. Lester started to laugh like a hen cackling after laying an egg. 'Hihh-hihh-kiff-kiff-hehhhnnn!' he laughed. 'But Milton, suppose the damn cow fall' down offa the ladder and drop something in the woman' face?' I told him that would be really bad; and that I had never seen a cow that colour, and I knew cows because my godmother had five. 'My father told me,' Lester said, 'that when he was a little boy coming to this very same school, the old woman was still pushing the cow up the ladder. And you know what, Milton? The blasted cow didn' reach the roof then, neither. You think it going reach the top before we finish school, Milton?' 'Who make these books we reading out of?' I asked him. Lester knew everything. 'Englant!' he said. 'They make in Englant!' 'Englant?' I said, in astonishment; because I was told by the headmaster that the wisest men and women and the best things came from Englant. 'Englant, old man! Everything we reads, every word... whatever we writes on, everything we sing, even the clothes we does wear, they make up in Englant! Englant could do any and everything. You don't see the signs on the back of the inside o' this shirt-collar I wearing now? Look! You see, Milton? It say "MAKE IN ENGLANT". Or if it ain't really and truly *make* in Englant's soil, it make by Englant's toil, and in that case, they write down, "ENGLANT MAKE", instead o' "MAKE IN ENGLANT"; Vicar Adamson told me so, and he is a' English-man 'cause he come' from Englant. That is why he know' so much things that you nor me, nor Blackman the headmaster nor Willy-Willy don't know to exist. He has tell me that in the olden days, Englant went in Africa and free' all the Africans and teach them how to hold a knife and fork and eat mashed potatoes, and one time a' African-man eat the potatoes with the handle o' the knife. Hee-hee-hee! But I glad I is not a' African, though, Milton. You glad, too? 'Cause being a' African, it mean' you can't go to a school like this one we going to now, and they ain't no books in Africa – Vicar Adamson told me so – and in Africa, as a' African I couldn't attend the Queen's Birthday parade on the Garrison Savannah, nor... nor...' And I had to confess, because I knew no different, that Englant must be a very pretty, powerful country, full of vicars and learned men. And Lester said Englant was real big and powerful; that that was the reason the Queen chose Englant to live in. 'But Lester, you know why Englant made the cow a red-and-white cow? And why the cow climbing up a ladder to eat grass offa a house, when they is grass on the ground?' And Lester said, 'Milton, the cow climbing the ladder and it is a red-and-white cow becausing it is a' English brand o' cow. A cow cannot reach the grass by climbing *down* the ladder, man!' And I was very confused by what he said, and I told him that. My godmother had cows, but her cows were black cows, brown cows, brown-and-white cows, but never a red-and-white cow! Lester said Vicar Adamson told him they had everything up in Englant. 'And I want to go to Englant when I grow up to be man,' he added. 'Me too,' I agreed, 'but man, red-and-white cows? We going see so many blasted red-and-white cows up in Englant, it going to be a shame!' 'That ain't nothing, though! Vicar Adamson told me he have seen a cow what was red-white-*and*-blue!' And I laughed out then, and the headmaster looked up, stopped laughing himself, and came to find out why.) And looking back now over all those days in my mind, I forgot again and I laughed out, and my mother who was not accompanying me in this escape of the mind, yelled at me, 'Milton, is you dreaming again, boy?'

'No, Ma.'

'Ain't I ask' you to help me look for Daniel in the lion's den?'

'Yes, Ma.'

But all I was hearing was the thunder and all I was seeing was the lightning. I was looking at my mother holding the Book, but I was seeing the green pastures in our village stretching far far out to sea all the way across the ocean to Harlem New York City, America.

'What I have here?'

'Lamentations, Ma.'

'Lemen – heh-heh… lamentations? You ain't pulling my leg is you, boy?'

'No, Ma.'

'You not laughing and joking in my face, is you, Milton? 'Cause I know I have great tribulations and lamentations in my life, but I not asking you to relate my suff'rings to me, eh. You hads better mind your manners in front o' me boy!'

172

'Yes, Ma. But Lamentations… Lamentations is the name of a book in the Bible, Ma. That's why I say Lamen—'

'Yes yes yes, that's true! Yes! Lamentations!'

'And after Lamentations is Ezekiel, and after…'

'Is who, you say?'

'Ezekiel.'

'Heh-heh-heh, boy! You is a real genius like the headmaster say you is! Well well well! my own little boy-child know all this 'bout Ezekiel!'

'And after Ezekiel is Daniel, and then…'

'*Who?* What? Not *the* Daniel we was looking for all this time?'

'But Ma, I didn't know if Daniel-in-the-lion's-den was in Daniel' book, Ma. But after Ezekiel comes Daniel, and…'

'Good Jesus Christ, boy!… look how you make me take the Lord's name… Oh Christ, Milton! You have keep me down here on my bended knees all through this damn storm looking for Daniel in the lion's den, and you didn't have the insights to know that if I want to find Daniel in the lion's den, then it must be found in Daniel' book? Where have you expect' to find Daniel? In Lamentations? Heh-heh-heh! Look, boy, you ain't no true-true genius in truth, eh?'

'But Ma, the headmaster told us they is *two* Daniels. One, the Daniel what went into the lion's den. And two, the Daniel what *come* outta the lion's den. One and one is two, Ma. Two Daniels, Ma, and either one o' the two o' them Daniels could be the Daniel we was looking for, either one o' them two Daniels could have been the Daniel in Daniel' book, so, Ma, you can't get vexed with me, the headmaster told me so.'

'Heh-heh-heh! That headmaster want' something doing to his brains, boy!'

And then there was a knock on the part of the house where my mother slept.

'Ruby? This is Nathan. Open this blasted door, I drowning out here in this storm, man!'

'Nathan? Nathan!'

'Open, Ruby! I drunk as hell and the rain falling…'

'Milton! Has you not heard your father out there in the rain? Open the door and let in your father, boy!'

173

And I went to the door, to open it. And when I opened it, the wind tugged it wide open, and only the rain came in. I could hear Nathan walking away through the water. And I was glad.

'Where' Nathan, boy?'

'There isn't nobody out there, Ma.'

'Must be a damn rotten ghost, then. Close the door quick!'

11

All night long, I lay cradled in the crux of my mother's belly and thighs, as we tried to fall asleep and forget the rain and the fear, like two soup spoons fitted into each other. But the rain came in on us, dropping on the bed through the sieve of the roof and splattering on the floor. I could see rivers glistening on the floor like streams of dewdrops on a leaf. I began to beat a drum in my mind to the rhythm of the raindrops. But each time I had composed a symphony of sounds, the rain would change its tune; and I had then to search in my mind throughout hymns ancient and modern and contemporary, for some new melody to wrap around the droning of the raindrops. My mother sucked breath through her mouth with her teeth clenched, and said something very awful (she thought I was asleep) about poor black people. But that did not make the rain stop wetting us. I was thinking of the lonely white woman who lived out in the Front Road, in her house which did not leak. But she was alone. And I wondered why she could afford a house which did not leak. And I wondered why that was made so, why my mother who worked harder than six white women, seven days a week, had to spend this unholy night in a sieve... Tomorrow, tomorrow it would be like the day after a flood. The chickens would be drowned, the tomatoes and the cucumbers which helped feed us, would be killed and ripped off their vines, and they would be floating like buoys in a topsy-turvy sea. And tomorrow would be Saturday, the day for ironing clothes – only three days after I had run away. Tomorrow, Lester and I would be running across the road, naked in the drizzling rain, all across the road but we would remember to stop before we crossed the rubicon of the white world, the Front Road corner. And if Miss Brewster or Girlie are in sight, we would have to hide between the raindrops and put back on our clothes… and I was thinking of sailing ships made from the shingles blown from the houses, with sails made from the leaves of the large grape trees, and watching them sail like the ships of the Vikings all along the coasts of undiscovered England, all along the white cliffs of Dover which Bing Crosby talked so much about in croons; watching my men and Lester's men get off the ships and climb ashore and conquer the English, men and women like our white Sunday School teacher. And then jumping back aboard and sailing for home. And then the feastings and the rejoicings and the dances and the music playing and the roasts of goat and sheep and cows that were not red-white-and-blue cows, and something which our headmaster called 'venisome'; all this food with large red big grapes like the grapes which Nero and Peter Ustinov ate in the movie about Nero. And I would make myself King of all England; and I would come back one night and raid England and take away their Queen for my wife, because I was the King; and the King can do no wrong. Our headmaster told us so. And I would take away all the English women as slaves as the Romans did in the olden days in Latin books; and I would leave the men behind without any women because they would die off; and because, too, our inspector of schools was an Englishman, whom our headmaster called 'a blasted limey bastard' behind his back one day when he gave our headmaster a bad report for conducting his school…

'This damn rain! This damn damn rain, though!' It was my mother. I thought she was travelling through dreamland; but apparently she too was counting sheep.

…and on that day, once a year as his custom was, the Englishman came to inspect our school to see whether we had learned anything in the three hundred and sixty-five and a quarter days since he last appeared. And I remember that on that day he came as he always came, dressed in the white of colonial power: white shirt with the short sleeves exposing the copper-wire sprigs of hair on his bony arms; white cork hat with green undersides, white short pants with white threequarter stockings and white leather shoes which he never cleaned. And he had a funny smell on him. A smell none of our teachers ever had, an essence which none of our men or women in the village ever carried on them. But it was a smell which some of the women from the Front Road used to have when they attended Sunday matins in their morning-service-Sunday best; and it would be lingering on their lace handkerchiefs – a smell of whiteness and richness, a woman's smell also. And the inspector inspected us, and looked into our ears to see if there was any wax there, to see if we were healthy and whether the headmaster had given us our due of the biscuits and the Carnation milk which our government and the Queen of England had given us to help us through the afternoons of undernourishment because we were the Queen's citizens – and most of which our headmaster took home to feed his family. The inspector pushed a long lead pencil through my hair and the pencil broke, and he laughed and he expected the headmaster to laugh, but the headmaster did not laugh. 'This boy should use Brylcreem, Mister Headmaster,' the inspector had said. But the headmaster only turned his head aside in shame. And I remember the inspector would send the headmaster across the Front Road for his lunch, because he did not like buying any food from the shops in our section. The lunch would consist of a large jug of lemonade with small glaciers of ice in the jug; and it would not be coloured lemonade, not lemonade made with brown sugar which our village could only afford; but it was *white* lemonade – lemonade made with white sugar. And he would sit high on the school platform (although the headmaster swore to kill any boy who dared to eat inside his school!) and eat his sandwiches; and the sandwiches would be thin like a holy communion wafer which Vicar Adamson snapped in quarters on Sunday; and their edges would be trimmed off, and there would be leaves of lettuce sticking out of them. And we small boys, hungry and hawked-and-crowed, would watch the inspector and water at the mouth, while our stomachs clinched with starvation and contracted with the pangs of hunger, and follow each slow, deliberate, frightened twist and turn of his mouth. And then the small, carefully chewed lump would move towards his swallow-pipe, and we too would swallow; and I would look sideways to see if anybody had seen me swallowing, and I would see Lester swallowing, and with tears in his eyes, swallowing and finding nothing to swallow. But he would laugh quickly and nervously, and call me a starved-out animal; and I would laugh, and we would all laugh. And there, on the platform, contradicting the eating rules of our school, the white inspector, a world away, would wipe his pink lips, tap-tap-tap! with a shining linen napkin like one of the many my mother washed for the princess out the Front Road; and he would ball the greaseproof paper in which the sandwiches were wrapped and preserved from the hands of our headmaster and the dust of the road, into a very small tennis ball of a ball, and put it back into the large biscuit tin which he used as a sandwich box. Never in my life, never in Lester's life, had we seen such a beautiful tin. It was made of tin, and painted gold and black and silver, and there was an embossed design on it and letters written by Englishmen in the olden days, letters like those I saw once in the large Bible in our church. And none of us in that classroom had ever eaten these imported featherweight biscuits which came to our island in ships from England. They were ENGLISH-MADE biscuits; and they belonged to the Front Road. But sometimes we were lucky. We would find an empty, discarded ENGLISH-MADE biscuit tin in the Santa-Claus-Christmas-stocking garbage cans of the people who lived in the Front Road, and among the exotic wrapping, the silver foil and the strange delicious almost sickening smell of the richness of the biscuits, there would be one biscuit which the wrapping had concealed from the eyes of the rich; or which they had purposely left in the tin for the man who collected garbage in a donkey cart, or for us to find. And the inspector would belch ever so softly as if the pipes in his throat were made of paper, so softly that you could not really call it a belch: it was so different and repressed, so different from the eruption which rushed out of Blackman after a hearty meal of steamed breadfruit and red fish. And then he would smile. But the second or third time he made this smile, I realized it was not really a smile, but rather the twisting of his face in the agony of indigestion. Perhaps he, too, spent a lot of money at the Mister Smith's Doctor Shop, buying Eno's Fruit Salts, and Dodd's Indigestion Pills!... the rain is still falling falling and my mother is moving from side to side, grunting and cursing the rain... and our headmaster would be given the empty sandwich box to clean, and he would return it

178

smiling and sparkling to the inspector. Now the inspector, full of lunch, would ask us the most difficult questions because, as it seemed to me, he wanted to show us how much he knew, and how little we knew. And he would stare at us coldly, through those steel-grey eyes that looked like bayonets; and we would cry; and he would borrow the headmaster's whip, thinking that we were crying because we were fools, not knowing, and not being able to know, that we were crying because he sat in front of us and ate, while we were starving. And without a word, without a muscle moved, without any feeling, without even seeming to breathe, he would pour that whip into our black backsides as if he were still in the midst of slavery. Melting in tears and shame (it was very disgraceful to have the inspector flog you; and the headmaster said it reflected badly on the school) we would plan to pour gravel in his gas tank or put pins in his car tyres. But we never did any of these things. He was the inspector of schools. And when the inspector patted his white cork hat on to his head, and went down the driveway in his small black Prefect Ford, the headmaster would rant and rage on the platform, shouting and yelling, with a large loaf of bread that had a slab of fried dolphin rammed into it, in his hand, and curse us and call us black animals because we had let him down in front of the 'blasted white man', and that 'Gorblummuh, next time, he going have to get a servant to go for his lunch out the damn Front Road!' And after the storm, there would be singing of Negro spirituals and those soothed us and soothed the headmaster, and he would call us perfect gentlemen and geniuses before the last bell rang for four o'clock, and we jumped over the benches and desks and trampled the assistant masters out of our way…

'Milton, you hear a knocking?'

'Yes, Ma.'

'Open the door, Milton. I hear Nathan knocking. It is your father out there all this time?'

'Yes, Ma.'

'Get up get up, and open the door!'

Nathan has returned. And my mother has accepted him. She has opened the door for him, and that means she has welcomed him back. But I did not welcome him. I hated him still. I could not understand why she would want him back now, when an hour ago she could have killed him. Now, her hands are outstretched to greet him. And although the wounds which she had inflicted upon him were still wet with blood and the memory, yet she wanted him. And the terrible nature of the night seemed to have increased her desire for having a man she could call her man. I opened the door, and Nathan came in. When my mother heard him, and heard his breathing and his footsteps as belonging to Nathan, she sat upright in the bed, and a new peace rested on her face. Relief came back to her movements, and joy was present.

'Praise God, Nathan, you come back!'

'Ruby, why the arse you didn't open the door when you first hear' me knocking? Man, be-Christ, I could have been drown', you don't know?' He stomped his feet on the floor and little pools of mud formed. He then slapped his hat against his thighs and the hat turned into a water sprinkler which I saw Lester using in the vicar's garden. 'Jesus Christ! I have never see' waters so high, waters so rough, waters so blasted cruel in all my borned days! I have never see' death take a toll in a village' backside as I have see' tonight with my two eyes! And Ruby, you know what happen'? Guess what happen'?'

'Girlie' paling fall-down?'

'No! Guess again.'

'The Front Road wash' away?'

'Gorblummuh! that would never happen! 'Cause the man that send' the rain is one o' them! But what really and truly happen' is that Willy-Willy floating 'bout out there by the Bath Wall, swell'-up like a pig bladder, dead and drowned!'

'Willy-Willy?'

'Dead! Dead as a nit!'

'Lord have mercy!'

'The bastard drowned! Willy-Willy that blasted fowl-cock thief dead and drowned... and I hear' from a certain fellar that the police was looking for Willy in connection with the church, and blowing it up, and...'

'It is a blasted good thing that he did blow it up, though.'

'Ruby, what you saying?'

'I say the church should have been blowed up –'

'Jesus God, everybody in this village gone mad? Everybody gone stark-staring-arse-hole mad! Eh, eh, eh?'

'You have come back, Nathan, you have come back. All right, you come back.'

'Be-Christ, I not too sure! I not too sure I shouldn't have stay' with Medlin, and…'

'I do not have you handcuff'!'

'All right all right all right! All right, Ruby! I los' my head just now, all right.'

But all my mother did was stand there and look at Nathan as if she were looking at a mirror. I could see the sadness, the grief and the weakness. But Nathan could not. He did not know what his words meant to her; or perhaps he did know, and he had chosen to say them in such a way as to hurt her. I was feeling her grief with her. Willy-Willy is dead. Nathan is alive. My mother has a man. And I, a 'father'.

Nathan stood looking at me for a long time, pinning his eyes to mine. And when he got tired, and before he would bring himself to wink and let me see him wink, he looked off and laughed. It was one of those laughs which made you wonder whether it was a laugh of love; or a laugh of hate. He laughed again, and then walked to the rocking-chair. My mother was in the bed, sitting up, and I was standing stupidly, waiting to see what was going to happen to me. The rain was still falling, although not as steadily as before. It was very very late at night, sometime between the end of the night and the beginning of the day. We never owned a clock, and so we lived by guessing at the time.

Nathan was rocking in the chair, and smoking a cigarette, and puffing on it, and watching the smoke circle around his head like clouds.

'How it went at the horspital, Nathan?'

'Ruby, I hungry as arse. You got any food outside? I could eat a blasted horse and a half, man.'

'I sorry sorry that the bed has got wet, Nathan, in all this rain, and that you going have to lay-down in a half-wet bed. This house ain't no decent house, if yuh ask me. This house is a blasted fish net.' She climbed down from the bed, and she went and placed her hands on his head to see how wet it was. 'Milton, go and start a fire! You don't see your father starving, boy?'

'Yes, Ma.' And I went outside into the swimming kitchen.

'How the hand?' I heard her asking him.

'It still join-on there!'

'It break bad?'

'It didn' break, Ruby. It did not break. And you hads better praise your Saviour real good for that! 'Cause be-Christ, if it did really and truly break, gorblummuh!' And then I heard a slap. But I did not hear her voice after that. He went on talking. '…and you would have been dead by now.'

'I sorry, Nathan, man.'

'Sorry? You say sorry? You was not sorry when you throw that clothes-iron at me! You only sorry you didn't break my blasted hand…' They stopped talking when they heard me returning. The fire was going. My mother went into the kitchen, and I was left standing alone with my 'father', alone with him for the first time in my life. And I did not know what to do. He sat there in that rocking-chair, not rocking, so quietly, and he continued to look at me as if I was a centipede, and he was deciding how best to stomp out my life. To be so near to him, and knowing that in future every day and every night I would be going to bed and waking up and he would be there, terrified me.

He ran his hand over the mound of white bandages on his forehead, and the large one around his forearm. He passed the same hand over the bandages twice; and he did all this without once taking his eyes off me, and I could not take mine off him, for I did not trust him. But I tried to take my mind off him. I tried listening to the rain, to the distant thunder and the water running down the gutters at the sides of the road, and I tried to listen to my mother singing in the kitchen, and to the plates…

'You see this, you little bastard?'

It was his bandaged hand which he thrust out for me to see. I crept away from him, although he had made no effort to grab me. He was so still, so menacing! I sat on my mother's bed, yearning for the sun to come up, for morning to come and release me from this prison. Lester and I would be playing in the drizzling rain, and sailing our ships all around the world, discovering worlds and countries and happiness like Columbus; and perhaps, if the day was long enough, I could even reach as far away from this village and from Nathan and my mother, as Harlem New York, America...

I heard his voice saying, 'Tomorrow morning bright and early, you march your arse with me up in that rock quarry, and me and you going cut limestone, you bastard!'

...and I knew I could leave them all, because I had defeated them all. I had defeated Nathan, in particular. I had set him back years in his return to my mother's love. She would always distrust him, always keep him on the bottom shelf of uncertainty. But sleep was taking charge of me, and I was soon dozing off.

'Get up get up! You not sleeping in my bed now, Milton,' my mother bellowed. 'I going make up a bed for you on the floor.'

Nathan giggled. My mother placed the food before him, and he ate it with his hands although there was a large worn soup spoon near the plate. Every now and then, he wiped his hands on the seat of his trousers.

'Take these,' my mother said, giving me three washed-out sugar bags. 'Now don't lay down in the rain. Move over in the dry part.' But she kept the bags and spread them on the floor herself, away from the target of the raindrops. All the time Nathan was eating, I was crying. But he did not see me crying; and my mother could not see me crying. The tears ran down my cheeks and nobody knew. The tears washed my heart right out of my body and nobody heard, nobody heard the sorrow. I lay on my stomach, pressing my grief against the damp sugar bags, while the raindrops plunked into the tin tots and the large flowered chamberpot which my mother had placed on the floor to catch the water. And the water was making five different sounds as it hit these containers. Tink!... teenk!... dreep!... tint!... plink! Before she pulled the bags over my head, she emptied the containers, and immediately I heard the music of leaks again.

'Jesus God, that was good, though!'

'Yuh like it, eh, Nathan?'

'It feel' real' good down here!' He slapped his fat stomach many times, and my mother giggled. 'Now! Bed. Sleep taking a heavy toll in my backside.'

'Nathan, I have a clean new-brand pillowcase 'pon the pillow for you to sleep on. And I just spread a clean new sheet 'pon the bed where you going to sleep. You must really be damn tired, man. Come, take off them wet clothes and lemme rub you down in some bay rum and limacol… and pass my hands over them wounds o' yours.'

'Another time, Rube, darling love. I too damn tired now for that shit. Is sleep what weighting-down my mind, girl. I sleeping in my clothes the same way I dress'… but hey! Isn't you carrying the white woman' clothes in the morning?'

'Clothes, you say?'

'Tomorrow is Sa'rday, clothes day.'

'Tomorrow is Sa'rday, but it ain't clothes day 'cause I ripped up every-blasted-piece o' old rag that woman give me. You had me so damn vexed, Nathan! You had me so vexed, I ripped up every-blasted…'

'But, Ruby, is you mad, or something?'

'I not mad, Nathan. I free. I free. I never have feeled so free in my life as when I ripped up every-blasted-piece o' rag and shift what that, that-that-that… that *lady* own'.'

'Ruby, something gone wrong with you, eh, girl? You doing some funny things here of late!'

'Never have I feeled so good and free in my life, Nathan. In the morning, I will worry 'bout clothes and white people.'

'Gorblummuh! well, goodnight then, I hitting this damn sack, pronto!' And his heavy body crushed the bed. And the old rusty springs bellowed. I heard him sigh. It was a pleasant sigh, a sigh of relief, a sigh of conquest. And then my mother got into the bed, and she too sighed, but her sigh did not say satisfaction. It was a sigh that represented a putting down of her troubles for the night, until the next day. She romped slightly in the bed, getting into the best shallow trough for her rest. When she was settled in her briar patch, Nathan passed gas, hard and aloud, and he did not say, 'Excuse,' as my mother had taught me to say when I did that. And my mother did not ask him to say, 'Excuse.'

'Milton?' she called. I pretended I was sleeping. 'Milton?' I pretended I was dead. I wished she would spend the rest of the night calling me, and I was not going to answer. But soon, I heard her hoofbeats trampling towards me. She shook me; but I was not afraid, for my hate for her and Nathan had clothed me with a new courage. 'You heard me calling you?'

'Yes, Ma.'

'Wake up, and say goodnight to your father.'

'Goodnight,' I said.

'You better learn manners, eh, boy!'

'Yes, Ma.'

'Leave him to me, Ruby. Leave him to me. Bright and early tomorrow morning, I going have his arse in that rock quarry, and he going have a' iron drill in his hand blasting rock stones!'

'And we was wasting our time planning high school for this, this-this-this… this…'

'Chain-gang for you tomorrow morning, boy. School wiped outta your life from tonight!'

My mother pulled the blind to, and I was left outside their world, in a world by myself. I listened to their voices giggling and laughing, and to their grunts and to their smothered happiness. And then, the same rhythm as the rhythm I had heard when I was under the cellar came back to me… perhaps I was in a dream… but I could hear springs creaking in that same one-two-one-two rhythm; and then the springs stopped talking suddenly, and the bed stopped shaking and their voices returned, this time very low, very lifeless, very softly… and then I heard the rain again, pouring down around the house. When my ears grew accustomed to the noise of the rain, I heard the drumming of the raindrops falling in the tin tots and chamberpot a few inches from my bed. And I started to count the drops until the drops turned into sheep and I counted them too, counting and counting until there were millions of sheep falling headless into tots and chamberpots which filled the room, and the sheep of raindrops started to dance… waiting and listening for the sun to rise, for the cocks and the birds and the infants in the village to tell me that the sun is in the sky… waiting for morning to come, to run away, to play with Lester, to get out. But all I could hear in that long terrible, tearful night, was the grumbling voice of Nathan, raging because the house was leaking; and the voice of my mother, trying to soothe him and make him remain with her, at least until tomorrow.

'Rain rain rain!... this blasted rain!... this blasted rain!... looka, this blasted rain, though!... be-Christ! I had better been standing under a shower in the Bath!...'

'Patience, Nathan. Morning soon come, morning soon come, man. So, patience.'

'But look at this blasted rain, though!'

'Tomorrow going to be another, diff'rent new day, man. Patience... this night ain't got long to last, man.'

ABOUT THE AUTHOR

Born in Barbados in 1934, Austin C. Clarke was educated at Harrison College and became a schoolteacher before moving to Canada in 1955 to study at the University of Toronto. Beginning in 1959, Clarke worked as a freelance broadcaster for the CBC, for which he recorded a series of interviews and documentaries on racial issues in North America and Britain. This began a prolific period in Clarke's career, during which he wrote several short stories and the novels: *Survivors of the Crossing* (1964), *Amongst Thistles and Thorns* (1965), and *The Meeting Point* (1967); followed by the novel *Storm of Fortune* (1973) and a collection of short stories entitled *When He Was Free and Young and He Used to Wear Silks* (1973). In the mid-1980s Clarke published two collections of short stories, *When Women Rule* (1985) and *Nine Men Who Laughed* (1986), as well as the novel, *Proud Empires* (1986). Returning in the early 1990s to the short story form, Clarke published the collections, *In This City* (1992) and *There Are No Elders* (1993). In 1992, in response to a riot, Clarke produced the pamphlet, *Public Enemies: Police Violence and Black Youth*. Also in the 1990s, Clarke wrote *A Passage Back Home* (1994), a memoir of his friendship with the Trinidadian writer Sam Selvon, and *Pig tails 'n Breadfruit: The Rituals of Slave Food* (1999), a "food memoir" that combines recipes with memories of Clarke's formative years in Barbados. Clarke's 1997 novel, *The Origin of Waves*, won him the inaugural Rogers Communications Writers' Trust Fiction Prize in 1998. Clarke's memoir, *Growing Up Stupid Under the Union Jack* (1980), won the 1980 Casa de las Americas Prize for Literature. His novel, *The Polished Hoe*, won the 2003 Commonwealth Prize and the 2002 Giller Prize (Canada's most prestigious literary award). Over the course of his career, Clarke has held many political, professional, and academic positions, including: Cultural Attaché to the Barbadian Embassy in Washington, D.C.; General Manager of the Caribbean Broadcasting Corporation in Barbados; and visiting lecturer in creative writing and African American literature at Yale, Brandeis, Duke, the University of Texas, and the University of Western Ontario. He lives in Toronto.

CARIBBEAN MODERN CLASSICS

2009/10 titles

Jan R. Carew
Black Midas
Introduction: Kwame Dawes
ISBN: 9781845230951; pp. 272; 23 May 2009; £8.99

This is the bawdy, Eldoradean epic of the legendary 'Ocean Shark' who makes and loses fortunes as a pork-knocker in the gold and diamond fields of Guyana, discovering that there are sharks with far sharper teeth in the city. *Black Midas* was first published in 1958.

Jan R. Carew
The Wild Coast
Introduction: Jeremy Poynting
ISBN: 9781845231101; pp. 240; 23 May 2009; £8.99

First published in 1958, this is the coming-of-age story of a sickly city child, sent away to the remote Berbice village of Tarlogie. Here he must find himself, make sense of Guyana's diverse cultural inheritances and come to terms with a wild nature disturbingly red in tooth and claw.

Neville Dawes
The Last Enchantment
Introduction: Kwame Dawes
ISBN: 9781845231170; pp. 332; 27 April 2009; £9.99

This penetrating and often satirical exploration of the search for self in a world divided by colour and class is set in the context of the radical hopes of Jamaican nationalist politics in the early 1950s. First published in 1960, the novel asks many pertinent questions about the Jamaica of today.

Wilson Harris
Heartland
Introduction: Michael Mitchell
ISBN: 9781845230968; pp. 104; 23 May 2009; £7.99

First published in 1964, this visionary narrative tracks one man's psychic disintegration in the aloneness of the forests of the Guyanese interior, making a powerful ecological statement about man's place in the 'invisible chain of being', in which nature is a no less active presence.

Edgar Mittelholzer
Corentyne Thunder
Introduction: Juanita Cox
ISBN: 9781845231118; pp. 242; 27 April 2009; £8.99

This pioneering work of West Indian fiction, first published in 1941, is not merely an acute portrayal of the rural Indo-Guyanese world, but a work of literary ambition that creates a symphonic relationship between its characters and the vast openness of the Corentyne coast.

Andrew Salkey
Escape to an Autumn Pavement
Introduction: Thomas Glave
ISBN: 9781845230982; pp. 220; 23 May 2009; £8.99

This brave and remarkable novel, set in London at the end of the 1950s, and published in 1960, catches its 'brown' Jamaican narrator on the cusp between black and white, between exiled Jamaican and an incipient black Londoner, and between heterosexual and homosexual desires.

Denis Williams
Other Leopards
Introduction: Victor Ramraj
ISBN: 9781845230678; pp. 216; 23 May 2009; £8.99

Lionel Froad is a Guyanese working on an archeological survey in the mythical Jokhara in the horn of Africa. There he hopes to rediscover the self he calls 'Lobo', his alter ego from 'ancestral times', which he thinks slumbers behind his cultivated mask. First published in 1963, this is one of the most important Caribbean novels of the past fifty years.

Denis Williams
The Third Temptation
Introduction: Victor Ramraj
ISBN: 9781845231163; pp. 108; May 2010; £8.99

A young man is killed in a traffic accident at a Welsh seaside resort. Around this incident, Williams, drawing inspiration from the *Nouveau Roman*, creates a reality that is both rich and problematic. Whilst he brings to the novel a Caribbean eye, Williams makes an important statement about refusing any restrictive boundaries for Caribbean fiction. The novel was first published in 1968.

Roger Mais 2010/11 titles
The Hills Were Joyful Together
Introduction: Norval Edwards
ISBN: 9781845231002; pp. 272; December 2010; £8.99

Unflinchingly realistic in its portrayal of the wretched lives of King-ston's urban poor, this is a novel of prophetic rage. First published in 1953, it is both a work of tragic vision and a major contribution to the evolution of an autonomous Caribbean literary aesthetic.

Edgar Mittelholzer
A Morning at the Office
Introduction: Raymond Ramcharitar
ISBN: 978184523; pp. 215; May 2010; £8.99

First published in 1950, this is one of the Caribbean's foundational novels in its bold attempt to portray a whole society in miniature. A genial satire on human follies and the pretensions of colour and class, this novel brings several ingenious touches to its mode of narration.

Edgar Mittelholzer
Shadows Move Among Them
Introduction: Rupert Roopnaraine
ISBN: 9781845230913; pp. 352; May 2010; £10.99

In part a satire on the Eldoradean dream, in part an exploration of the possibilities of escape from the discontents of civilisation, Mittelholzer's 1951 novel of the Reverend Harmston's attempt to set up a utopian commune dedicated to 'Hard work, frank love and wholesome play' has some eerie 'pre-echoes' of the fate of Jonestown in 1979.

Edgar Mittelholzer
The Life and Death of Sylvia
Introduction: Juanita Cox
ISBN: 9781845231200; pp. 362; May 2010, £10.99

In 1930s' Georgetown, a young woman on her own is vulnerable prey, and when Sylvia Russell finds she cannot square her struggle for economic survival and her integrity, she hurtles towards a wilfully early death. Mittelholzer's novel of 1953 is a richly inward portrayal of a woman who finds inner salvation through the act of writing.

Elma Napier
A Flying Fish Whispered
Introduction: Evelyn O'Callaghan
ISBN: 9781845231026; pp. 248; December 2010; £9.99

With one of the most delightfully feisty women characters in Caribbean fiction and prose that sings, Elma Napier's 1938 Dominican novel is a major rediscovery, not least for its imaginative exploration of different kinds of Caribbeans, in particular the polarity between plot and plantation that Napier sees in a distinctly gendered way.

Orlando Patterson
The Children of Sisyphus
Introduction: Kwame Dawes
ISBN: 9781845230944; pp. 288; November 2010; £9.99

This is a brutally poetic book that brings to the characters who live on Kingston's 'dungle' an intensity that invests them with tragic depth. In Patterson's existentialist novel, first published in 1964, dignity comes with a stoic awareness of the absurdity of life and the shedding of false illusions, whether of salvation or of a mythical African return.

V.S. Reid
New Day
Introduction: Norval Edwards
ISBN: 9781845230906, pp. 360; December 2010, £10.99

First published in 1949, this historical novel focuses on defining moments of Jamaica's nationhood, from the Morant Bay rebellion of 1865, to the dawn of self-government in 1944. *New Day* pioneers the creation of a distinctively Jamaican literary language of narration.

Garth St. Omer
A Room on the Hill
Introduction: John Robert Lee
ISBN: 9781845230937; pp. 210; November 2010; £8.99

A friend's suicide and his profound alienation in a St Lucia still slumbering in colonial mimicry and the straitjacket of a reactionary Catholic church drive John Lestrade into a state of internal exile. First published in 1968, St. Omer's meticulously crafted novel is a pioneering exploration of the inner Caribbean man.

George Lamming
Of Age and Innocence
Introduction: Jeremy Poynting
ISBN: 9781845231453; pp. 320; January 2011; £11.99

In one of the most insightful explorations of race and ethnicity in colonial and postcolonial societies, Lamming reaches far beneath the surface of ethnic difference into the very heart of the processes of perception, communication and coming to knowledge. In a novel that is tense and tragic in its denouement, Lamming has written one of the half dozen most important Caribbean novels of all time.

Classic poetry titles 2010/11 titles

Wayne Brown
On the Coast and Other Poems
Introduction: Mervyn Morris
ISBN: 9781845231507; pp. 112; November 2010; £8.99

First published in 1972, *On the Coast* was a Poetry Book Society Recommendation in the UK, and established Brown as one of the finest young poets of the post-Walcott generation. This collection include all the poems of 1972, with those of *Voyages* published in 1988.

George Campbell
First Poems
Introduction: Kwame Dawes
ISBN: 9781845231491; pp. 172; January 2011; £9.99

A profound influence on Derek Walcott, George Campbell's *First Poems*, published in 1945, announced the arrival of modernism in Caribbean poetry. These poems of nationalist ferment in Jamaica celebrate blackness, the working class and the beauties of the Jamaican landscape.

Una Marson
Selected Poems
Introduction: Alison Donnell
ISBN: 9781845231682; pp. 160; March 2011; £8.99

Alison Donnell aims for a representative selection that reveals the complexity of Marson's scope – from *Tropic Reveries* (1930) to unpublished work written in the 1950s: a range that establishes a significant poetic achievement.

Titles thereafter include...

Austin C. Clarke, *The Survivors of the Crossing*
O.R. Dathorne, *The Scholar Man*
O.R. Dathorne, *Dumplings in the Soup*
Neville Dawes, *Interim*
Wilson Harris, *The Eye of the Scarecrow*
Wilson Harris, *The Sleepers of Roraima*
Wilson Harris, *Tumatumari*
Wilson Harris, *Ascent to Omai*
Wilson Harris, *The Age of the Rainmakers*
Marion Patrick Jones, *Panbeat*
Marion Patrick Jones, *Jouvert Morning*
George Lamming, *Water With Berries*
Roger Mais, *Black Lightning*
Una Marson, *Selected Poems*
Edgar Mittelholzer, *Children of Kaywana*
Edgar Mittelholzer, *The Harrowing of Hubertus*
Edgar Mittelholzer, *Kaywana Blood*
Edgar Mittelholzer, *My Bones and My Flute*
Edgar Mittelholzer, *A Swarthy Boy*
Orlando Patterson, *An Absence of Ruins*
V.S. Reid, *The Leopard* (North America only)
Garth St. Omer, *Shades of Grey*
Andrew Salkey, *The Late Emancipation of Jerry Stover*
and more…